The Rebellious Countess

The Scandalous Sisters

HELENE MATHESON

OLIVERHEBERBOOKS

The Scandalous Sisters were born while driving on a castle tour of Scotland with my friend and fellow author, Jerrie Alexander. As I muttered left, left, left, to ensure I stayed on the 'right' side of the road, the Blair sisters came to life. Thank you, Jerrie, for being my navigator and pushing this series into being.

To my editors, Jill and Martha, many thanks for the hours of hard work, guidance, and lessons in etiquette. You are the perfect governesses for me, and my ladies and gentlemen who were born without a proper bone in their bodies.

To the original scandalous sisters—I love you just the way you are.

"La vie est une fleur dont l'amour est le miel."
  Life is a flower for which Love is the honey

— VICTOR HUGO

Prologue

Dear Sir Williamson,

Much to my ~~horror~~ chagrin, I find myself ~~facing a firing squad~~ married. The Scotch merchant would not allow ~~a Sassenach pirate~~ an Englishman to purchase his liquor. He said, ~~and I quote, "Tek yer honkin' Sassenach arse away til ye marry a wee bonnie lass of good breeding." Translation,~~ if I didn't marry a Scottish lady and quickly, I would not be able to purchase the Scotch needed to bribe the ~~wicked witch~~ tavern keeper at The Happy Hag. Without that Scotch, the ~~damnable~~ Hag refused to set up my meeting. Without a ~~blasted virgin~~ bride, the entire plan to recover the package would be ruined.

In this particular region, ladies of quality are ~~bloody~~ difficult to find. When I happened across one in town, I ~~knocked over two lads and their grandfather~~ managed to obtain an introduction. As gratuitous as it may sound, it turned out to be a ~~disaster~~ minor problem. I did not know the identity of her brother-by-marriage until after I proposed, and by then it was too late to find another bride. Yet with no alternatives, I had to make a decision which ~~would~~ could create a ~~war violent enough~~

~~for Robert the Bruce to dig out of his grave to fight~~ bit of a scandal.

The young lady's sister is the Duchess of Ross, bride to none other than Nashford ~~bloody~~ Harding, ~~the bastard~~ Duke of Ross. Unfortunately, the duke and I are previously acquainted. ~~He broke my damned nose when he discovered me in a compromising position with a lady.~~ I will leave the details of our acquaintance to your imagination, but it is safe to say it was over ~~his mother~~ a woman he held in the highest esteem.

I have no doubt the duke will be in contact with you shortly, if he has not already. Please know, the plan was to leave her in Dumfries, ~~disappointedly~~ untouched, but then the seller wanted to meet the lass at the docks and I had no choice but to take my ~~bloody~~ wife aboard The Maribelle. When we arrive in Le Conquet, I will send the ~~temptress~~ young lady to Plymouth immediately. ~~The siren~~ She may be a bit confused as to her identity, since I had to use an alias. She will probably shed ~~fathoms of~~ a few tears and claim to be Lady Máira Collins, Countess of Dorset. If you could ~~take the damned shackles off my ankles~~ arrange for an annulment upon her return, I would greatly appreciate the assistance. I will keep her safe from the crew and myself ~~hopefully~~ throughout the voyage. She is a ~~passionate~~ spirited girl who could use some assistance finding a husband after everything she has endured ~~from me~~ for her country.

My apologies for the ~~black eyes the duke will deliver~~ difficulties this will create. You have my word as a ~~rogue who wants nothing more than to introduce Miss Blair to the sweetest carnal delights this side of heaven~~ gentleman, she is untouched.

When our package is secured, I will send word.

~~Pray that I can honor my word,~~
Regards,
E

*—An edited draft report to Sir Robert Williamson, War
Office London, England from an unidentified agent of the
Crown, Dumfries, Scotland. It was written while the agent
angrily awaited a Scottish smuggler, and edited later that
night as he stared at his wife's unconscious form lying across his
captain's bunk aboard his ship, The Maribelle. Her undefiled
breasts nearly bursting from the neckline of her wedding gown
were a display that would tempt the best of men—especially
men like him.*

T his was her life. She was on the honeymoon trip of a
debutante's dreams. Passionate kisses, festive glasses
clinking, raucous laughter spilling through the seams of
the building and...

...A drunken sailor falling at her feet.

"Ummpf." His fetid breath filled the air, and the condition of
his rotting teeth made a shudder crawl through her body when he
rolled over and grinned at the sight of her. "Beggin' yer pardon,
missy." Suggestive eyebrows waggled, and the *gentleman* tipped an
imaginary hat on his head, his two front teeth displaying more filth
than she'd seen in her lifetime.

She cringed and scooted further under the table. Cheap ale
spilled over the edges, filth covered the floor where she cowered like
a...a rat? A gasp was torn from her lips. Was that a rat?

Drat and double drat! She crossed her arms over her knees and
brought the skirts of her soiled wedding gown closer to her body.
Her safe haven should have been the strong arms of her gorgeous
husband wrapped around her body as she playfully dodged his
public advances. Instead, she was shooing away a beady-eyed
rodent who only stared at her as if *she* were the one who needed to
vacate the premises.

The rat, on second thought, was much more appealing than
the two-faced, good-for-nothing blackguard she'd married. That
rat had abandoned her on the docks with no money, no luggage,

and no way to find her way home. Just some cryptic message passed on by a member of his crew as he'd pointed down the street of the dockside town.

"Talk to Hag. She'll give you passage."

It was as if Ellison had dropped her off in a foreign land, to be rid of her once and for all. She hadn't even had her wedding night...

No. The only passionate kisses she'd witnessed were between the buxom barmaid and the beaver-toothed sailor currently crawling on his hands and knees toward the exit. Máira winced as a handful of the barmaid's strawberry blonde hair dropped to the floor and got lost in the shuffle and scuffle of the men fighting throughout the tavern.

The woman cursed, glass shattered and sprinkled to the floor in a storm of profanity. "May the devil take ya, ya dirty ol' rum gagger." A man staggered in front of her, his boots kicking the ball of hair closer to Máira.

"How did my honeymoon end in The Happy Hag tavern in France? France! Aren't we at war with France?" Máira asked.

Her question went unanswered. No shock there. Like the last several days, she was the last person on anyone's mind. From the time she awoke aboard a ship, she had one alarming experience after another. There had been no plans to board a ship on their honeymoon. There had been no plans to meet a pirate. And there certainly had been no plans to end up in the middle of a brawl in a bloody tavern in France.

To make matters worse, every rotten thing that occurred to her could be traced back to the moment she had said "I do" to the Earl of Dorset, the bloody blackguard who'd ignored her the entire voyage to France. A voyage that should have taken less than a day, but had been interminably long. On the very first day, she'd been lost and disoriented. With each roll of the waves, her stomach had done three. When lightning cracked and thunder roared, she'd sworn her head split in two and bounced off the walls. Her roaring megrim evidence of her being stuck in a hellish nightmare. She'd finally crawled out of the cabin and to the ladder to make her way to the deck. The rain then pelted her face and soaked her dress like a second skin to her body. As she'd shielded her face with her hands and looked up to the where she thought a captain of a ship might be—there *he* stood, wearing pirate clothes. *Pirate clothes.*

If her face had any color to it at all, it leached from her cheeks when she looked around and saw the hard men manning the decks. It only proceeded to get worse when her husband's beautiful head of hair turned in her direction and his handsome face delivered an angry scowl. His icy glower held enough menace to pierce her heart with ten daggers, like the one he wore strapped at his waist. In that moment, she felt a fear like nothing she'd felt in her life, and she'd felt plenty of fear before boarding that ship. Her life had not been made of tea cakes and fripperies.

Yet the gorgeous, strapping, sweet, doting Earl of Dorset who had worshiped the ground she walked while they'd been on dry land in Dumfries, had turned into a cold, arrogant bastard pirate aboard ship. A bastard who leapt over the railing onto the deck in front of her before she could run back to her cabin and bolt the door.

"What the hell are you doing up here?" he'd bellowed. It could have been rain splattering on her face, but she'd imagined it to be angry spittle. That along with her sudden memory of her older sister Iseabail lecturing her. "You can't possibly know him well enough to marry him!" had been enough to make her toss her accounts all over his shirt. She'd waited for a backhanded blow that never came.

Instead, he'd looked down at his shirt, rolled his eyes, and ripped it from his body. One minute it was there, and the next she was staring at the broad expanse of a naked chest with too much muscle. Flawless skin sculpted into the ideal embodiment of the male species. Michelangelo would curse his perfection.

"Bloody hell," she cursed his perfection.

Ellison blinked at profanity, then tossed her over his shoulder like a basket of fish.

She hadn't fought him. She'd let him carry her below deck, into the cabin she'd occupied where he unceremoniously tossed her onto the bed and left her without another word. Then he'd bolted the door shut—from the outside! The ship had rocked and swayed violently as she'd stared at the door. If it took on water, she'd go down to Davey Jones's locker without anyone the wiser. Despite knowing the furious pirate was the same man she'd married, she hadn't recognized the man who'd secured her in a room with no lifeline. He hadn't the time, nor the inclination, to deal with his sick wife.

She had hoped things would change, return to normal when they'd docked in the port of...port of...bloody hell. She didn't even know what port she was in, and now she was cursing like the sailors around her. Would she have to fight as well?

A man bent over and looked under the table, his eyes met hers and her blood curdled under his scrutiny. His coat was clean, his trousers that of a nobleman, and his manners gave the appearance of a gentleman as he reached out to take her hand. Only a fool would believe he meant to rescue her from the melee. And despite the evidence to say otherwise, Máira was no fool. She scooted back in the corner, pushing the rat out of his home and the man's grin grew.

"You like it rough, *chérie*?" His aristocratic polish and refined English were completely out of place with the street-born curses of the Frenchmen fighting around them. Yet deep in her marrow, Máira recognized the evil within. Not for one moment did she believe they would bond over shared nationalism. This man was evil down to his toenails.

"I will make you scream and beg for mercy," he cooed.

He thought she was French and didn't understand. To a naive miss who didn't speak English, he would probably appear as a debonaire gentleman coming to her rescue. Máira knew differently.

She understood more than she cared. His brown eyes spoke of a lost, soulless man who hadn't felt anything other than disdain for another human being in years, if ever.

He lunged for her ankle and she screamed, but there was too much noise for anyone to hear. She kicked and punched, striking him on the temple which only seemed to feed his violence as he dragged her out from under the table and wrenched her arm behind her back. She screamed once more, as her face slammed into the floor.

"I'll teach you to strike your betters, bitch." She felt his breath on her ear as he attempted to slam her face against the floor a second time, but she twisted her body, sacrificing her shoulder as her arm wrenched higher.

A scream vibrated through the air, and Máira wasn't sure if she was screaming or someone else was making the unholy noise. Her attacker's grip went suddenly slack and he fell onto his belly next to her. Arms underneath his chest and his head turned to the side, he looked directly at her. He didn't smirk, or talk, or even crawl away on his knees. He laid there bleeding with a knife the size of Cook's meat cleaver buried in one sightless eye.

Máira bit the back of her hand to hold the scream in her throat. She had never seen a man die before. She had experienced tragic loss multiple times, but this was gory and horrifying. Tears of blood streamed across the bridge of his nose and cheek and down onto the floor.

She wished the man at her side was her husband—the dirty Lothario who'd left her to this fate. *This* was what her sister had warned her about, the life of a woman who took a chance and married a stranger.

Bloody hell. "I swear I'm going to kill him."

One

Dearest Nash,

I have good news to report about Máira which may come as somewhat of a shock. She has met and married Ellison Collins, the Earl of Dorset. I warned her against a whirlwind romance, but she said I, of all people, should know how quickly one falls in love. I couldn't exactly argue the point, however, since I fell in love with a man I'd hated my entire life. You are the exception to the rule when it comes to rogues, darling. I did counsel her on having a long engagement. Another argument I lost. She said if I didn't give my blessing, she would run off and marry the earl anyway. They were married the 1st of June in the chapel at Caerlaverock and have left on a month-long honeymoon trip.

Oh, how I look forward to our own overdue honeymoon. I am counting the hours until your return.

Our son misses you almost as much as his mother does. This morning, he looked to your side of the bed, and I swore he called for his "da-da" after he finished feeding. Mary just giggled and said all children make that particular noise, and that his first word would be "mum." Regardless, he looks for you everywhere, as do I.

All my love,
Iseabail

—A letter from Iseabail Blair Handcock Harding, Duchess of Ross, to her husband, Nashford Xavier Harding, 8th Duke of Ross, regarding her younger sister Máira Blair's marriage to Ellison Collins, Earl of Dorset, June 1812

Where the devil was he? Odors assaulted his senses. Those faculties that weren't reeling in disgust, were quaking with pain and nausea. One minute he'd been walking down the street to meet his contact, and the next he was here—wherever *here* may be—with a godawful smell permeating the pain in his head. Considering his head hurt like bloody hell, his stench was the last of his worries.

Which meant only one thing—he was recognized some time before he'd met his contact and after he'd secured fare back to Scotland for his bride. She belonged there, riding across the countryside without a care in the world, not here, in the middle of a blasted war.

Elias purposely kept his eyes closed, his breathing slow as he attempted to identify his surroundings. The first scent was obvious: manure. By the caked, dried feeling on his cheek and the flies buzzing around his face, he suspected someone had dropped him in a pile of shite.

Beautiful, just bloody beautiful.

Getting that off his skin would take a thorough soaking. To think he'd spend six days aboard ship, drenched to the bone from dodging the British and French Navies by entering the squall that nearly capsized them, and the first time he'd been dry in a week, he was covered in shite. He'd probably have to shave his head. His hair didn't mean much to him, but she'd adored running her hands through it...

This was turning out to be honeymoon trip of a man's nightmares—no buxom bride to bury his cock inside, just a shite of a mission no one could know about and—hell. Where was his bloody-damned bride!

His jaw tensed involuntarily. He had to get out of this mess to save the damned chit who'd turned his mission into a disaster. He started taking stock of his injuries only to realize his hands were bound behind his back and his feet were tied at the ankles.

Bloody fanfuckingtastic.

Other than the fetor of animal waste and the obvious lump on the back of his head causing nausea to grip his innards, he was in pretty good shape. Cheap wine hit his senses next. He suspected it had to be pretty bad if he could smell it through the odorous horse excrement. Footsteps fell to his left, and his nose twitched from the sudden tickle on the tip of his nose. He suspected either something had been kicked upon his face, or a fly found it to be a cozy landing spot. The tickling continued, circling the tip of his nose as if a bug had indeed found a juicy meal in the shite painting his flesh.

Bloody hell. If he were still passed out, none of this would bother him. As it were, he was going to sneeze. "Ahh—chooo!"

"The Cap'n's awake, is 'ee?"

Elias opened his eyes, blinked at the light threatening to crack his skull in two, and looked up at the two men standing over him as recognition set in. He'd know those black teeth anywhere. He allowed himself to slip into the language these two would understand. "Billy, me boy. It seems I got meself tied up and tossed in a bit of muck." He grinned and tugged at the bindings that held his arms behind his back.

"This particular wench's perfume not to yer standards, Cap'n? I be thinkin' she's not quite as sweet as that bit o' flesh ye had back on the *Maribelle*, tho, is she? When we're done here, we be meanin' to show yer lady a bit o' fun, right Billy?" Jack nudged

Billy in the ribs with his elbow and the man responded with a vile grin. In that moment Elias decided he'd kill Jack first for suggesting this man even think of touching his wife...right after they told him where he could find her.

He winked at Jack despite every muscle in this body wanting to tear the blighter limb from limb. "Jaaack," he let the man's name drag out on his tongue the way he'd make the man die—slowly and painfully. "Ye know I've been without that morsel the entire trip. Me cock isn't very fond of a wife too sick to swallow. Now cut these bindings, and let's go find some real whores who like it deep." He thrust his hips in a crude gesture these two could appreciate.

The two of them laughed humorously. "Now Cap'n, I'm 'fraid those days be o'er for ye. We just be needin' to know where ye stashed the chit."

"Who? What the devil is going on? Enough games," he growled. "Untie my damned hands and I'll let you off with a couple lashes. If you don't, I'll see you swing."

Jack reared back and kicked him in the ribs. It was all the answer he needed. He was at war, and these two picked the wrong enemy. Whoever tied his hands didn't know a stopper knot from a clove hitch knot. He rolled with the impact, his speed and momentum overtaking Jack. He was down on the ground with an "Umph."

Still moving, Elias threw the rope clear of his hands and grabbed Jack's pistol before Billy even realized he was loose. Eyes wide, Billy desperately fumbled for the knife at his waist.

"Don't do it," he cautioned.

Billy ignored the warning and pulled the knife from the sheath.

"Billy..." Elias used the stern tone he used with his crew, hoping to leave no doubt in the other man's mind that he would do what was necessary. But Billy was new. The voyage to France had been his first with the *Maribelle* crew.

And his last.

Billy raised the rusty blade to shoulder height, his eyes targeting Elias's chest.

Elias pulled the trigger. The blast reverberated off the walls as smoke swirled in the air and the scent of gunpowder mixed with blood. Billy's sightless eyes stared at him as the bullet hole between his eyes began to seep. The knife dropped to the ground, followed by the hollow thud of Billy's body.

"Dammit," he cursed. He turned his attention back to Jack as he struggled to stand up. The pain in his head not letting him forget the beating he'd taken. It rolled through his skull like a licentious storm on the ocean, and he swayed as he reached for his satchel on the table.

Jack scurried across the floor, crawling over his partner's body, and grabbed Billy's knife. By the time Jack looked up, he was already beaten.

Elias shrugged. "You left my pistol." He nodded toward the empty leather satchel lying on the table as he pointed the gun on a now cowering Jack, who held his palms extending outward in a gesture meant to placate. "Don't be shoot'n, Cap'n. Just a bit of fun we be havin'."

"I don't think Billy finds your idea of entertainment very diverting." He rubbed at the back of his neck. What day is it?" He asked. He'd come ashore on Tuesday morning, but he had no idea how much time had passed.

"Wednesday," Jack answered, his gaze traveling to Elias's bound feet. The addled brain was concocting a foolish plan of attack.

Elias growled. "Drop the dagger and move over to the empty stall."

The small dagger dropped in the filth as Jack began to stand. "Crawl on your hands and knees," Elias ordered. "Then lie on your stomach in the middle of the stall."

"But—"

Elias cocked the pistol.

"Aye, Cap'n," Jack obeyed the order without further complaint.

Elias grinned and patted one of the nags on the neck as she ambled out of her stall to see what all the fuss was about. He would have thought she'd run at the sound of the shot, but somehow the old girl was more curious than frightened. He supposed a life on the streets would do that, even for an animal.

"You get used to the wench's *sweetness*," he told Jack, as he crawled through shite. It was a lie. He couldn't wait to dunk his head in a trough and get the shite off his body. "Who's the chit you were wanting information about, Jack?" It had better not be his wife.

"Yer wife, Cap'n."

Elias delivered a nasty taste of Jack's own medicine and kicked the man in the ribs, making sure he cracked ribs with the first blow.

Jack curled in on his injury and grabbed his side with a moan. "Please, Cap'n. We wasn't goin' to urt 'er."

"What were ye going to do with her then, Jack? The two of you aren't known for treating the whores particularly well."

Again, Jack curled in on himself as if Elias had delivered a second blow. He hadn't. Which meant the arse was going for the blade in his boot. "If you want to keep your foot and not be called *Stumpy* for the rest of your miserable existence, I suggest you leave the blade inside your boot."

Jack froze, the fingers of his left hand lost to Elias's view somewhere in between his calves.

Elias raised the pistol. "It's not a particularly good day to die... according to Billy." He smiled, every bit of the deadly desire to pull the trigger visible to the man in front of him as he thought of what Jack had planned for Máira. "I suggest you lie flat on your belly with your hands spread wide, palms up."

Jack showed more intelligence than he had the entire time Elias had known him. He obeyed with a gasp of pain as he straightened his torso.

"Count the pain you're experiencing as the blessing it is, because if you don't put those arms straight out away from your body, you won't be feeling anything ever again." With his directions followed, Elias tried again. "What were your plans for my wife?"

"A toff promised twenty pounds each if'n we delivered 'er to 'im."

The price was more than his crew would have received for this voyage. "What toff?" he asked.

"Ah dinnae ken, Cap'n. Ah swear it. Billy, he be makin' the deal in Dumfries."

Elias growled his frustration. "It seems I killed the wrong arse."

Jack's eyes widened as if he saw his death warrant on the wall. "No Cap'n, you dinnae. I can take you to 'em. The spot I ken well."

"Why did you ask me where my wife was? You know bloody well I left the ship without her."

"After you left, Peter brought 'er ashore. We figured ye wanted a fuck."

"If I wanted a fuck," he nearly spat. "I'd go to Hag." It wasn't true. If he wanted to fuck, he would have done what he'd been doing since this blasted mission began. He'd have used his damned hand, not his virgin wife.

"Where's Peter now?" He asked to keep his mind focused on what was important, locating his wife, who was becoming a major hinderance to the job he was supposed to be doing.

Peter was one of the few men who knew Elias's real identity. They were working this mission together, and if he brought Máira to shore, he'd had a good reason.

"'Ee came back without 'er."

"Did you ask him where she was?"

Jack shook his head, another automatic reaction that hurt to his core and back. "'Ee wouldn't answer our questions," he continued. "Said 'twas none of our damned business what ye and yer wife be doin'." He shrugged and then winced when the movement was too much for his broken ribs. "When night fell, we came ashore."

"Then what?"

"We waited outside The Hag. When ye arrived witout 'er, we took ye instead."

Wonderful. Just bloody wonderful.

He'd had some time to waste before meeting his contact, and he'd spent it buying a change of clothes for his wife. She couldn't return home in her wedding dress, it would cause a scandal. He'd had the local dressmaker send the items to the merchant ship Máira was to take back to England the next day. No, that ship left today.

Blasted. She missed her damned ship home, and because he'd been distracted with thoughts of her and had gotten himself kidnapped by these two idiots.

While carting him off, they undoubtedly spooked his contact, and now the mission was at risk. His two *former* crew members were trouble through and through.

"Did Hag know you were part of the crew from the *Maribelle*?"

Jack shook his head with caution, no doubt wondering if his answer would get him shot.

"Where were you going to take my wife?"

"Let me stand and I be showin' ye."

"Ye be telling me, now," Elias replied through gritted teeth.

Jack smirked. "Think not, Cap'n. Otherwise ye be killing me sooner rather than later."

Bloody hell. He'd have to take the arse with him. His damned wife was turning out to be more trouble than she was worth.

Two

Dearest Iseabail,

I am hoping your letter regarding your sister's marriage to Ellison Collins, Earl of Dorset, was written in jest of the disastrous season Máira endured. If you check our copy of Debrett's Handbook in my study, you will find the Earl of Dorset to be an extinct title. The last Earl of Dorset, Lionel Sackville was made the Duke of Dorset in 1720 by King George. The line, however, went no further than his son, when he died in 1790 without an heir.

If these comments were not a display of witticism, please send me everything you know. Forrester should be there soon, and he will track down the blackguard and hang him in short order. I shall be home within the week after this session is complete. Give our little one a big kiss for me—I will deliver yours personally. I cannot wait to hold you both in my arms.

Your loving husband,
Nash

—A letter from Nashford Xavier Harding, Duke of Ross,

to his wife, Iseabail Blair Handcock Harding, Duchess of Ross,
regarding her sister's wedding to the Earl of Dorset

N O.

Máira closed her eyes. Why had she wished for an adventure? She wanted to go home. She wanted tea cakes, and parties. She wanted the ton.

That might be going a bit far, but she wanted her sisters and cold drafty castles. She wanted thistles and blustery winds blowing her bonnet away and her coiffure into a rat's nest.

Okay, no rats. An empty nest. She didn't care, anywhere but here, where the barkeep was suddenly two women approaching her with pistols in their hands and the people around her were fighting as if a dead man wasn't bleeding out onto the floor. She couldn't see straight, her head ached worse than ever before, as she put her hand to it and felt a knot the size of Scotland forming on her forehead. She tried to shake the dizziness away, and then there were *four* women with guns walking in her direction.

She jerked when an explosion tore through her hearing, becoming suddenly mute to everything but an incessant ringing, as smoke filled the tavern and her lungs. Yet for a mere moment, there was only one menacing barkeep starring down at her, and a bloody hole in the back of the dead man next her. Máira coughed, and the motion churned her stomach as she tried to scurry away, more blood staining her dress even further.

The look on the woman's face was pure malevolence, until she surveyed the silent crowd frozen in place around her and began to laugh.

Laugh.

It was only then that the raucous crowd cheered the barkeep like a hero, not a murderer. What world was she living in? Máira clutched her head as the people around her went back to their mugs of ale as if the brawl and subsequent homicide had never occurred. The barkeep closed the distance between them, keeping her bold, territorial gaze fixed on Máira as she stepped on the dead man's shoulder, bent over, and pulled the knife from his face, the moist sound seemingly silent to everyone but her.

The woman was a cold-blooded killer.

She wouldn't have believed it if she hadn't witnessed her walk up and shoot the man in the back while he laid dead on the floor. Was it necessary to kill him twice?

Afraid to move, Máira stood still and waited for the woman to look at anyone...anyone other than her. She had thought her beautiful when she'd first arrived and seen her running the bar with authority. Her cat-like green eyes filled with mischief as she toyed with the sailors waiting for a pint. With those same eyes now scrutinizing her from head to worn slipper, there wasn't a hint of mirth.

"Do you have a problem with Hag's justice?" The woman asked in a heavy French accent, as she cleaned her bloodstained knife on the dead man's shoulder.

There was no humor, no camaraderie, nor a hint of compassion in her question. Nor were there any answers as to how she knew Máira did not speak the native language of the village occupants. Nothing but wariness, and judgement that Máira suspected found her lacking.

She shook her head in response and instantly regretted the move as her head pounded and her stomach lurched, yet she'd been unable to even contemplate a response. Standing in front of the woman she was supposed to seek out for assistance, Máira was fairly certain Hag was the last person she would ask for help, even though she needed help desperately.

Hag turned to say something in French to a huge man on the other side of the bar, and Máira didn't wait for it to translate into murder. More specifically, *her* murder. It didn't matter if the woman had been defending her or had killed the man because he was merely a man in her bar, Máira needed no further proof that hesitation meant death. She was not going to be next on Hag's list for disposal.

Grabbing her skirts, she ran for the door, only to bounce off the stomach of a large, sweaty man entering.

"*Pardonnez-moi, mademoiselle*," he said, as he started to steady her, only to pull back at the sight of her bloodstained dress.

Máira looked over her shoulder and stumbled against the door frame, her head striking the frame and her vision blurred with the pain. When her vision started to clear, Hag was watching her and she didn't wait for her to order the man to grab her. She ran into the bustling streets where merchants were heading home and sailors were heading for the tavern and more unsavory places, where women sat on windowsills and displayed more skin than Máira had exposed to her maids.

Men leered and said things no young lady's tutor would teach a young student, but their meaning was loud and clear, and suddenly Máira knew she was in a bog with little leverage to extricate herself from the muck and mire. Instead, she grabbed her knees and retched in the middle of the road.

God in heaven, where was she to go?

A butcher shop across the street still had its lanterns lit, and she ran for it. She hit the door with a loud thud. It slammed open and into the wall, only to bounce back, nearly striking her in the face. The man inside took one look at her and began yelling in French while pointing a meat cleaver in her direction. His yelling may have frightened her five days earlier, it certainly assaulted her splitting head today, but it was the cleaver that sent her back into the streets, heart pounding, breath coming in short gasps and her head throbbing with so much pain she didn't want to go on.

She remembered her sisters and the pain they had known when each of their parents died. She refused to bring even more tragedy to her family, and tried the dress shop next with a little less force, then the fripperies store, and finally the baker. Each one took one look at her and sent her right back out the door without a *by your leave.* Even the workers had kept their heads down as if she were insignificant.

She should be grateful for the burnt biscuit the baker had thrown in her direction as if she were a dog. She certainly clung to it just as greedily, slipping it into the pocket of her gown to eat after she was safe.

Lost, with her head throbbing and nowhere to turn, she spun in circles in the middle of the street looking for any route of escape from this nightmare. Until a man on a horse nearly ran her over. Stumbling backward across the cobbled stone, she fell on her backside and cowered as his horse snorted hot breath in her face. The cursing rider shook what appeared to be three fists in her direction as he trotted down the street and out of sight.

There were no gentlemen in France.

For all she knew there were no gentlemen outside of Scotland. She certainly hadn't met any during her season in London, and her husband—he was the worst of them all. She looked up to see Hag leaning against the door jamb of the tavern wearing an inscrutable stare. Máira jumped to her feet as a group of unsavory men approached her. The look on their faces was anything but friendly as they smiled and once more tried to educate her into the less savory aspects of the French language.

"Messieurs, c'est parti pour une soirée de divertissement," a woman yelled, and the men looked toward the tavern. Once more she ran when opportunity arose. Her head pounded with every wobbly step she took. Máira glanced over her shoulder to see Hag still in conversation with the sailors, that engaging smile somehow luring them inside without any promise of sexual wares. But it was the sailors coming ashore that made her turn toward an alley next to a closed fish market to hide. The stench of dead fish permeated the air, and she gagged as she slumped against the wall, out of sight.

A cat gnawed on a fish head, and her stomach turned once more at the noises the feline made in its rush to consume dinner before something or someone took it away. Would life ever be easy again? She swore if she made it back to Caerlaverock, she would never look twice at another man as long as she lived. Other than her nephew, of course. A tear ran down her face as she looked up to the darkening sky and thought of her sisters at home spoiling the future Duke of Ross as they gathered in the library.

A violent quake of nausea nearly knocked her on her arse, and she decided to sit before she fell over from the waves of dizziness. Her body then began to shake uncontrollably. Whether it was from cold, fear, shock or the injury to her head she wasn't certain. She needed a plan. Now.

Except she couldn't think. The ringing in her ears hadn't subsided and the drumming of pain to her injured head was beginning to grow louder than ever. She turned and found a drier spot to sit, crawled over and wrapped her arms around her knees. She gasped in pain when she tried to rest her head on her forearms and then turned her head sideways and closed her eyes to quell the nausea threatening to take over once more. Pain radiated throughout her body, and all she could do was close her eyes.

She would rest. Let her head stop hurting and her shoulder stop smarting and her stomach calm. Just close her eyes and let the darkness shroud her with visions of a happier time and place. Just a few minutes rest, and she would find a safe place to spend the night.

A loud crack startled her awake. A horse whinnied and Máira blinked several times before realizing she had been asleep, her face resting on her hands as she lay on the hardest bed of her life. She looked up to find an orange tabby cat looking down upon her.

"Meow."

She blinked again but the cat was still there. She wasn't dreaming but her head felt as if she'd been kicked by a cow. When had an orange tabby shown up in the barn?

She reached for the feline, but it scurried away, exposing her surroundings. An alley. No. *The* alley. No. No. No.

She was home. In Scotland. In the barn where they had horses and kittens. She was not lying in a stinky alley in France. God, the smell. Was that coming from her? It couldn't be, it was awful.

Slowly sitting up, nausea threatened and she touched her head where it hurt most. A fig-sized knot was in the middle of her forehead. Taking in her surroundings, she tried to remember why she was there. Something had happened that sent her running. Broken crates and tipped-over barrels littered the area. Next to her sat an empty barrel that smelled distinctly of fish waste. Hadn't that been full?

If it had, that meant someone had been here, and she hadn't noticed.

Oh. Oh. Fear threatened and she recognized the terror wanting to take control. She checked her person to make sure no one had done the unthinkable. Nothing felt off or different, other than her entire existence. It was the one spot of luck in the entire nightmare. Her head hurt, along with her shoulder and knees, and everything else, but it was her heart that felt bruised and battered.

And her pride. She'd been a fool of the first order. Falling for the first blackguard to speak prettily to her. Misery threatened to take over, until she remembered her sister's final goodbye. *"Remember you are one of the Blair sisters, and we bow to no one, unless we choose to show them deference."*

She would not bend to fear and despair, certainly not to her bawbaggin' husband. A smile threatened and she surveyed her surroundings. She had at least learned some colorful alliterations to toss his way.

The sun would soon be rising—she looked toward the entrance of the alley to gauge the position of the sun. It couldn't be. How could it be setting again, it wasn't possible. It had already set by the time she'd closed her eyes last night. There was no way she'd slept through an entire night and most of the day. Yet the sky was telling her otherwise. Her body was screaming the truth. She hurt everywhere, not just her forehead, and her bladder was talking loud and clear.

The rumble of a cart traveling down the road captured her attention. She needed help and that may be her only opportunity to get—somewhere. She slowly rose to her feet, lest more nausea overtake her, and leaned on the stone building for support. The whistling cart driver grew closer, the melodic tune causing her chest to squeeze with recognition as she stood. Except the closer the wagon got, the more the song caused her back to stiffened. She peered out of the alleyway to watch the cart driven by a farmer stop in front of The Happy Hag.

It couldn't be.

It wasn't possible.

He was a pirate, not a farmer.

Yet he'd been an earl before he was a pirate.

Her Scottish blood began to simmer. The mettle of her ancestors wronged by backstabbing, licentious English bastards was rising to a call so deeply ingrained in her soul, she wanted to fight. It didn't matter her mother was English, she was a Scottish bastard through and through as far as the ton was concerned. One of the *scandalous sisters*. Even Iseabail's marriage to a duke hadn't been able to stop the label from spreading. Máira's good-for-nothing husband had just added to her family's ruination by making her a walking, talking scandal of the worst kind.

It *was* Ellison. There was no doubt. It didn't matter that he wore clothes she didn't recognize, or that a hat sat low over his brow hiding most of his features. It didn't matter that the sun was going down and the only light in town was coming from the windows of The Happy Hag. It didn't matter that she'd somehow slept the night and day away probably due to the bump on her head.

She knew it was Ellison by the tune he whistled and poetical way he performed it. He'd whistled that same tune the night of their wedding. How she remembered that she wasn't certain, but it was him, of that there was no doubt.

He could whistle like no one she'd ever heard in her life.

Melodic, and sorrowful, his song spoke of love found and lost. It spoke to her soul, and she wanted to punch those sinful lips for making her feel anything but hatred.

Máira crouched down low behind the empty barrel that reeked of fish waste and watched as her husband, sitting on the wagon seat, stopped the horse in front of the stone tavern located in the middle of the block on the opposite side of the street.

The dark wood siding of The Happy Hag stood in stark contrast to every other white-washed building in the village. Now, it was the noise erupting from inside the tavern that drew the attention of anyone left on the streets, including Ellison.

She prayed the night didn't end with another dead body.

"The bloody fool is going to get himself killed," she muttered to the cool ocean breeze. She shouldn't care. She didn't care. She wanted to be the one to insert the dagger in his black heart.

She should steal his cart and go...but she was in France, and the only English-speaking people she'd run into were the sailor who tried to share her space under the table, and the man who'd attacked her under that same table.

Then there was Ellison...and the ruthless beauty who'd killed without a care.

Memories of the dead man made her body shudder from head to toe. She should stop Ellison, save him, and then maybe he'd take her home.

Except he'd had his first mate deposit her on shore with nothing. *"The captain said your marriage was a mistake. He was going to sell you to the highest bidder this evening. Go to The Happy Hag. Hag is the pretty redhead who owns the place. She'll make certain you arrive back in Scotland safely."* With those parting words, the man she'd known as Peter had jumped back in the dinghy and rowed away. Leaving her standing on the docks with nothing but a few words that tore her heart in two.

When they'd headed for shore, she'd hoped Ellison was waiting in the village with a bath, a bed, and an apology. She would have stupidly forgiven him. When Peter abandoned her, she'd thought him to be back on the *Maribelle*, avoiding her as he had for the entirety of that miserable voyage. Now, she wasn't certain where he'd been. The only thing she knew without a shadow of a doubt, was that her husband had deserted her, and she wasn't going to risk her neck for a man who had thrown her to French wolves.

The ship, however, was still anchored in the harbor and it remained her only means of transportation home. It wasn't as if she was going to ask Hag for safe passage anywhere. The woman was a merciless killer.

Her heart dropped. Had that been Ellison's plan? To have her gutted by the barkeep in order to be done with her?

She shook the ridiculous notion from her head and nearly lost her balance. It didn't make any sense. Why marry her in the first place if he was just going to kill her? Or had he planned to collect her dowry without having the burden of a wife? If she died, Nash would still owe him her dowry.

She watched as Ellison jumped down from the seat, his feet surprisingly bare. He patted the old swayback horse on the neck and then walked around toward the back of the cart. His hair, no longer tied back, fell loosely on his shoulders and was visible despite the hat he wore. She remembered the one time he'd allowed her to release it from its queue. Ellison had almost looked pained at her request, but when she'd bit her lip and said, "*Please*," it was as if he could refuse her nothing.

In that moment she'd felt powerful. The Earl of Dorset had given in to the request of a mere slip of a girl who'd failed at her first season. And she'd marveled at the thick, luxurious mane that was too long for fashion and yet so entirely masculine in its beauty. It was softer than she'd imagined. The rich chestnut locks felt like silken threads in her hands as the sunlight captured streaks of gold in its length. She didn't think any man could possibly have sensual locks, but her husband did.

Their innocent picnic near the lake had turned into so much

more. Staring up at a perfect azure blue sky, and pointing out bears and cats and chariots forming in the clouds. It had been the most intimate, magical moment of her life when she'd made that request. He'd leaned over and tentatively kissed her, as if he didn't want to frighten her or hurt her. One taste of him, however, and she'd been lost and had pulled him down for more. She'd been brazen, and he turned the kiss into everything she'd ever wanted. When he'd torn his lips away breathless, and asked her to marry him, she knew he'd felt the same.

What a bloody fool.

She eyed him for hints of the real man underneath the facade he'd worn for her. He was tense despite the carefree music he made with those beautiful lips, his shoulders were tight, and his gaze jumped from one shadow to the next. For a moment she could have sworn he spotted her, that his gaze caressed her cheeks the way it had that day in the meadow, but then he turned back toward the cart and pulled a man from the bed, his arms and legs bound.

The man cursed him loudly. The mumbled profanity filled with anger and animosity underneath a gag secured tightly in his mouth. She recognized the prisoner as one of his crew, and she wondered what the man had done to warrant being tied up. Neither one of them looked clean, in fact they both appeared to be rather sodden.

She'd never known Ellison to be dirty...

How would you know if the man bathed in mud or water, you fool? You don't *know* him. You met him less than a month ago and married him. You married a complete stranger.

Who may want you dead.

Yet she could tell Ellison was uncomfortable. He had a restlessness about him that wasn't just from his guarded manner. His clothing irritated his skin and grated on his nerves. Literally. He scratched his arm, his neck, his—she blushed when she thought about what his hand surreptitiously adjusted, then he pulled and yanked at his shirt. His beautiful hair wasn't beautiful. It was drab and matted, if the image she was seeing by the light from the windows could be believed. What had he done to those gorgeous curls?

Ellison pulled his prisoner up to the front door of The Happy Hag and Máira ran across the street to get a better look, her head swimming with each step she took. Her blush-colored wedding slippers were no longer delicate or pretty. Nor did they do a good job protecting her feet on the cobbled streets. Like her dress, they were stained, tattered, and ugly. She looked exactly like the type of woman this filthy version of Ellison would marry.

Yet she wouldn't have cared about the condition of their clothing, if Ellison loved her.

What a foolish ninny.

He didn't love her and she needed to get that silly romantic ideal out of her head. Tomorrow was a new day, a new start to her future. She just needed to figure out a path to get home to that new future. Alive.

Ellison looked back once more. His gaze prowling the streets as if he were searching for someone important, someone like...

Stop it. She was being a child thinking of him in that manner. He was a pirate, nothing more.

The noise from the tavern spilled into the streets as Ellison opened the door and dragged his prisoner inside. When the door closed behind him, it was as if the barrier had silenced everyone within. Máira scurried to the window, the wind chilling her to the bone as it howled through the night. She lifted to her toes and peeked inside. Every face was turned toward the door, watching Ellison and his prisoner. Hag pushed her way through the crowd, a trail of chatter in her wake as she pointed a handgun in the air, the elbow of her gun arm resting in her other palm. This woman was more comfortable with a firearm than anyone Máira had ever known. Her brother-in-law would call her reckless, yet Máira couldn't help but admire the woman's defiant skill.

Her auburn curls were alight with torment, or so it seemed to

Máira. Her eyes were narrowed on Ellison. Her angular face, sporting the fine lines of age, remained expressionless. Máira guessed the woman to be in her forties, but she couldn't be certain. She wasn't quite sure how the woman had earned the name Hag, but it was not because of her looks or her figure. She was beautiful yet hardened by the life she lived. Still, there was a timelessness to her beauty that irritated Máira.

It was either that, or the grin forming on Ellison's face was making her teeth grind. She knew that grin. It was the look Ellison delivered right before he kissed her at their wedding. Máira wanted to cast up her accounts on the spot. Instead, she forced herself to watch and learn.

Ellison said something she couldn't make out, and all the people in the tavern broke out in laughter. Even Hag's lip quirked with mirth, but her response brought back sobriety. Quiet reigned once more.

Blast.

In order to hear, she was going to have to step closer to the door or go inside. She chose moving closer.

With a growl of frustration, she opened the door a mere inch, and pain shot through her shoulder. Even on a good day, when she wasn't hurting from her arm being twisted behind her back, the door was too heavy to hold open. She stuck her foot in the opening, gritted her teeth to bear another source of pain, and listened. They were speaking in French, but after almost a day of wandering through the French village before the murder, the teachings of her tutors kicked in enough to catch parts of their conversation.

"You're still as beautiful as the day I left."

"And you've started bathing in the shite that spills from your mouth."

Ellison was the first to laugh. "I do find myself in need of a bath. Perhaps you could allow me to use your chamber to get out of these sodden clothes."

He spoke French! And not just any French, but the fluent and beautiful French not found in any Scottish drawing rooms. Ellison spoke French as if it were his native language. She couldn't see his face, but she recognized the teasing tone he was using. It did things to a woman's insides. Hag's response brought her focus back to the tavern and the drama unfolding inside.

"I find the thought of you in my chamber dressed as you are a bit repulsive, Elias."

Elias? Who in the world was Elias?

"What happened to your shoes?"

"My boots were stolen by this maggot. He tossed them out." Ellison nodded toward his crew member and things started to make a bit of sense.

Ellison's prisoner muttered something excitedly into his gag.

Ellison, however, was not dissuaded by the other man's interruption. "Perhaps I could bathe first, and we could...*talk* afterwards."

Anger burned deep inside her. She was hurt. Her body was hungry, even if she could not stomach the thought of food. She was thirsty, and she was dirtier than she'd ever been in her life. Not to mention her husband was propositioning another woman, a woman who had cold-bloodedly killed a man in front of her.

She had to admit the man Hag killed deserved to die. He did. She didn't believe she would have survived much longer if his assault had continued. It was a sobering thought. Who knows how many times he would have cracked her head against the stone floor as punishment for her defending herself. Believing he deserved death, however, and seeing the callous disregard for life, were two different things.

Everything she had gone through all boiled down to one event —her marriage to Ellison Collins, and by God, he was hers. Not Hag's, not any other woman on this continent or England or any other place the *Maribelle* took him. Ellison belonged to her as long *as they both shall live*. Period.

She had no doubt about the meaning behind Ellison's words

to Hag or the raspy tone in his voice that she'd loved up until this very minute. Despite her resolve to return to Scotland without a husband, Máira would not allow her husband to sleep with another woman while she was mere feet away.

She stood up straight and pushed her way into the tavern, head held high as if she was a member of court. "No one but your wife will be tending to you tonight, *husband*." She ground out the word *husband* with so much venom, she saw several men back away. Good. They should fear a woman scorned.

Hag's grin spread across her face, bigger and brighter than ever before. Everyone in the room was captivated by what that smile did —everyone except Ellison. He stared at Máira as if she had three horns and the barbed tail of the devil.

"Elias, I'd say your *wife* has different plans for your bath this evening." Hag threw back her head and laughed then retreated to behind the bar. "Drinks are on Elias tonight, gents!" Hag's announcement caused the entire tavern to break out in a boisterous cheer.

Had she heard her correctly or had she missed something in translation?

"Elias?" She whispered, stunned as she searched his face for the truth and came up empty when he wouldn't meet her gaze. Her anger disappeared as her heart truly ripped in two. She didn't care that he wanted to be rid of her, or that he even possibly plotted to kill her. But lying about his name...

That meant he'd lied about his identity on their very first meeting in Dumfries. His bow and the brush of his lips against her knuckles after he'd recovered her dropped parcels. It had all been an act. Their entire courtship, their kisses, his proposal, that romantic moment she thought she'd tell their children, had been nothing but a ruse. A cruel and heartless game she had blindly played to win...and lost.

Three

My dearest Nash,

Máira is gone. She and her husband were to spend their honeymoon month at Drumvermar Castle. My missive, however, was returned with the message that Máira Collins was not in residence. Nor were they expecting her or the Earl of Dorset anytime soon.

The man we've known as the Lord Ellison Collins, Earl of Dorset, had advised he rented the home from the Duke of Braeberry for the summer. He described the castle down to the last stone, and even told the story of the long, beautifully landscaped drive being made specifically for the Prince Regent's visit. He went into detail about how angry the duke was upon Prinny's cancelation of the trip. I suppose there is enough local lore for anyone to learn the details surrounding Drumvermar, but it still vexes me to no end that we were so easily duped by the earl. As I do not know what else to call him, I will continue to address him as Earl, since I can think of no other polite form of address for my sister's husband.

My next step is to visit the registrar and view the marriage license to discern any information I can. It is a long shot, but Forrester and I are determined to leave no stone in Scotland unturned.

Our son misses you almost as desperately as I. Please come home soon.

All my love,
Iseabail

—*A letter from Iseabail Blair Handcock Harding, Duchess of Ross, to her husband Nashford Xavier Harding, Duke of Ross, regarding her younger sister Máira Blair's marriage to Ellison Collins, Earl of Dorset, June 1812*

"Máira..." He took a step toward her, wanting to take her into his arms and erase the horrors she'd experienced in the hours since he saw her last. The way she quickly moved to keep distance between them, nearly gutted him and he stopped before he made her run out the door she'd just entered. "You look as if you fought off the demons of hell and somehow won. Are you alright?" He asked.

The noise she made was decidedly unfeminine and nothing like the woman he knew. Somewhere between a snort and a growl, it was attached to a sneer that only hatred could form. "I'm breathing, if that's what you're asking."

"Breathing?" Holy bloody hell. What had he done? He was going to kill Peter and every one of his crew for not looking out for her. "I meant, do we need to fetch a surgeon?" He spoke softly, as if that would keep their conversation private in the middle of a tavern with every eye and ear observing them with avid curiosity. If he were lucky, only Hag, her henchman, and Jack spoke English.

"Are you worried about my reputation? My virtue? My life? Or are you worried that I still stand on this green Earth?" Her hand rose to her chest in a display of mock distress. It succeeded in drawing every eye in the place to her damned feminine curves.

He glared at the men around him, some looked away sheepishly, others didn't care. They would look their fill unless he challenged each and every one of them. In his current condition, he didn't think he'd be able to survive one fight, let alone ten. He felt almost as bad as she looked.

He'd never expected to hear such bitterness in her voice. Anger and regret for their marriage, yes, but this was something so much more than that. It was deeper and filled with anguish and betrayal and despair...and hatred. His heart jumped and screamed and drummed the beat he'd always heard in her presence from the first moment he laid eyes on her. This time it pounded on the drum harder. She was beautiful—and broken. He had done that.

He moved toward her, but she backed away once more and he winced at the pang her mistrust caused. "What happened to your head?"

"You." Venom dripped from her voice.

"Me?"

"The condition of my lovely gown, my perfectly coiffed hair, and my dainty slippers, along with this knot on my head and the nausea I can't seem to control are all thanks to you." She delivered the last three words as if each one was its own separate punch to his gut.

"Let me take you to a room, and I'll fetch a surgeon."

She laughed as if the situation called for humor. "Do you want to share our marriage bed now?" Her voice held a fighting spirit he'd not known she possessed, as she cocked an angry brow at him that only made him want to throw her over his shoulder and toss her into a bath where he could soothe all her aches and anger away. She was even more appealing than the fresh-faced innocent who'd furiously blushed when he'd first brushed his lips on her knuckles. It was the last thing he needed to notice.

"No. I want you to remove the layers of shite you're wearing as if it were part of a trousseau." The sparkle in her eyes died, the light no longer glimmering and he knew he'd hit the target that would stiffen her spine. Because even if he could win her back, he couldn't have her. He cleared his throat and turned to the woman he'd come to see as he pushed the bound and gagged Jack forward. "Hag, if you would be so kind as to take care of my friend while my wife and I have a word. In private."

"Does that involve me bathing and tupping him?" Hag asked, as she lifted her chin in Jack's direction. Returning the conversation to French pleased the crowd, who broke out in laughter. Hag only tupped one man. She had a few private meetings in the back with others, but never of a sexual nature. Those meetings were strictly business.

He sweetened the deal. "I'll throw in an additional barrel of Scotch."

"You'll throw in five extra barrels of Scotch." The crowd whistled and Elias rolled his eyes.

"Three and not a pint more."

"Done. Would you like him cleaned up and fed? That will cost you a pound."

His headache wanted to split and multiply. He'd had enough with difficult women. A pound for food and bath? He wouldn't be paying that much for his own comforts and Hag knew it. She was rubbing salt in the wound she sensed the moment Máira walked through the tavern door.

His gaze traveled to the beautiful blonde standing with her back to the doorway, wounded and nearly broken. She braved his observation without realizing the danger her position posed. A hunted man wouldn't stand in front of an open door in the manner she had adopted. Máira, however, didn't have an inkling about the hidden perils of the world she entered. Her vulnerability was even more evident by the way Jack looked at her, the same way every other red-blooded man in the place did. They were cataloging her assets, from her plump lips to her long neck and the delectable twin mounds of flesh he wanted to devour, while completely ignoring her filthy hair and attire. Every man in the tavern wanted his wife the same way he had the moment he set eyes on her. Except he wanted to catalog her injuries and soothe her pain. While Jack wanted to douse the fire in her lovely eyes then turn her over to Billy's business partner.

For that look alone, Elias put his foot in front of the man and gave Jack a shove. Máira stepped forward in a futile attempt to catch the bastard, but was too late to stop his fall. Jack twisted his body mid-air, in time to keep his nose from hitting the floor. The muffled grunt he released caused Máira to flinch and a few men in the bar to raise their glasses to toast the nasty bugger's predicament.

She turned on him, eyes flashing as if she suffered the same brutality. "Do you think treating a member of your crew with violence will earn my trust?"

"You don't understand what he wanted to do to you."

"The same thing you wanted to do to me?"

He snorted. "Not even close. I was defending your honor."

Máira looked down at her torn and soiled dress, then lifted a limp curl from her shoulder. "You do it well."

His guileless bride didn't understand Jack's evil intent, nor did she appreciate Elias's manner of defending her honor.

He ground his teeth. She was sizing him up like she had never done before, and he had to school the anger seeping through the facade of polite concern he'd worn since the moment she'd walked into the bar and he'd seen her battered face. She knew warm-hearted, polite Ellison Collins, Earl of Dorset, not Sir Elias Drake, ruthless killer, spy, and recovery agent for the Crown.

As a knight, he would be accepted in some circles of *ton*, but as an earl, all levels of society would open their drawing room doors to him, and they had. Máira had been ripe for the picking from day one. She'd been innocent before she'd met him, desperate to prove she was good enough to wed a member of the *ton* of her choosing. She had been the perfect mark. Again, his chest pinched, but he ignored it.

He turned and addressed the woman he hadn't seen in several years. "Pour a pint down him and he'll be happy in the cellar. Mind you, Hag, don't give him an inch. He'll put a knife in your back the size of Gibraltar."

Hag shook her head. "I've never seen Gibraltar."

"Nor have I. What is it?" Máira added.

It figured Máira would seize the opportunity to bond with Hag. That was the last thing he needed. "It's a large pointy rock neither of you want buried in your back."

"I believe I had one put in my back while I naively stood at the altar in my family's chapel." Máira's voice was calm and matter of fact.

Hag smirked. The men in the area who continued to listen out of boredom, snickered. They couldn't possibly understand what she'd said, but her tone, and the expressions passed between her and Hag were enough for them to understand Elias was the object of their ridicule.

"I deserve your rebuke and more, but I will not discuss it here."

She eyed him as if she were thinking about how to put something sharp into his back. She was entitled to her rage, but so was he.

"Let's go, Wife. I'm in need of a bath." He wouldn't tell her about his need to ensure that she had not been hurt in more ways than he could see. Elias walked toward the steps where Hag had rooms for let.

"Not in one of my tubs, Elias."

He turned around and Hag was still smirking.

"What is that supposed to mean?" He asked.

"It means there's a trough out back you need to use first. Once you've rinsed the stench off your person, you can take a flowery bath with your wife. She may need one more than you." She walked around the back of the bar and began serving her customers once more, and the man named Thomas took control of Jack.

Máira inhaled sharply, her lips pressing together.

"It's taking all of your self-control not to give her a scathing retort, isn't it?" he asked.

"If she wasn't correct, I would, but days of being violently ill onboard your ship with nothing else to wear has taken its toll on my attire. Not to mention the assault I suffered, the murder I witnessed, and the night I slept in an alley."

Merde! What had he done to her?

"Oh, and the items you purchased for passage on the ship were dropped off here," Hag yelled from the bar.

"Here?"

"The captain of the *Confiance* said he had no use for the shite. By the looks of things, I'd say she does."

The cornflower blue dress he'd purchased for Máira wasn't the height of fashion, nor would it fit her as well as her own clothing he'd left behind in Dumfries. It was for a fresh-faced country girl who welcomed picnics from the man she was falling in love with, and the moment he saw it, it reminded him of the day he'd proposed.

He hadn't meant to ask her that day. The picnic was a prelude to a chaste kiss he'd planned to place on her cheek before he'd returned her home. The next day was to be the proposal, but the fresh-faced girl who'd secretly met him in the meadow wearing a simple blue dress, had given him a taste of everything he didn't want—a responsive, passionate, virgin bride. And the blue dress he'd purchased in the shop across the street, had been meant to symbolize her new beginning—a beginning so much different than the day he'd altered her life in a meadow with a kiss neither would forget. Her, because it had been her first. Him, because he'd never wanted anything so much in his life, and he hadn't even known just how much until their lips met.

He tossed the memory out of his thoughts. It would do him

no good to reflect upon the bond he'd destroyed, because her butter-cream gown looked like aged, moldy cheese now. "Is that dried blood staining the front of your gown?" He stepped toward her, intending to grab her arms and scour her body for any hint of injury. The flare of his nostrils, however, reminded him of his own stench and it forced him to search her person from a distance.

"It's not my blood." Her voice was flat, as if any emotion she'd felt had been extinguished, but her eyes looked haunted.

"Whose is it?"

"The man who indelicately adorned my forehead with a knot the size of our Queen's most beautiful amethyst brooch. My jewel, however, should never be worn by the Queen. On anyone other than myself, it'd be garish at best." It was the type of response he would have expected while in conversation with a man.

"No woman should have such a gem."

"It sounds as if you find it valuable."

"Valuable in a sense that the person who gave it to you should pay with their life."

It was the slow blink of her left eye as her vision clouded and she no longer saw him standing in front of her, that nearly undid him. He wanted to wrap her in his arms and whisk her away from this awful time and place he'd created. An act of mercy he couldn't perform for many reasons. So, he did what he did best and maneuvered her forward with cold hard words.

"Is he dead?"

She lifted her gaze, and it flashed to Hag before it landed on him. "Yes."

"Good."

She slowly nodded in agreement, not quite certain she believed him.

"If he weren't already dead, I would kill him with my bare hands. It would not be the quick and painless death, as I suspect he received."

Her lips quivered and once more it took every ounce of

willpower he possessed not to capture her in his arms and make her forget.

"What happened to your shoulder?"

Hag interrupted before Máira could answer. "While you were playing around in horseshite with Jack, she was fighting your *friend* for her very life—in here."

"It happened here?" His gaze swung from Máira to Hag then back to Máira.

"A man grabbed me during a fight in here yesterday. Hag killed him."

His eyes shot to the barkeep, even though the movement made it feel as if the bullet was traveling through his bruised brain. "You killed him? My friend I was going to meet?"

"I did," Hag said. "He won't be meeting you anytime soon. Not unless you visit him in the unmarked grave in the cemetery. He had nefarious intentions and he was knocking her head against the floor as if he was pounding down the gates of hell to drop her inside. I threw my knife and then finished him off by shooting him."

"The gun was a bit overzealous," Máira added.

Hag shrugged. "I had to be certain."

His contact had attacked his wife, then Hag had killed him and disposed of him.

"Thank you, but why didn't you keep her here?" he asked, because he was incredibly grateful she had stopped his *friend* from hurting his wife further.

"She took off as if those gates had opened up and the hounds of hell were chasing her."

And now his mission was in jeopardy. A month ago, he would have been furious. At the moment, he found himself relieved Máira was safe. She was safe, yet still in more danger than he'd ever realized.

Directing his attention to Hag he asked, "Do you have a razor? I want to shave my head."

"What?" Máira gasped. "You can't shave off your hair."

"Whyever not?"

"Because I lov—" She stopped as if she couldn't bear to finish. She *loved* his hair. She'd confessed that fact on multiple occasions, and he had to admit, the one time he'd released it from its queue for her to run her fingers through had made him as hard as the Rock of Gibraltar.

"If you try to shave it while it's..." Her nose wrinkled as she carefully chose her next word. "Dirty, every cut, nick or scratch will cause a fever."

"What are you talking about, Wife?"

Máira scowled at his use of the word 'wife.' "I don't know what it means, but I have found dirt in a lesion on a cow can become red and enflamed. Sometimes the cow even gets a fever and dies."

"You work with cows?" Maybe he didn't know his wife as well as he thought he had.

"I did, back on our nursemaid's farm."

"And now you're comparing me to a cow?"

She lifted her chin and spoke to him as if she were an authority on the subject. "There are several similarities between people and livestock."

Oh, this he had to hear. "What other similarities are there, Máira?"

Her cheeks stained pink, as he knew they would. "What cows will do while filthy, I will not."

He couldn't help his laughter. "I wouldn't dream of touching you while covered in shite. After my bath however..."

"I will wash your hair, but that is it. I do not want to be married to you, but I don't want you to die, either."

"Why is that?" he asked, knowing he shouldn't.

"Because you're my only way back to Scotland!" She nearly stomped her foot and he grinned. He really liked this fiery side of her.

"Hag, could you put the clothes I bought for my wife in our room? And I could use a change of clothing and shoes as well," he asked, without releasing Máira from their locked gaze.

"That'll cost ye another barrel of Scotch."

He bit his tongue. She was trying his patience, when all he wanted to do was get a bath and then touch Máira to ensure every bit of her was okay. "Fine," he muttered.

"You bought me clothes?" Máira asked.

"Yes." It was his turn to be embarrassed, except he was so filthy, no one could tell.

Her tone softened. "When?"

"Yesterday." He frowned trying to get the time back that was lost to him. "I think it was yesterday. When I came ashore."

He didn't want her to soften toward him. It wasn't safe for either of them if she did. He needed to send her back to her family at Caerlaverock. Untouched. To do that, she needed to believe him to be a scoundrel of the first order.

He inserted a bit of crassness in his question by grabbing himself where he never had before in the presence of a lady. "Now let's get to that bath, shall we? I find myself in need of my wife's attention."

She stomped past him toward the back door, but her body swayed a bit as if she, too, had trouble keeping her balance after the beating she'd received.

He pretended good humor and winked at the lads in the tavern who cheered him on. After all, a beautiful woman was going to give him a bath...how could he not enjoy that?

"Ow! Bloody hell, woman, you're going to kill me."

"If I was going to kill you, I would have hit you harder and you'd be dead instead of whining."

"Are you sure I'm not dead?"

"You smell as if you were."

She tossed the scrub brush into the water. He ignored it as he grabbed the back of his shirt and pulled it off over his head. The wet shirt landed with a splash at her feet.

Máira jumped back with a squeak. "You did that on purpose."

"I have never been accused of being a good sport."

She snorted. "Of that I have no doubt." She tried not to look at his broad shoulders, which were unfashionably sculpted in a manner to make a woman swoon. On board the *Maribelle* she'd been too stunned to truly take note of all the dips and valleys defining his musculature. But now...now she had to swallow the lump in her suddenly parched throat. She'd seen farmers in nothing but trousers as they worked in the fields and stables on particularly warm days, but none, and she meant *none*, had been built like Ellis—

Elias. She dumped another bucket of water over his head and refused to watch the rivulets caress his muscular back as he sputtered.

Elias pushed the filthy water out of his eyes and glared at her. She crossed her arms over her chest and jutted out her hip, a smirk of satisfaction lifting the corners of her lips.

Then she froze when he reached under the water and started unbuttoning the falls of his trousers, all the while watching her.

"What are you doing?" she asked, her voice sounding ridiculously breathless.

"Getting undressed."

"You can't do that here!" she hissed, her composure completely gone.

"What is the point of taking a bath if one doesn't get naked?"

From his tone, it was evident he was getting quite a laugh at her expense. She wanted to hit him with the bucket, but thought better of it. She still needed him to get home. So, when he lifted almost completely out of the water to remove his trousers, Máira turned her back.

He'd betrayed her and their vows, she needed to remember that.

His pants sloshed to the ground at her feet and she jumped. "What are you doing? You're getting disgusting muck on my gown and slippers."

"This way I know you'll take a bath as well."

She stomped the filth from her feet. "I planned to bathe and burn this dress. But I hardly want the rot you're covered with on me."

"Ah, so we will have our honeymoon after all."

"Alone! I'll be taking my bath *alone*."

He chuckled. It was that sound she absolutely adored. The throaty vibration traveling deeply through his chest. She closed her ears, eyes, and heart to the sound. "It is my understanding that if one participates in a wedding ceremony under a false name, the wedding is not binding."

He stopped laughing. "I wrote down my legal name on the church registrar."

She turned around so fast, she nearly stumbled into the bath with him. "I would have seen that!"

His smile was a bit sad. "I distracted you."

She let her memories come into focus...standing in the back of the church, ready to sign the register, feeling the happiest she had in her entire life, Elias had kissed her, repeatedly as if he couldn't stop...and she realized Elias was speaking the truth. Ellison had lied during their wedding, but Elias was not lying now. He had distracted her in the most sensuous manner. His hand had tickled her backside as she'd bent over, and she'd nearly jumped out of her slippers. As it was, her own signature was less than legible when she was finished. Elliso—Elias had been talking to the vicar about the renovations to the chapel at Drumvermar, all the while his hands were casually positioned behind his back...and on her. He looked innocent to everyone but her—and Iseabail. Her older sister had caught a glimpse of the entire thing and that had only served to make Máira blush further. Luckily, her other sisters and the vicar had not seemed to notice. If they had, none of them had been brazen enough to quirk a brow in her direction as Iseabail had. And after signing, she had never again looked at the register.

"You sir, are a rat."

"A rat you like to kiss."

"A rat just the same."

"We're married, Máira. It's legal."

"It's not."

He gave her a sad smile again, as if she were a delusional wife who needed to be institutionalized. Dear Lord, was that his plan?

As if sensing her unease, he replied. "It is legal, but I will ensure you receive an annulment." Elias continued to scrub his body and then dunked his head under water and scrubbed it hard.

When he came up, she asked, "Why the subterfuge?"

"I needed a *wee bonnie lass* of a wife to prove my business intentions were honorable."

She scoffed. "You wouldn't know honor if it slapped you in the face."

The candle flickered in the warm breeze. "I kept you safe and pure for six days, did I not?"

"You kept me locked in a cabin!" An emotion she refused to recognize made her voice raise an octave.

"Or you could say, I kept everyone else locked out. Considering Jack, in there, had a bounty on your head. I'd say I did you one helluva favor." He nodded his head in the direction of the tavern.

She froze. A bounty? She had a bounty on her head? Whatever for? "You're lying."

"I'm not."

"Then why did Peter convince me to run from you and then immediately dumped me ashore with no way home?"

. . .

He looked up at her, his face devoid of expression except for a tick in his jaw she'd never seen before. No, that wasn't completely true. She'd seen his jaw tick with anger that first day aboard ship when she'd staggered up to the deck and discovered her husband was a pirate captain. This look, however, was something much more dangerous. It was deadly.

Four

My lovely wife,

Unfortunately, I have nothing good to report. I contacted the War Office about our imposter of a brother-in-law. Sir Williamson had little information regarding the earl, as a matter of fact, he departed without divulging anything more than what we had already known—the title expired in 1790. His manner seemed...a bit guarded. The more I ponder our exchange, the more I suspect he knows more than he shared.

I also met with the Duke of Braeberry, who assured me his country estate was not available for let, by an earl or anyone else. He was so concerned, he left for the country with a gaggle of footmen immediately after our meeting.

I'm sorry I was unable to discover more. After meeting with Braeberry, I hired the best Bow Street Runner in the business, Mr. Johnathan Payne. He came with the highest of references when I was attempting to locate you last spring. He found you; however, Edward discovered his investigation first—and paid him off. I do not resent the man for that mistake in judgement, as I am unsure of where the two of us would be now had we met under different circumstances. I have no doubt I would have loved you, yet I fear your love for me may not have flourished the way it did. Because of that, I will give him the benefit of doubt. If he double-crosses me again, however, I will have his head.

I will do everything in my power to bring Máira home safe and sound. If need be, I will secure a husband for her. My dear friend Astley is in need of a bride. He and Máira get along very well and are constantly conspiring to bring your sister Caillen out of hiding. He will make the best of husbands for Máira, and as an earl, he can minimize the scandal.

Please do not fret, dearling. I cannot wait to hold you and our son in my arms once more. If I am delayed next week, it will be due to following a lead to bring your sister home safe and sound.

All my love,
Nash

—A letter from Nashford Xavier Harding, Duke of Ross, to his wife Iseabail Blair Handcock Harding, Duchess of Ross, regarding her missing sister, Máira Blair Collins, Countess of Dorset, or Mrs. Máira Blair Drake, or the ruined Miss Máira Blair

H e would kill Peter. No, that was too good for his first mate. He would draw, hang, and quarter him. Watch as the man's blood stained the decks of the *Maribelle* as a lesson to any man who put his wife in danger. That was the punishment for treason.

Except he'd married her under subterfuge, and he had no doubt her family wouldn't recognize it as legitimate, despite the Duchess of Ross and four of her sisters attending the ceremony. Damnation.

He had assumed the loyal, incorruptible Peter had been over-powered by Jack and Billy. Caught unawares at worst. But betrayal? It was like one's brother turning around and stabbing you in the heart—the one place you allowed in only the few who were deemed worthy. Peter had been one of those people for the past ten years. They had gone on mission after mission together, saved each other's worthless necks countless times. It made no sense.

It was the last bit that made him pause. He stood up in the trough, naked as the day he was born, and Máira's eyes nearly popped out of her skull before she squeezed them shut. He did notice she only did that *after* she took a long look at the part of him that longed to be buried deep inside her.

His lips quirked. He couldn't have her, but the urge to corrupt her drove him to distraction. He grabbed a horse's blanket from a peg on the mews wall and covered his lower body. "Tell me every-thing that happened after I left the ship yesterday morning." His voice was calm and devoid of emotion and brooked no argument.

"Peter told me he was taking me ashore to help me escape, but when we arrived, he left me in the street with no means to find passage home."

"Why would you think you had to escape?" He'd had no plans of hurting her or placing her on shore in France. He had every intention of transporting her directly to the *Confiance* and return her safely home.

"I don't know, maybe because you turned out to be a pirate, who treated me as a prisoner. Then when he told me you planned to sell me—"

"Sell you!" Damnation. Every part of him wanted to believe she wasn't telling the truth.

She nodded and warily continued. "Once we were at the docks, he said I should go to The Happy Hag and ask to speak to Hag."

Frustration simmered through his body, threatening to send him into a rage. His pounding head kept his voice low. "Why the bloody hell would you believe such a story and not create a scene for me to hear?"

She bristled at that. "Because you were the reason I was imprisoned on a pirate ship to begin with! Who or what was I supposed to believe?"

Elias grabbed her wrist and pulled her toward the kitchen's back door. Máira squealed and attempted to drag her heels in the mud. He lifted her up and tossed her over his shoulder then picked up his gun and dagger. Hopefully he could secure Máira safely upstairs in a locked room before any further violence erupted.

"Ellison—Elias! Put me down!" She pounded on his back in time with the pounding in his head. It was as if she could hear it, too, and wanted to make godawful music to torture him.

"Be quiet, Wife. Or everyone will hear us going through the kitchen to the back stairs and know exactly where we're going. Unless you feel safer with the men in the bar knowing exactly where you are?"

He could almost hear her thinking as she pondered his question, wondering which path was the safest one to choose. He breathed a tired and thankful sigh of relief when she chose not to fight him further and entered the kitchen.

The cook looked up from the stove and stared.

"Send the maid up with enough food for the two of us. Then my wife will need water for her bath. We'll be in Hag's room. She was good enough to offer it up, seeing as how we're newlyweds."

"*Oui, monsieur.*" The cook didn't bat an eye at his request. She did ogle his naked chest and legs that dripped with water with each step he took, until her eyes snagged on the cockstand he couldn't hide. The bloody thing had been wanting his wife for too bloody long. He winked and the older woman grinned, her sagging cheeks turning the slightest bit pink before she turned back to her stove.

He felt a pinch on his backside and couldn't help but laugh at the minx in his arms. "There will be time enough for that when we get to our room, Wife."

She pinched him harder and his cock responded in kind, as he thought about her bare hands on his buttocks, nails biting into his flesh while he drove into her tight, sweet cunny. If his head wasn't splitting, she would be in danger of losing more than the filthy clothes she wore. As it was, all he wanted to do was take another bath and fall onto a mattress. Any clean mattress would do.

It was the lie he kept telling himself. His traitorous cock, however, was the only honest bone in his body.

At the top of the stairs Máira spoke. "Hag won't be happy with you taking her room."

"It will be *us* taking her room, not me."

"Same thing."

"Not even close. If it were just me, she'd shoot me."

"Like the man she shot yesterday?"

Her question spoke of fear and shock, and so much more that a gently bred woman should never be forced to endure. Yet he could tell she wanted him to believe she was as comfortable with their conversation as she would be if they were discussing the weather while she lounged in her library doing needlepoint. She deserved more truth than he could give her, and knowing that only caused the pang of guilt to squeeze harder.

He would make certain she was safely returned to her home, but it was up to Sir Williamson to repair the damage to her reputation.

Elias looked down the darkened hallway and listened for any source of danger among the other guests. Normally he stayed in the first door on the right. Since he was taking Hag's room he went in the opposite direction, to the left. Once they were inside, he could slip the drawbar into place, sealing the heavy wooden door like a medieval castle. If they needed to escape due to the tavern being under siege, or Peter bringing troops to take them into custody, the drop from the window would be soft enough to survive without breaking a limb. To climb into it, however, would take a man with the capabilities of a spider.

At Hag's room, Elias made his way inside, kicked the door closed and set Máira down on her feet before turning to slide the heavy drawbar into place. He lit a candle and glanced around the room. "Hag has been doing very well for herself as of late."

The bed was large, with a deep luxurious mattress and bedding made of the highest quality linen and deep burgundy silk that glistened in the dim light of the fireplace. In the corner near the window was a screen hiding a copper tub fit for a queen, or at least a duchess. The ornate desk and chair on the opposite wall of the bed was as opulent as the furniture sold out of the Palace of Versailles, and Elias wondered if Hag had bartered for the piece the same way she had maneuvered him out of more Scotch whisky. He walked over and checked the desk drawer but found it to be locked. It wouldn't take much to break into it, but he couldn't do it without destroying the drawer and lock which would defeat any attempt at stealth. If it were any other mission, he would take his chances. Discovering Hag's secrets, however, was of personal interest, not the Crown's.

A table and singular chair sat next to the fireplace. He stared at the scene and imagined the small, stern redhead, capable of killing a man in cold blood, eating alone while looking out the window into a back garden that hadn't been tended to in a decade. He, of all people, knew Hag had chosen this life for herself, but it still didn't make it any less tragic.

Shaking off memories that threatened to engulf him with melancholy, Elias pulled the desk chair over to the table and offered it to Máira. "Have a seat. As soon as our food arrives, we'll eat and then you can take your bath."

She nodded and did as she was told, which spoke of how hungry and tired she had to be. "Start with yesterday morning and tell me everything that happened to bring you here tonight."

She sighed. "As I said, Peter came to my cabin after breakfast. He said we were going ashore, but I had to hurry and be quiet, lest one of the crew saw us and reported my escape to you."

"Report your escape? He said he was helping you escape—*me*?"

"Yes."

His teeth ground together. "Continue."

"When we got ashore, he helped me out of the dinghy and told me to go to The Happy Hag. He said you would be at the tavern later that evening, so I should not lollygag around if I wanted get transportation back to Scotland before you arrived. I was to tell Hag I was your wife, and she would help me get passage on another ship."

That was true. It would take some work on Hag's part, but she would get it done and then charge him the price of his ship for her help when he came into the tavern in the evening. But Peter knew he was going to meet the captain of another ship before his meeting at The Happy Hag. He had made arrangements for Máira's trip home first thing when he'd come ashore.

"What time did he bring you ashore?"

"It was seven o'clock. I know, because my meal arrived promptly at half past six every morning I was on the *Maribelle*, and several of the crew were awake."

"I had left the ship by then and was already making arrangements for you to be on a ship home this morning."

Her blank stare said she didn't believe him. He didn't blame her. His first mate would have no reason to lie to her. Even he couldn't see a reason why Peter would fabricate such a story. Why had he circumvented Elias's plans? Had Peter known he'd been kidnapped?

No. That couldn't be. Jack and Billy had thought he'd hidden Máira somewhere in town, so Peter had left the ship with Máira prior to Jack and Billy kidnapping him.

He needed to speak with Peter and find out if the mission was in jeopardy, then kill him if treason was the reason for his deception. "Did you make your way directly here?"

Máira shook her head, attempting to hide the fatigue a young lady of society was not allowed to display, the back of her hand covering her yawn. "No. There was a group of questionable men going into the tavern at the time, so I decided to walk down to the market and see if I could find anyone there to help me."

Elias didn't want to think of the danger she'd been in while walking around the seaside port. For the most part, the town was safe—for men, but when sailors came ashore, anything could happen to a young woman walking alone.

A sharp rap at the bedchamber door caused Elias to draw his pistol and cock it before answering. A tavern maid about the same age as Máira stood there with a tray of meat pie and a pitcher of ale. She took one look at his bare chest and her grin grew saucy. The twinkle in her eyes and the proposition on her tongue were a thing of beauty. Not as pretty as his wife, but if he weren't a married man, he'd be damned tempted to invite her for a tumble. As it was, he smiled, winked, and opened the door wide enough for the maid to enter.

The maid and Máira were a dichotomy of womanhood if he ever saw one. Whereas the maid was tall, thin, and graceful, dark hair and eyes to match, her experience in the bedroom was obvious in every single movement. From the pout of her mouth to the way she walked across the room with the food and ale, her hips swaying in a manner to catch a man's eye. Máira, on the other hand, was as innocent as the day she was born. Blonde, blue-eyed, petite, dainty, with feminine curves that drove a man batty. Her jealous fire as she watched the maid set the tray down and then walk to the door made him harder than he'd ever been before.

Of course, the maid noticed his condition, licked her lips and winked. "That will be all," Máira said and gave the door a kick to slam it shut.

"That was rude," he teased.

"You're married. Remember?"

"But the lady was enjoying the view."

"The *lady* will have to enjoy other views downstairs."

He shouldn't enjoy her jealousy as much as he did. She was not his to keep. He would not ruin her, as much as he wanted to. He should take what the tavern wench obviously offered, but he wouldn't do that, either. He was married, even if it was in name only. He had made vows to Máira he would keep until the annulment was procured. He owed her that much, and more for taking advantage of her the way he had.

Again, his chest twinged, and he rubbed it to make the blasted feeling go away. Then the aroma of the meat pie hit him, and his mouth began to water. "That smells like heaven."

"You know what heaven smells like?" she asked, mockery lacing each word as she stood at the wash basin cleaning her face and hands.

"As a matter of fact, I do." He said the words the same way he'd said them during their wedding, full of meaning and genuine sincerity.

She froze for a moment, hiding any expression behind the cloth she'd used to dab her cheeks dry as her eyes connected with his in the mirror. Then she turned around and glared at him. "Don't. You've already made a mockery of me. Don't act as if it meant something."

He nodded and gave her what she needed to hear. "My apologies." Then he moved toward the table and took a seat.

She didn't need to know he'd meant the vow from the moment he spoke and looked into her cornflower blue eyes during the ceremony. He'd had to tell himself countless times their marriage wasn't real. He couldn't have her in the manner a man bedded his wife. Their marriage would be his first, and his last. She would be his only bride. A man like him had no business subjecting a woman to his life. One day he might not come home, and no one would visit his wife to tell her why. If she went in search of him, contacted shipping company after shipping company, none of them would know the captain she believed him to be. Even if one day she stumbled across the crew of the *Mari-*

belle, they would respond as if he never lived and she a candidate for Bedlam. They would make her believe she was a mad woman searching for a ghost. He would just cease to exist and she wouldn't know why.

No, he would not leave that fate to any woman or child the way his own father had. It was only a stroke of luck that he'd learned of his father's fate.

As she filled his plate with the best-looking meat pie he'd seen in ages, he said, "Thank you." It took everything he had to remember his manners and wait until she was seated—his stomach, however, wasn't as polite. It growled as if it caged a magnificent beast.

The corner of her mouth quirked. "Go on, eat your food. Don't fret about your manners and I won't worry about mine. I feel as if it's been a fortnight since I ate."

"When did you last have a meal?"

"I had a biscuit last night."

"That's it?"

"Yes, so you better eat up before I eat it all myself." She grinned and filled her fork with the biggest bite he'd ever seen a lady take.

He joined her with a monster-size bite that made hers look like it was a wee bitty bite for a faerie. He grinned at her, stupidly enjoying this time as if it were a memory they would share for a lifetime—instead of a memory he would cherish alone.

Elias folded his hands across his bare stomach which didn't look at all like he'd just consumed large quantities of food. It was as flat and rippled with muscle as it had been prior to their meal. How did he consume such mass quantities of food and still look the way he did? It was beyond comprehension. She felt as if she might roll out the door, down the steps, and go splat.

"It's time, Wife," he said.

"Time for what?" she asked, her stomach completely content. Her nerves, however, were bouncing off the walls. She couldn't look at him. He was too tempting. Sitting next to her gorgeous and well-formed husband, while he wore nothing more than a horse blanket was more enticing than any dessert. The young miss in her wanted to squeal...the lady in her took bite after bite of her meal while not tasting a thing. She needed the nourishment for what life threw at her next.

"For your bath."

She nearly sputtered. "I'm not taking a bath in the same room as you!"

He grinned. "It's my right as your husband."

"It'll be your bloody damned death!"

He smirked at her profanity, and she wanted to throw her ale in his face. The knock at the door saved him. How dare he act as if they were on their wedding night! Elias—the name suited him she thought, much better than Ellison. Elias Drake, the Earl—blast him! Was he an earl? He'd tricked her into marrying him, so why wouldn't he have lied about his title?

Her glass smashed against the wall next to the door before she even realized she'd thrown it. Elias flinched, but opened the door to two boys carrying a pair of buckets, each full of steaming water.

Her husband said something in French to the teens that sounded very much like, "My wife will be needing a broom to clean up the mess I made." Then he winked at them as if they understood how things were between men and women.

The boys laughed, then looked at her angry face and cast their gazes downward as they made their way to the tub. They knew Elias hadn't broken the glass. It was obvious to everyone and sundry that she had lost her temper. She had let the drama of the afternoon get the best of her and allowed Elias to turn her into a shrew. She wasn't a shrew. Yet she'd acted like one. Everyone at The Happy Hag thought she was one. And she strongly suspected they believed her husband was the man to tame her.

She closed her eyes and took several calming breaths, counting to ten as she did with her youngest sister in the midst of a tantrum. She didn't need taming. She was the calm sister. The one to soothe and heal the surliness between siblings. Yet somehow the man she'd married brought out the worst in her.

"If you could bring my husband some clothes, that would be wonderful. He would like to go down and have a drink with the men while I freshen up." She smiled sweetly at the boys. Elias would not win this battle. He was not going to use the lack of clothing as an excuse for staying in the room with her while she bathed.

"*Nous ne parlons pas anglais.*" The oldest bowed his head to her when he finished emptying his buckets into the bath.

"*We don't speak English.*" Of course they didn't. No one in the blasted village did. She'd used a similar phrase countless times in the past twenty-four hours. Máira closed her eyes, searching for patience to find the proper words in French. She'd studied the language as a girl, but the only conversations she'd ever experienced in French before this nightmare of a honeymoon involved fripperies, bonnets, and gowns.

She repeated her request for clothing in a choppy mixture of English, French, and a language she'd obviously created from the look on the boys' faces. Her French had gotten better since landing on shore, but her request was as foreign to her as it was to them. The older of the two, who couldn't have been more than fourteen, nodded as if he understood. Elias stood at the door, his arms crossed over that gorgeous chest of his, his face a mask of humor as he watched her struggle.

"Your French isn't bad," he said, after he closed the door behind the retreating servants. "Although I think you would prefer I wear a shirt and trousers, not a night shirt." He grinned that devilish smile that could melt the drawers off a seasoned courtesan, and she wanted to hurl another glass in his direction. As if sensing her temper about to boil over, he took another tack to gain the upper hand. "Could you see if Hag has a pair of socks I could put on so I don't cut my feet."

"Of course." She searched through the wardrobe and found one pair of mended men's socks, and she suddenly wondered if he knew they were there because they were his. Determined not to show how the discovery affected her composure, she grabbed them, along with a chair so he could sit to put them on.

"The chair wasn't necessary, but I appreciate it."

"You're welcome."

They sounded like strangers. Before their wedding, conversation had always flowed freely between them, yet now it was as if everything they had in common prior to exchanging vows, never really existed, kind of like Ellison Collins.

"Are you an earl?" She asked,

"No."

"No?"

"No."

"No. That's it. You're not going to expand on that and tell me why you lied to me?"

"It's the same reason I told you my name was Ellison Collins. In order to complete a business transaction, I needed a Scottish wife and a title. The gentleman would only deal with members of the *ton* with Scottish brides. Rather a short-sighted fellow, considering how few members of the *ton* marry Scottish ladies. My decision to lie about my identity was strictly business."

She tried not to flinch, but his words stung. While she had been falling in love, he had been calculating a business deal. She could have been any of her sisters—no, that wasn't true. Her two youngest sisters were too young, Iseabail was married, and Caillen was at the country home of Simon Clark, Earl of Astley, visiting with his mother and sisters. That left Máira or Ailsa. She asked herself if either of them would do, or if it hadn't really mattered as long as he snared a Scottish bride in his trap.

"Why not the blacksmith's daughter?" she asked, and he

looked pained. *She* was pained. He could answer her bloody damned questions.

"A gentleman of the *ton* would require a lady."

"Why me?"

"Why not you?"

"Because I'm one of the Blair bastards."

"I didn't know that."

"And if you had known?"

"I would have chosen you anyway."

"Why?"

"Because you dropped your package."

His response stung, but not any more than knowing she was part of a scheme to buy Scotch. "I was convenient."

"Convenient and too beautiful to pass by."

Oh, how she wanted to believe that. "Do you have a title?" Her drive to prove to the *ton* that Iseabail's marriage was not a fluke, that the Blair sisters belonged in society, had been her real undoing.

"No. Sorry."

He didn't sound sorry. He sounded like the whole scenario was an inconvenience, to him and no one else. It was a prevalent trait of the *ton* she despised. "You're a mister?"

"No, I'm a knight of His Majesty's kingdom. Sir Elias Alistair Drake, if you please. Of course you are a lady, as my wife."

"Well, I suppose it's better than being a butcher's wife."

He winced and refused to meet her gaze.

There was something in that evasiveness, that gave her pause. "Are you a butcher?"

"Of course not."

"But—" she prompted.

"My father was, before he met my mother and moved from his home to take up her family trade."

"What trade was that?" She asked.

"It's irrelevant now."

Wonderful. She'd wanted to help her sisters on the marriage mart this season, not hurt them, and now they weren't just bastards of a businessman who lost his home to a gambling debt, but they were sisters to a charlatan who happened to be the son of a butcher.

They wouldn't be able to secure marriages in Covent Garden —thanks to her.

If she had remained a miss, waited for her second season, and allowed Iseabail and Nash to work their love-match magic on the *ton*, her sisters could have been a success. Except Iseabail and Nash's marriage had been tainted with scandal, and this would only further it. Plus, her sister Caillen had eloped, only to find herself a widow within the week of her marriage. She had not returned home since. The scandal sheets had run out of fodder to print on the tragedy. The article, *Baron Buried After Eloping with a Blair By-blow*, had been a society favorite in the rag sheet *Whispers of the Ton*. It had been unseemly, especially since Caillen had eloped prior to Iseabail's marriage to the Duke of Ross.

Elias downed his ale when another knock sounded at the door. The same two boys brought in four more buckets of steaming water and emptied them into the tub. Elias spoke quietly to the eldest, and she was almost certain the boy had said something about his size had made finding appropriate clothing difficult. Elias would have to wait a bit longer for them to find suitable clothing. She was so preoccupied with thoughts of bathing while her husband stood by and watched, it barely registered when a maid entered the room and swept up the broken glass.

Elias tossed a coin to each boy and they left without another word.

"They said they haven't found any clothing for you."

"Correct."

"You can't leave this room while I bathe." Even to her ears, her voice lacked inflection.

"No." In that moment, she believed he wished he could leave.

"Move the screen in front of the tub. Then position yourself at the opposite end of the room."

He bowed his head and did as she requested. Never once flirting or behaving in an untoward manner as he moved the screen, picked up the chair, and crossed the room, where he sat down and crossed his ankles, his long legs jutting out into the room. "When you are done, I will finish my toilette."

He should look ridiculous sitting there wearing nothing more than a horse blanket wrapped around his waist. It did absolutely nothing to hide his masculine prowess. She wasn't certain anything could hide the hard planes, the lean sculpted muscle and sinew, once a woman was exposed to them. She also didn't believe a real gentleman would be that comfortable dressed as he was in front of a lady. Yet she was his wife, and as his wife she would see everything...

Looking at his strong muscular thighs barely hidden from her view reminded her of him suddenly standing up in the trough behind the tavern. The lighting had not been the best, but it had been good enough. Naked as God intended him to be, Elias was glorious. In that moment she swore it was not the serpent that tempted Eve, but rather Adam himself, because when she caught sight of the power of Elias's manhood, stiff, strong, and proud, her body had instantly readied for what a man and woman did on their wedding night.

"A penny for your thoughts?"

Máira looked up and caught her husband grinning. He knew where her thoughts had gone.

She was a virgin, but she was far from ignorant when it came to bed sport. Her sister Iseabail might be the Duchess of Ross, but she had made certain Máira understood everything there was to know about what happened between the sheets and otherwise. The best of the *ton's* courtesans could not have gone into their professions with a better education than Máira had going into her wedding night. Yet her marriage was not to be. Elias said he would return her to Scotland untouched, just as she wished.

"You can tease me all you want, Husband, but I know you want me." She nodded toward his blanket.

Elias's grin grew. "A man's body reacts to a woman's, just as a bull reacts to a cow."

She snorted. "Fine."

"Fine." He repeated her words, but his tone was much different. Whereas hers had sounded pinched and succinct, his drew out with humor.

It was quite annoying.

"I need help with my gown," she announced to the room at large, unable to look him in the eyes. If she'd been looking at him, perhaps she would have been able to discern if the hitch in his breath was her imagination, or if it came from a man who knew his limitations when it came to touching her.

"Come here."

She did as she was told, her body aching for his touch with each step she took, which was ridiculous. He'd betrayed her. Lied to her. Used her for a business deal. And made fun of her. He did not want her the way a husband wanted his wife. He might want her the way a man desired a whore, but she was no whore.

He pulled in his legs as she approached then twirled his index finger around to indicate that she should give him her back. The chair creaked as he stood, and her body warmed with the heat of him. She remembered how hot his body was to the touch, so different from her own. Now she could feel the outline of him heating her to the core, and imagined his thighs pressing into her backside and his cock brushing against the upper cleft of her buttocks. She closed her eyes when his nimble fingers finally touched her gown and she swore his breathing increased as much as her own. She wanted his lips to caress her neck, trail a path to the pulse point that betrayed what he did to her.

"Done," his voice rasped a whisper into her ear.

She nearly moaned before she realized what he'd said. *Done.* He had finished unbuttoning her gown while she fantasized about his body joining with hers.

She hurried behind the screen, too embarrassed by her reaction to his proximity to care if he sensed how he flustered her. Heart pounding, she pulled the front of her gown down and flushed at the thought of being naked with him on the other side of a taut piece of linen...

"You can't see, can you?"

"The shape of your breasts as you pull your gown down over your shoulders?"

Her breath hitched. There was only one way he would know that—

He chuckled, deep and sultry, a sound that vibrated through every erogenous point of her body that she wanted him to touch. "No, Máira, dear. I am just quite good at painting a picture in my mind."

"In your mind?"

"Didn't you explore your fantasies as a child? Walk into the stables as if it were the palace itself and have every man fawning for your attention?"

No, she'd dreamt of helping children be born so that mother's might live, of healing broken souls so that fathers struck with the tragedy of losing a spouse might be able to go on for the sake of his children. Death and grief had broken her family, and her sister Caillen was suffering again due to the loss of her new husband.

If she had been with Caillen and her beloved, maybe she could have saved him after highwaymen had left him beaten and broken, with a gunshot wound that never healed. If she had been there, perhaps she could have kept his fever at bay and brought her sister joy, instead of the heartache and sorrow Caillen could not seem to escape long enough to come home.

Of course, Caerlaverock was Iseabail's home, not the Blair

family home, but Caillen would have been surrounded by sisters, not strangers.

"Tell me what you dreamed of," she said, as she stepped out of her gown and then her undergarments. Her stockings were riddled with holes and her slippers could never be repaired. She had planned to save her wedding gown, cherish it as one of the happiest days of her life. Its current condition, however, made it more appropriate as a symbol of the miserable state of her marriage; it was in shambles and was never meant to survive.

"My dreams were of a more lascivious nature."

Her skin flushed. "As a boy?"

He laughed. "I don't remember any of my boyhood dreams. What I recall are the dreams I had as a young man."

She stepped into the hot bath and had to catch herself from moaning. "What dreams do young men have?"

He laughed at that, and again she felt it vibrate through her body as if he were with her behind the screen, touching her.

"Do you really want to know?" He asked his voice barely above a whisper.

"Yes." Máira grabbed the bar of soap and began scrubbing her arms. "I find the differences between men's and women's wants and desires fascinating."

Five

Dearest Nash,

We have discovered the most distressing news. Máira's husband is not Ellison Collins, Earl of Dorset. He signed the church registry as Sir Elias Alistair Drake. How this slipped by everyone until now is beyond my comprehension, except to say that Elias Drake is a conniving blackguard of the first order. I'm not even certain that is his true name. He could be anyone at this point. My fear for Máira's safety is compounded by how easily Caillen was duped into believing her husband married her for love, not her dowry. Have I failed yet another sister?

Please come home with the utmost haste.

All my love,
Iseabail

—A letter from Iseabail Blair Handcock Harding, Duchess of Ross, to her husband Nashford Xavier Harding, 8th Duke of Ross, regarding her younger sister Máira Blair's marriage to Ellison Collins, Earl of Dorset, or rather Sir Elias Alistair Drake, July 1812

F*ascinating.* His wife found his desires fascinating. That's what he'd heard...it wasn't, of course, what she'd meant. It was an innocuous statement of a naive young woman who'd been sheltered away from men like him. He shouldn't indulge her, or more to the point, he shouldn't indulge himself, but temptation was too great not to give in to just a taste of corrupting her.

"My favorite fantasy as a young man was one where I stumbled upon a virgin taking a bath." Damn, but he could use the cup of ale sitting on the table at the other side of the room. It taunted him with one more pleasure out of his reach.

"Really? What would you do?" Her voice didn't sound aroused, but rather amused and somewhat curious. While he sat on the other side of the room, unable to touch her, see her, with his cock standing tall—demanding attention. He pulled the scratchy blanket away from his body and allowed himself to tell her exactly what he wanted.

"I would come home from a long ride, dreaming of the most beautiful young woman I'd ever seen, with hair the color of golden wheat blowing in the wind."

"Wheat?" She choked. "That's a terrible description of a woman's hair. It's coarse and brittle."

"Close your eyes and imagine the bigger picture. Field after field of it, swaying in the breeze, a sea of silken threads of amber, cream, and honey, the rich sun causing a glow of cascading waves flowing down her back."

When she said nothing, he continued.

"I open the door to my room, and she gasps, shocked by a man interrupting her most intimate moments. Yet she's in *my* room— surely, she had to know I would come in."

"What if she didn't? Would you be a gentleman and leave?"

He laughed softly. "This is my dream, Wife. You asked what young men dream about."

"But if it really happened. Would you behave as a gentleman should?"

He rolled his eyes. She was attempting to derail his fantasy. "Of course, I would back away and beg her pardon. While I savored the memory and prayed the view would be burned onto the inside of my eyelids until my dying day."

"Scoundrel," she muttered.

He couldn't help but laugh again. "Are you telling me you wouldn't treasure the memory if a handsome man walked in on your bath?"

"No, I would not! I would be mortified."

"You're lying, Wife."

"I do not lie."

"Everyone lies. It's human nature to lie. To make oneself more appealing in the eyes of others. Did you not just lie and say you wanted me to leave, when deep down you wanted us to share this intimacy?"

The water splashed in angry waves, yet she said nothing, and he let the silence linger in the air between them.

"Fine. Is that the end of your dream?"

If she had been able to see the smile spread across his face, she would recognize the satisfactory gleam of the cat not only catching the mouse, but devouring it. He had no doubt, however, that his voice conveyed the message clearly with its husky undertones.

"Hardly. Would you like me to continue?" Please, let me continue.

"If you'd like. It matters not to me."

He let her admission slip away, because he wanted to share this fantasy he would never allow himself to experience with the one woman who'd inspired it. "Our eyes would meet, and her cheeks would turn a gorgeous color of country rose, just like the flowers blossoming at Caerlaverock. Wild and free, but cultivated into the perfect shade of a desire she could not deny."

"I didn't know you were a poet."

"A woman's body can turn any man into a lyricist."

"Hmmmm."

That noise alone would turn a priest's cock hard. Good God, this was torture. "I should probably stop. I do not wish to corrupt you." It was the biggest lie told to date. He wanted to corrupt, debauch, ravage. Bury himself deep into her body over and over until the lust between them had run its course.

He could not.

"Do not do so on my account. I have been well-versed on the happenings between a man and a woman."

Something like jealousy sprung to life in his chest. What man had dared to educate his wife? It wasn't as if he believed she should be virginal—experience would make their first time together less worrisome for both, but still...jealousy burned.

"She would not hide her beauty as that blush traveled down the feline curve of her neck and collarbone, only to disappear into the water of her bath. I would not follow that blush despite it being my every desire. Instead, I would gaze at her face. Shy, yet eager. Apprehension in her eyes, as she watched me close the door and turn the key. The snick of the lock securing us together. Alone.

"I would walk over to her and take the soap from her hand. Of course, she would attempt to hide her luscious curves and gasp in shock and perhaps a bit of fear. I would soothe her nerves as I enticed her body. Running the creamy bar of soap over her shoulders as she covered her breasts from my view."

"What if she didn't want your attention? What if she wanted you to leave?"

He paused for a long moment. "I would leave, guard over her while she finished, and never see her again." Was that what she wanted? To never see him again?

"And if she wanted you to continue?"

A slow smile spread across his face as her voice became breathy. She wanted him as much as he wanted her. He had known she wanted him while they were in Scotland. Once they boarded the *Maribelle*, however, it had been a completely different chapter in the story of their relationship. He'd been uncertain, until now. "I would dip the bar of soap in the water, brushing the tips of her breasts, now budding with need. The water would caress her, encircle her sweet tips the way I wanted to tease her with my tongue, but I wouldn't because she wasn't ready."

The slosh of the water in her bath was driving the fantasy, pulling him in so deep, he had to encircle his cock with his fist. He had no choice but to embrace the need coursing through his veins. He stroked up and down as he listened to her wash. Imagined her taut nipples peeking above the water line, begging to be touched. His jaw clenched at the image he painted in his mind, his cock hard with a drop of his pleasure seeping from the tip.

"Her skin is as soft as a rose petal, and I can't resist kissing the nape of her neck exposed for me to devour." He could hear her breathing, her effect on him almost too much to bear. "I would put the soap in her palm and cover her hand with my own, guiding her to rub the smooth bar in circles around her breasts. Moving closer toward the center with each turn, making her wait for the soap to trail over her where she wanted it most and when it finally touched her pebbled nipples, she gasps in pleasure. Her back arching, pushing against the soap as she yearns for my touch just as much as I crave to caress her.

"Are you touching your nipples, *mo ghaol*?"

The water stopped licking the edge of the tub as if she'd frozen. He cursed his use of the Gaelic term of endearment, praying it didn't freeze her as well. When he'd first used the translation for *my love*, he had done it to woo her, and it had worked. Since that day, however, it was always on the tip of his tongue when he thought of her. Not that he loved her, he couldn't do that, but if he'd had the freedom to choose a woman to spend the rest of his life with…he would let his heart travel where it wished. There was no doubt it would lead to Máira.

He continued, hoping she would as well. "Feel how they reach for my touch. Distending, demanding to be pleasured. Do it for me, Máira. Touch yourself. Pleasure yourself. Give in to the ecstasy your body needs. As you stroke one breast with the soap, roll the nipple on other between your thumb and index finger. Swirl around the tip, pinch it, learn what makes you lose yourself to the bliss of sensation."

His cock ached. Burned to be buried deep inside her, especially when he heard the feminine moan on the other side of the screen. Bloody hell this was torture.

"What would you do next?" With her question, he knew she was in as much misery as he.

"Let me show you." He was going to hell. He swore he wouldn't do this, but Máira, she needed this as much as he did.

"Promise me you won't look."

"I promise." He spoke almost as fast as a child being told he could have cherries if he ate all his carrots. He wanted her cherry with everything he was made of.

"Alright but leave the candle over there."

"As you wish." He picked up his chair, stopped by the table to take a fortifying drink of ale and walked to the screen, leaving his blanket behind. He wanted her to see him, know how much he desired her, but trust that he would not ruin her. He walked to the screen, inhaled deeply and exhaled before he joined her on the opposite side. Her back was to him, her blonde tresses down around her shoulders as she glanced at him and gasped.

He closed his eyes. "I'm not unaffected by you. I think you're quite lovely and you will make some man a wonderful wife. I want you, but I won't do anything without your consent, and I will not ruin you."

"And if I want to be ruined?"

He shook his head. "I am not the marrying sort."

The smile in her voice was sad. "Just the lying sort."

"Exactly. I am being honest when I tell you I will return you to Scotland with your maidenhead intact."

"Thank you."

He nodded. "May I open my eyes to sit down next to the tub?"

"Yes."

Her arms covered her breasts from his view and her knees were bent obscuring her sex, just as he had described in his fantasy. "You are the loveliest thing I have ever seen."

"Th-thank you, but you weren't supposed to look."

He bit back a smile and looked at the floor. "Of course. Forgive me. I have always found you entirely too diverting."

He positioned the chair behind her head and spread his legs wide around the tub, almost as if he sat in the tub with her and the view became too tempting by far. He meant to steal a glimpse of the top of her breasts, but the bruising covering one of her delicate shoulders snared his attention more strongly than a trap could hold a wild boar. His hand was immediately drawn to it.

"Does it hurt?" he asked as he lightly traced the hues of blue and purple adorning her skin. "Can you wash your hair?" He was suddenly quite certain her injury would not allow her to raise her arms easily if the deep colors marring her flesh were any indication.

"No, I was going to ask the maid—"

"I'll do it."

"Do you know how to wash a woman's hair?" She looked over her shoulder and he quirked a brow at her question, then shook out his own hair.

She let out a self-deprecating laugh. "I see." She grinned and handed over the soap.

"I need you to scoot down and dunk your head."

"Of course." She disappeared under the water and when she came up, her arms were no longer covering her breasts, and she rose much higher than she'd been before. Elias tried not to look, he really did, but he was a starving man being tempted with cherries —bloody cherries. He wanted to eat all night long.

He cleared his throat. "You might want to sink down a bit. I need my eyes open for this part."

"Oh." If the lighting had been better, he would have probably compared the color of her cheeks and chest to be the color of his favorite fruit, but they were both saved from that imagery by the candle flickering on the other side of the screen.

He lathered the soap working the creamy foam in between his fingers before handing the bar back to her. He stopped a moment, uncertain if he could trust himself to touch her and not take her.

"If you would rather I ring for the maid—"

"No. If I did that, our status of newlyweds would be put in question."

"Oh." There was a pain in her voice, and he suspected she misinterpreted his hesitation.

"I'm trying to get my body under control. You are the worst kind of temptation."

She stiffened. "The worst kind?"

He squeezed his eyes closed. "That's not what I meant. What I meant to say was, it is very hard not to touch you in other ways."

"But you said you would show me, and I said you could show me."

"I've changed my mind. That's not something I can do and maintain the proper distance between us. But I will wash your hair for you."

"I see," she said, as she lathered up a sponge and began rubbing it across her nipples.

He hesitated, his gaze glued to what she was doing.

"I don't want to leave you with cold water."

He needed the cold bath. His body demanded it...or satisfaction. One or the other. He wanted the other. He couldn't have the other, dammit.

"I will make it quick." He put his hands in her hair and immediately regretted not calling the maid. He'd washed his own hair plenty of times. The feel of long hair sliding through his fingers should be nothing new, but he'd never washed a woman's hair before and somehow this was much more intimate than he'd imagined. She pressed her head back into his fingers, making little noises as he massaged her scalp, and he found himself hoping that bar of soap in her graceful hand would travel lower.

Those thoughts sent him straight to hell. He didn't know how she knew, but her hand circled her navel and the slight indentation of her stomach. He shouldn't watch, he told her he wouldn't, but he'd also told her he was the lying sort, so when her hand went to the swell of her hips and down the outside of her thighs, he watched every stroke.

"Do you mind if I lean forward to wash my feet?"

He cleared his suddenly parched throat. "No." It was all he said, the only word he could force past dry lips, and as she bent forward to scrub her toes, he looked his fill at the globes of her of arse. It was truly formed for male hands, not small and tight, but round and full, sending all kinds of erotic images into his head. Bending her over and spreading her cheeks wide as he stroked her forbidden entrance and buried his cock deep in her sex. Pumping in and out of her, thrusting his thumb into the forbidden rosette as she cried out in pleasure.

"Are you done washing my hair?"

The mocking tone of her question shattered the vision. He brought his gaze up and found her smirking at him over her shoulder. She was a minx, through and through. He liked that about her. Loved the dichotomy of innocence and vixen that belong solely to Máira.

"Lean back, *mo ghaol*."

She did so with her little smile in place, and her hands covering her breasts from his view once more. He rinsed her hair, keeping the water from the delicate features of her face. He traced the arch of her brow with a wet thumb, ran his index finger down the length of her elegant nose, to her prominent cheekbones and around the elfin curve of her chin only to focus on her plump bottom lip. She nibbled on his flesh, and he could see his cock disappearing between those luscious lips.

She was so bloody beautiful he felt as if he could hear angels singing sonnets to her. Certainly, there had to be birds chirping, stars falling, men dreaming—all in hopes of being close to her. Bloody hell! He sounded as if he were writing a love ballad.

He finished rinsing her hair and helped her sit up in the bath, averting his eyes from every delectable curve he wanted to devour. "I'll get your linen." He walked around to the other side of the screen, his legs feeling like leaden weights as he paused and let his head drop forward. He thought of guns and swords and bloody wounds to make his cock relax. Nothing worked.

He interlaced his fingers behind his neck and looked to the heavens for assistance. The angels weren't helping either.

"Elias?"

"Yes." His voice was as strained as his control.

"Were you getting my linen?"

"Yes." He grabbed the white linen folded on the dresser and returned. Holding it up in front of him, waiting for Máira to step out of the tub and into the towel. In another place and another time, he would dry every curve, stroke every plane, and tease every nub until the only moisture left on her body was from their mutual desire. With that in mind, he switched places with her and pushed her to the other side of the screen. He'd wanted her to see how much he desired her, but now, he needed to escape her curious gaze, because in the depths of her scrutiny, were the embers of lust he wanted to ignite, yet needed to extinguish.

Instantly he stepped into the tub and sank in the water, wetting his head and shutting out the noises of Máira on the other side of the screen. When he came up, he reached for the bar of soap and found her on the chair he had vacated.

"What are you doing?"

"I'm going to wash your hair."

He scoffed. "I'm not injured."

"No, but you spoke of shaving it off because you didn't think you could get it clean. I am here to make certain that you don't shave it."

"Most ladies of the *ton* find my hair unfashionably long."

"Most ladies of the *ton* are fools."

He couldn't help but laugh. Despite her desire to be a part of society, Máira held most of them in contempt, as she should. He lathered up the sponge and handed her the soap, but whereas her bath had been slow and sensuous, he made sure his was quick and perfunctory. Scrubbing his body to near pain and not allowing her to luxuriate in his locks or massage his scalp. When it was time to get out of the bath, he waited for her to put on a borrowed night rail before taking the towel and drying himself off on the opposite side of the room divider as her.

"It's time to get some sleep," he announced. "We have a long day tomorrow. You can have the bed and I'll take the floor."

"Don't be ridiculous. I felt the lump on the back of your head the size of a goose egg. We'll both sleep in the bed."

"No," he argued.

"Fine. Then I'll sleep on the floor with you," she fired right back at him.

"I could tie you to the bed."

She grinned. "I didn't realize you were into that."

Jesus H Christ, he'd just got his cock under control, but images of her being tied to his bed—naked—well that was enough to make a man of the Cross go hard. "Tonight we can share, but not again." He could make it one night without touching her, couldn't he?

She had one night to see him, all of him, and no matter what the cost, she would see her husband the way she should have seen him on her wedding night. Not just his face in repose, or his...his cock in the shadows, but in all its glory. She would see the part of him that was made to pleasure a woman beyond her imaginings. The part that stood strong and proud at that very moment, proclaiming his manhood as it tented the towel he wrapped himself in, like a steeple on a church.

How many women had prayed to his steeple? Yet there he lay on the top of the covers, spread out on his back, arms resting under his head as if it didn't bother him in the least. Iseabail had said a man became hard when they were aroused, and Máira didn't think he would have been able to hide that all the time they'd spent together before they were married. So how did he sleep? Didn't it drive him to near insanity? The embroidery on the nightdress she was wearing was driving her nipples mad with the rise and fall of her chest. She dared not breathe, which made her wonder how the towel felt on the tip of his cock.

Her curiosity won out. She had to see all of him basked in light of the moon, not hidden in the shadows. He was her husband, and if she never experienced this again, she wanted to remember Elias as the man who loved her—even if he felt only lust, she deserved that much.

"Are you awake?" she whispered.

His breathing stayed steady and strong and she took the opportunity to pull the coverlet back and slowly rise from the bed. Her feet silently hit the floor, and she peeked over her shoulder to see if he'd stirred. Finding him unmoved, Máira tiptoed to the foot of the bed and froze when the floorboard squeaked. Heart pounding in her ears as loudly as her little sister banging on the pots in the kitchen, she held her breath while she waited and watched for any sign of movement. When she reached the silent count of twenty, she breathed a sigh of relief and continued around the footboard to his side of the bed where the light of the full moon illuminated his entire body.

She marveled at the curly strands of hair falling across his fore-head. Even still wet from his bath, she wanted to twist it around her fingertips. She let her gaze caress his prominent cheekbones and aquiline nose that contradicted his strong jaw, showcasing several days of whisker growth. She allowed herself to study his statuesque shoulders and broad chest, marveling at masculine growth of hair covering the contours of muscle and sinew. Her breath hitched as he moaned, and her gaze darted to his closed eyes as he shifted his leg out from under the bed cloth covering his lower body.

Even his large foot appeared strong and capable and oddly alluring, but it was the part of him that remained covered that she was curious to study. Where hair from his navel traveled downward as if paving a walkway for a woman's fingers to travel to his—cock.

Just thinking the word to herself made her cheeks fill with heat, or perhaps it was because his cock still stood tall and proud despite him sleeping.

Did it hurt? She couldn't imagine suffering something so uncomfortable while sleeping. She had seen his manhood twice now—the first time, she'd been too shocked to even know if she'd seen what she'd thought she'd seen. The second time when she'd been sitting in her bath, she'd been too embarrassed and averted her gaze. Now, she wanted to see him completely before it was too late.

It was her right as his wife, by fraud or by manipulation, it didn't matter. If he could use her in such a manner, then she had every blasted right to discover everything she possibly could about the male form. About his form. Glancing at his face to ensure he still slept, she carefully lifted the bed linen off his impressive cock and exposed him all the way down to his other foot.

Her breath hitched and became ragged as she examined him with wonder. They would never...ever fit. Even now, it seemed inconceivable that those powerful hips, defined by the V-line of muscle leading to his slim waist, could drive into her with so much force and cause no pain. He would tear her in two, and if she somehow survived, she would be so sore, walking would be difficult. Yet knowing all of that, even now her body prepared to take him just the same. Dampness built between her thighs, and her nipples hardened with anticipation.

When his hand stirred, she nearly yelped, then stood rooted to the floor as his long slender fingers wrapped around the thick base of his cock and stroked. He made a slight noise as if he was in pain and her gaze flew to his face, but still he slept. She watched as his hand moved up and down his shaft, squeezing and pulling until a small bead of moisture appeared at the tip.

She had seen the images in one of Iseabail's books of a woman's mouth over a man and the sudden urge to experience that very act, drew her closer. He smelled fresh and clean and something indescribably masculine that made her want to taste him even more. With another glance at his face to ensure he slept, she lowered her lips, paused once more as her breathing increased and then licked the pearl of moisture from the tip of his cock. He was salty and delectable, and a sigh of pure pleasure escaped her mouth. His hand hesitated, his body stiffened and she nearly ducked down behind the bed, until he resumed his stroking up and down his length. She lowered her head once more and took the tip of him into her mouth and nearly groaned with the sensation. His supple skin was smoother than anything she'd ever felt. It teased her senses, and she immediately thought of iron wrapped in rose petals. Elias's own analogy described his most intimate part.

Tentatively she explored him with her lips and tongue. Kissing and licking, she found his clean, masculine scent utterly intoxicating, making her want more and more. She encircled the head with her tongue, then lowered her mouth further and further, imitating the action she'd read about in the book. His breathing grew ragged, matching her own, and his cock jerked in her mouth. Suddenly he was grabbing her hand and placing it where his had been.

She glanced up to see if he was truly awake, but his eyes were still closed, his lips still parted as if she wasn't exploring his body in the most intimate way possible. With his hand covering hers, she wrapped her fingers around him and moved them up and down, following the motion with her mouth, and a groan escaped his lips. He released her hand only to grip the knot of hair at her nape as he guided his shaft deeper into her mouth, and his hips began to thrust upward as he forced her head down. She gagged once, and he eased the pressure on the back of her head, but not enough to allow her to pull away.

She didn't want to pull away. Something about this man had awoken a taste for carnality within her. She was lost in the passion and desire he alone had stirred to life. Wanting to give as much as she took, she swirled her tongue around the ridge, stroking the pulsing vein with the tip of her tongue before she flattened her tongue to take in the entire length of him. Again, she gagged, but found if she breathed through her nose, she could take him in deeper.

A low growl vibrated through his chest, and she moaned in response. She caught a glimpse of his other hand wrapped in the bedding and knew he was close to his pleasure. This entire act should shock her, instead it enflamed a desire to please him.

Her sister had wanted her to go to the marriage bed with knowledge, not blindness, and they had talked and discussed for hours. Iseabail had given her several books to read, and Máira had ended up with more education about sex than most married women of the *ton* experience in a lifetime—yet still, she remained untouched.

Máira cupped between his legs and gently squeezed, exploring every inch of him. A shiver went through his stomach muscles, he gripped her hair harder; controlling her movement, he thrust into her mouth, and she sucked in a breath. The motion seemed to drive his need out of control and his cock pulsed in her mouth. She sucked him harder, not knowing what to expect until thick cords of liquid shot to the back of her throat forcing her to swallow again and again, his salty seed spilling from her lips as he released her hair and his arm flopped over his eyes as if it had all been too much to bear.

A heavy sigh escaped his lips, and it was as if he never woke. She smiled. He wasn't the only one who could drive the other beyond the brink of control to exhaustion. She went to the wash basin and grabbed a clean cloth. After cleaning her face of the evidence of their sins, she returned to the bed and washed his body.

His cock was still long and thick and somewhat firm, but it lay against his thigh as if it too were completely satisfied. This was how she wanted to remember him. In her mind's eye she drew his form, strong and powerful, raw and replete.

"Thank you, Elias," she whispered, and lay down next to him and fell sound asleep.

Six

Dearest wife,

I know you are extremely concerned about Máira's safety, but I do have a bit of good news. I gave Mr. Payne the information you obtained from the registrar. It seems our brother-in-law is quite famous in the spy business; he is also known to be a gentleman. I can only surmise that he was on a mission and needed a wife, or he truly did fall in love with your lovely sister. It is not out of the realm of possibilities. I am not making excuses for his lies—we can only hope that he included Máira in the ruse from the beginning and that she is seeking an adventure as most young people do.

I have an appointment with Mr. Williamson day after tomorrow and will demand answers. I have no doubt he knows more than he let on in our first meeting and I vow to obtain the answers you require.

Please do not fret so. Our son needs you strong and healthy. I have only been able to make it through this wretched session because I know you both are well and he is in your hands. I am

*counting down the days and the hours until I hold you once
again in my arms.*

*You own my heart,
Nash*

*—A letter from Nashford Xavier Harding, Duke of Ross,
to his wife Iseabail Blair Handcock Harding, Duchess of Ross,
regarding her missing sister, Lady Máira Blair Drake, and her
scoundrel of a husband Sir Elias Alistair Drake*

Bloody hell. Where had a virgin learned to do that? She hadn't been an expert by any means, but she'd taken his cock all the way down her throat. Only the most experienced courtesans had been able to tolerate his size before tonight. She was the first virgin he'd ever—he'd never even touched her. He'd kissed her. He'd washed her hair, and he'd watched her touch her breasts, but he had never touched her. Fuck. He wanted to return the favor, but he couldn't. If he tasted her, he would take her virginity and then what would he do? What kind of life would he force her to live? A life with a husband who was never home and had very little to his name.

She deserved much better than he.

And he had a job to do. An important man to rescue. He'd already lost two days and his informant was dead. He looked over at his wife. His beautiful, giving wife who even slept with a smile on her face. He wasn't sure what to do with her. She'd missed her passage home and there wouldn't be another ship heading for England until he commanded the *Maribelle* back—or it left without him. Sailing these waters was dangerous, they were at war after all. For a woman, they were doubly so. Most of the men on those ships couldn't be trusted with pirated cargo, let alone someone as precious as Máira, with her cerulean eyes that turned the color of midnight in her passion.

Experiencing the change in her eyes as heat flared in her body had been one of the greatest gifts of his life. He didn't want her to lose it, despite his selfish need to be the only man to witness the transformation. That need, however, came secondary to her need to live a full and happy life. Even now as she lay next to him, her hair glistening in the moonlight as if sprinkled with angel dust, he couldn't imagine himself with any other woman.

His thoughts were dangerously close to ballads again. The woman was bloody dangerous without even lifting a finger. Elias got out of bed and did the only thing he could—he wrapped himself in the bed linen he'd discarded in the night, since he was loath to put the dirty horse blanket around himself again, and headed downstairs. He needed Hag—it was either that or go utterly mad about moon dust.

Elias made it out of the room and down the stairs without waking his lovely wife, and found Hag sitting at the bar, sipping a whisky with her back to him. The tavern was completely empty except for her loyal guard, Tomás, leaning against the doorframe to the kitchen. He'd never understood their relationship, but Tomás was always there, watching over her, taking care of the riffraff who inevitably came ashore from the ships. It was the one thing which puzzled him about Hag shooting his informant.

That was Tomás's job.

"Why aren't you taking advantage of my fine bed?" she asked in English, her accent a thing of beauty he had always admired.

"I needed to talk to you."

"I certainly wouldn't be down here if my bed was empty."

"You wouldn't have left it unlocked if you hadn't expected me to use it."

The corners of her lips drew up and she took a sip of her whisky. "Don't think I have a soft spot for newlyweds."

He drew back in mock bewilderment. "I wouldn't dare." He pulled up a stool next to her and reached over the bar for a glass.

"You're going to have to pay for that."

"Damn, but you are ever stingy these days." Elias reached for her bottle of Scotch and poured himself a drink. "I hear this is a very good year."

"Eh, it's about average. The Scots don't know how to let things age like we do in France."

He looked at the bottles behind the bar. "I can see you have some of the finest wine in France." He lied. She had some of the best wine on the Continent. "Any luck locating clothes so that I don't offend the fine ladies of France?"

"If you were afraid of offending, you should have sent your wife for clothes."

"My wife prefers me naked."

Tomás snorted and crossed his arms at his chest to eye him with a disdain he reserved just for Elias. The man stood as straight as a sarcophagus, and he was just as big as one, too.

"Your clothes will be here first thing in the morning."

"Thank you." He paused and got to the real reason he was here and not upstairs in bed with his wife. "Now that we're alone, are you going to tell me what happened?"

Hag swirled the contents of her glass, creating a miniature vortex of amber liquor. She watched each whirl of Scotch as if she expected something magical to appear. "You didn't ask your wife?"

"No."

"Why not?"

"We were otherwise engaged." He didn't want his wife to know about the meeting, let alone the importance it held.

"Your bride has been through much turmoil since your ship came into harbor."

"How much turmoil?"

"Tomás saw her wandering about outside early yesterday. She appeared lost and confused."

Damn Peter.

"I told him to watch her, but apparently at some point, she realized she was being followed. Tomás is a bit too big to hide sometimes."

"No one is too big to hide."

Tomás snorted. "This from a puny English dog."

Elias grinned, but kept his eyes on Hag. "What happened with my friend?"

"Your wife finally came inside, but as she did, some of the crew from the *Confiance* began to fight over Louise."

Elias winced. That crew manned the ship his wife was supposed to take back to England. Louise wasn't a bad-looking woman—her hygiene, however, left something to be desired. In all honesty, most sailors held a stronger foulness to them than Louise. "What happened?"

"Some pushing and shoving, then punches turned into chairs and glasses being thrown. You wife tried to hide under the table." Hag indicated the largest table in the front corner. "Your *friend* found her there."

"Where was he?" He pointed to Tomás. He knew Máira's well-being was not Tomás's concern, but Hag had told him to keep an eye on her. A sigh or a growl was released behind him. He didn't look. It was best not to engage a beast. He wasn't afraid of Tomás, he just didn't have the time or the energy to engage in a round of fisticuffs.

"*He* was doing his job and protecting my bar."

"It doesn't look as if he did a very good job." It was true. There was more damage to the tavern than Elias had ever seen.

"The damage you see was from the last group of Napoleon's men to travel through here. I was compensated with things I didn't need."

That explained the luxurious furnishings in her room. Hag's smile was sardonic. "What does a businesswoman need with fancy bedroom furnishings?"

He heard Tomás's feet shuffle behind him and knew the man was thinking about the things he could do in her room. It was obvious to everyone but Hag that Tomás pined for her. Elias returned to his questioning. "What happened to Máira's shoulder?"

"Your friend tried to force his intentions upon her. She wanted no part of him and resisted. When he could not persuade her, he wrenched her arm behind her back and slammed her head against the floor. He did it a second time and she screamed. I threw my knife, then grabbed my pistol and walked over to make certain he did not get up."

He nodded. He wouldn't have expected anything less, nor would he have wanted anything less to happen to the low-life pond scum who not only betrayed his own country for riches, but then attempted to force himself on a woman. If ever a man deserved what he got, Henry Greasley did.

He wished he could kill him again—he would have liked to do it after he got the information he needed, but Hag had done what needed to be done.

"I don't suppose you found papers on him?" He asked.

"Papers?" The expression on her face was more ambivalent than ever.

Dammit. "Hag, I know you went through his pockets."

"What would make you think that I would do such a thing?"

He stared at her. Waiting. Her mock innocence annoyed him and made a muscle tick in his cheek. She killed the bugger. She was as far from being an angel worthy of heaven as they came. She would be more aptly cast as Lucifer, himself. Of course, he was no saint either, and they would probably rot in hell together, along with Tomás.

Máira would not be with them.

"What did you find, Hag?"

She blinked. "Oh, you mean the part you didn't share with me? The part about Simon Clark, the Earl of Astley, traipsing through France on a mission from the English Crown, and the Frenchman who captured him?" Her tone was casual, but everything about this moment spoke of violence and secrets too important to utter aloud.

"I don't know who has captured the earl," he hissed under his breath, and looked over his shoulder to ensure no one else had come in before continuing. "You killed the man who was supposed to give me that information. So, stop playing cat-and-mouse and tell me what you found."

"The Minister of War and chief of staff to the emperor himself, has your earl. They should be at the Bastille of the Seas by now, since the correspondence was dated over a month ago."

Bloody hell. He had put his wife in a dangerous spot if the Minister of War had captured the earl. Chances of recovering Astley alive were slim at best. With that amount of time there may be too little left of Simon Clark to take home in anything but a small box.

He wanted to curse himself to hell for endangering her as he had. Yet it all boiled down to that one moment in time when he saw her in the streets of Dumfries and she'd captured his attention with her laughter. The graceful turn of her neck as she said something to her maid had thrown his stomach in knots and his cock had nearly pointed the path to her feet. He'd instantly decided she had to be the one woman he would marry. The only woman he would swear his loyalty to. It wouldn't matter if the town was full of nobles, something inside him demanded he select her as his bride, the dangers be damned.

Except he hadn't expected any real dangers. Certainly not like what Máira had already experienced. And he was afraid it was only the beginning. In essence, he had no one to blame but himself... and his damned cock.

Seven

Darling,

Your treasured brooch was sold to a French nobleman who collects American pieces of jewelry. I must say I have never heard of such an interesting, if not especially valuable, type of collection. It is said that he has pieces made by the natives who saved the ignorant wretches from the Santa Maria from starvation. I'm quite certain the fools from the ship should have been showering their hosts with gifts for saving them, not the other way around, but perhaps I am missing something to the story.

To retrieve your brooch, I must travel farther than I had previously planned, since the gentleman in question has retired to the country for health purposes. I will send word once I have met with him and your beloved brooch is in my custody.

Until then darling,
Simon

—A coded letter to Sir Robert Williamson, War Office, London, England, from Simon Clark, Earl of Astley, secret agent of the Crown prior to his capture in the Bay of Biscay.

She'd awakened as soon as he'd slipped from the bed and out into the hall with nothing on but a bed sheet. Had she been that terrible? She'd thought he enjoyed it. He certainly seemed to enjoy it. She had been prepared for his release, had known from talks with her sister what exactly to expect when a man spilled his seed. If she hadn't known, she would have jumped back with alarm—or worse—bitten him.

She shuddered at the thought. Educating women about bed sport prior to marriage would always rank highly in her opinion. Otherwise, she could have ruined it—ruined *him*. Another shudder shook her shoulders.

Except now she truly wondered if Elias had enjoyed it as much as he would have if they'd actually had intercourse. Why else would he leave their room with no clothing on? A sudden thought struck her and she sat up in bed.

"He wouldn't," she breathed, the air expelling from her nose in a rush, and she suddenly felt the anger a bull would feel if another male had stepped into his pasture.

Elias would not seek pleasure in the arms of another woman. If she hadn't performed to his satisfaction then he would have to teach her otherwise. As long as they were married, he would not be stepping outside of their vows. Máira slipped from the sheets, her new night rail bunch up around her waist as if she had fought the linen garment for hours. She pulled a wrapper around herself, opened the door a crack and listened. Faint voices could be heard from the tavern below. She made her way into the hall, turned and slowly closed the door, leaving it the slightest bit ajar to allow herself a hasty retreat. As she descended the staircase, a floorboard creaked under her bare feet. Unable to hear the voices due her own heartbeat thundering through her thoughts, she froze and held her breath. When she finally did hear something, it was the joy in Hag's laughter. She was laughing with Elias.

Had he really left their marriage bed to flirt with another woman? Pain, humiliation, and anger sliced her battered heart in threes. It dissected each section into minuscule pieces, leaving nothing to remain but irritation with herself for dreaming, hoping, seeing something that didn't exist. She was a fool to think a man like Elias would want her. She'd known the moment she met his deep chocolate gaze that he was out of her league.

He was no different than the dowry hunters of the *ton*. He said he didn't care that she was bastard born. She supposed that was true enough. In the bedroom he wouldn't touch her. He'd sworn he didn't want to ruin her, yet he'd also confessed to being a liar.

What had she done? How had she been such a fool?

Her face heated at the memory of how she'd behaved while in the bath, and out. Tears prickled, but she refused to let them fall. She would not let anything more happen between them. She would make him take her home to Scotland and disappear to Caerlaverock. She suddenly understood why her sister saw it as a safe haven from the ton. Last season she had been in all the scandal rags as one of the six Blair By-blow Bitches attempting to climb their way back into society's good graces. There had been a cartoon of five female hounds, teats engorged with milk, crossing the ancient drawbridge of Caerlaverock, with the Duke of Ross holding a pregnant bitch in his arms.

Iseabail had cried. Máira had laughed it off and said it was good to know what the *ton* really thought, yet deep down it had stung. Her sister did not deserve their scorn. Their parents may not have been legally wed, but they had believed their marriage to be binding by the law and the church. It was certainly all-consuming within their hearts.

Lady Elizabeth Sinclair had disavowed her inheritance, her standing in the *ton*, and her parents' threats to disown her if she married a mere merchant. Their mother had left with Duncan Blair for love. They had run to the border and married with all haste, and settled down in a castle they had called home for twelve years. It was after the death of her mother during childbirth that their lives had fallen apart. Their father drank his troubles away and lost their family home to a gambling debt. Then he'd done the unthinkable and thrown himself off a bridge in despair.

That was when the six sisters had been declared bastards. After their parents' deaths and proof of their marriage could not be found. Six young girls thrown from their home, and yet despite the scandal and their illegitimacy, Iseabail had married well.

She had thought she'd done the same. Love and a title were a rare combination, but now she knew her husband thought so little of their marriage and her that he would leave her bed to visit the bed of a tavern whore. Nothing had prepared her for this. She had incorrectly assumed Elias would remain true to their vows.

Determined to face the truth head-on, Máira crept down the remaining steps and stopped at the doorway to the tavern where she could hear their conversation.

"What do you want, Hag?"

"Elias, you wound me."

There was humor in her tone, but Máira could sense the tension in the air.

"I don't have the luxury of time to play games. What do you want?" Elias's voice was hard and clipped. Maybe he wasn't there to seduce the barkeep.

"I want my next shipment of Scotch for free."

"That's the talk of a crazy woman."

"I'd say that's the speech of a confident businesswoman holding every card in the deck."

Silence lingered, and Máira pictured Elias facing off with Hag. Neither backing down as Hag faced him toe to toe, nose to nose.

Maybe he wasn't there to cheat—

"I'll spend one week with you upon my next journey to Le Conquet."

Máira closed her eyes, the last bit of her dignity dropping to the floor for her husband to trample. She knew better than to hope. She knew better than to trust a man. Hadn't her father taught her they could not be trusted?

He had been the best of men, until their mother died. Then he'd shown how utterly untrustworthy every man was—yet there was the Duke of Nithsdale, her sister's first husband, and the Duke of Ross, her second husband. They were both good men. Honest and generous. Yet maybe they were all fools. Maybe no man was loyal or true. Maybe Elias was merely acting as all gentlemen did, and her ideas of love and marriage were just the romantic imaginings of a young girl.

"You have nothing to offer me now, Elias. You're married. You have responsibilities."

"I will no longer be married upon my return."

"Does your bride know that?" Genuine surprise lifted the tone of Hag's voice.

"She will when we return."

Máira couldn't take it any longer. She had to see her husband's face. She had to let herself absorb the look of interest in his eyes as he gazed upon another woman. She peered around the corner, her husband's profile in perfect view.

"We have an accord, Elias. Your next visit you are mine for one week."

Máira thought she was going to be ill as she watched Hag kiss Elias on one cheek and then the other. Her lips lingering on his skin as she caught sight of Máira.

"You're lucky that's one of my favorite pastimes," Elias said as he pulled away and looked Hag in the eyes. He never noticed Máira standing there watching them make a deal for his body, even though Hag and her big man standing at the door had.

"You men are all alike. Sex, fighting, and drinking. That's all you think about."

Elias laughed when she didn't think he would. Máira thought Hag had left one thing off that list—money. From her experience that was the first thing men prioritized.

"Not necessarily in that order, Hag. Besides you left out money," Elias said with a laugh.

And any last bit of hope Máira held fluttered out the door with her heart. She closed her eyes, her shoulders sagging with defeat.

"I need you to look after my wife."

Máira's gaze snapped up. Like bloody hell.

The fighting Blair sister spirit rose up in her chest. Her father had taught the sisters to fight when they were but bairns, and their mother had told them to embrace their anger and fight with courage. She'd also told them to keep a level head, but that lesson went out the door with Máira's heart.

"I will not be '*looked after*' by your mistress," she growled as she stormed into the room ready to take all three of them on if she had to. She would go home tomorrow on the next ship.

Elias dropped his head into one palm and began to rub his face.

"That's right, dear Husband. Your subterfuge is over." The way she spat out the term of endearment left nothing to the imagination about her feelings toward her spouse. A log in the massive fireplace shifted and sparked, sending shards of half-burned wood onto the stone hearth. Not one pair of eyes went to the firebox to ensure the log didn't fall to the floor. Hag and her man stared at her with interested amusement as she walked up to the bar and moved in between her husband and Hag. Their two stools were entirely too close for a married man to occupy with a woman other than his wife. She turned toward Elias, her back to Hag.

"Look at me," she demanded, when Elias refused to even acknowledge her presence.

It was as if she were a ghost of years past, attempting to talk to the living who had no idea she was present. Elias looked down at his drink, swished it around and downed the contents of his glass. She watched his throat constrict as he swallowed. Fumed at the way his eyes closed and he savored the burn of the alcohol. She had to bite her tongue, her teeth sinking deeply into her flesh, when he finally said, "Go back to bed, Máira. I'll be there in a moment."

His dismissal was all it took for her anger to explode. She

pushed him in the chest and watched in stunned fascination as he fell backward. His body hunched toward her, his free hand coming up to grab her wrapper. He caught the opening of her neckline and pulled her over the top of the stool with him.

Máira gasped. Their eyes connecting as the two of them went over like a tree in the forest. Glass shattered. Wood cracked and Elias hit the floor with a thud. She landed on top of him, cushioned by the hard planes of his body as he somehow wrapped around her in a protective cocoon.

She snorted. This man wouldn't protect her from a midge. Yet still as they lay there staring at one another, their eyes clashing like Titans, she felt his attraction to her grow beneath her belly, and her own body lit with a heat she couldn't deny. It was Hag's voice that broke the spell as they glared at one another.

"I don't think your wife cares to keep my company while you're gone."

"She'll do as she's told," Elias ground out.

Máira snorted again. "Like hell. I'm going home on the next ship."

"That would be the *Maribelle* in a fortnight's time, and I have business to attend to while we're here. You'll stay with Hag."

Máira frown. "Business? I thought you already did your business with Hag."

Her husband began to work his jaw and sat up while holding her biceps as he moved her to the side. "Are you injured?"

"No." Yes, can't you see my heart is bleeding out?

Elias got to his feet and then lifted her up to place her on a different bar stool that had all four legs intact.

"I expect you to pay for the stool. Clean-up is on me."

Elias didn't take his eyes off Máira as he responded to the tavern owner, who was grabbing a broom from behind the bar. "How generous of you, Hag."

"I aim to please." The woman's voice took on a sing-song quality that grated her nerves.

Elias huffed his disbelief, but didn't say a word to Hag. Instead, he addressed Máira. "You're supposed to be in bed."

"With my husband?" she asked with wide-eyed innocence.

"She has you there," Hag interjected.

"Shut up," Máira and Elias ground out in unison.

Hag laughed, and Máira heard the woman's bodyguard chuckle before he cleared his throat in a poor attempt to cover his laughter.

"What did you hear?" Elias asked, as if the other two weren't still in the room.

Máira crossed her arms over her chest, a motion that seemed to momentarily distract Elias as his gaze traveled to and lingered upon her breasts. His gaze turned her already heated response to him ablaze as her nipples hardened in anticipation of a wedding night that would never happen.

"Enough," she said to herself as much as she did to him. She couldn't afford the lingering attraction to a man who didn't deserve her desire, let alone her heart. But as his eyes reluctantly left the heaving breaths she couldn't seem to control, longing threatened to consume her, until his gaze met hers and every bit of emotion she'd witnessed in the past few moments was gone. Once again, she stood in front of the cold, ruthless pirate she didn't know. His green gaze as vast and unrecognizable as the depths of Galloway Forest. It made her wonder if he was plotting seven different ways to kill her and dispose of her body.

He could wrap his large, masculine hands around her throat and squeeze, slowing cutting off her air supply as he gazed into her eyes and showed her nothing of the man she'd believed him to be. He could grab the bottle of Scotch and bash her over the head. Crack her skull like one of those watermelons Iseabail had introduced to them on their first visit to Caerlaverock Castle. He could grab Hag's knife and stab her fractured heart.

Elias rolled his eyes. "I'm not plotting your murder."

"No?" She lifted her chin in open defiance. "You said you wanted to be rid of me. What better way to do it?"

His eyebrow quirked and she could swear he was laughing at her. "Are you suggesting that I *should* murder you?"

"I—I—"

He rubbed his chin as if he was contemplating it. "It would make my life much easier— your dowry would come in handy."

"I knew it!" She punched him in the middle of his chest.

"Ow!" He backed up, but Máira slipped off the stool and pursued him.

"That's the only reason you married me! You wanted my money! You blackguard!" Máira punched him a second time, but Elias didn't seem to want to fight her. Instead, he held up his hands to protect himself. If she'd thought about it, that wasn't the action of a man hellbent on murder. It was the action of a man who wouldn't harm her. But this wasn't the time to think, it was the time to act—

A piercing whistle stopped her assault.

"He's a spy." Hag doused the blinding anger soaring through her body with that one declaration.

Elias froze.

Eyes widening, Máira's head snapped in the barkeep's direction. "Pardon me?"

Standing behind the bar, Hag busied herself pouring two drinks as if she were preparing glasses of Madeira at a small gathering of ladies in a parlor of a Mayfair townhouse, the latest gossip on the tip of her tongue. Like a seasoned gossip, she held her audience captivated with her silence. Her expression one of serene indifference. Máira was beginning to believe the woman had fifty different masks she wore to hide her true feelings and wondered what she would look like if she trusted a person. Máira glanced at her husband to find a death glare leveled on Hag.

Máira asked again, "What did you say?"

"Nothing." Elias ground out between his clenched jaw. "Hag likes to cause trouble." The silent warning he delivered with his declaration made Tomás stiffen. Tension filled the tavern as if they had suddenly discovered a keg of gun powder hidden under the bar with a lit fuse attached to it. Each of them staring at the others as they waited for one of them to be brave enough to cut the fuse...or let it explode.

As the victim of a fortune hunter, Máira's anger was firmly seated in his hands.

Espionage, however, was a different story altogether. That was unpardonable treason. If she heard correctly, Hag was delivering a death sentence...to Elias—and to her as his wife. If anyone heard Hag's pronouncement, Elias would be dead within the fortnight. Her death would probably come much later, after experiencing unthinkable torture.

Dear heavens. Perhaps she shouldn't discount all the ways she could die a gruesome death.

"She's your wife. She has a right to know the type of danger you face, and what kind of vengeance she may face." There was something in Hag's voice that spoke from experience, as if she too had walked in the shoes of the spouse of a spy, and she'd paid dearly for her husband's profession.

If there was a bright spot—Hag was still alive.

"You're a spy?" she whispered.

Elias sighed. "Please stop saying that word before you get us both killed."

Eight

Mr. Greasley,

The Earl of Astley was captured in the Bay of Biscay. He was on board a merchant ship from America, and claimed to be traveling to France in search of a stolen piece of jewelry for his wife. I will be taking him to Le Mont-Saint-Michel. I need you to broker a ransom of fifteen thousand pounds. Your cut will be one thousand pounds. Once I receive the balance, your debt is paid and the earl will be returned to England—in a box.

Maximilien de Danton

—A letter from the Prince de Wagram, also known as the Minister of War and chief of staff to Napoleon Bonaparte. Recovered from the pocket of dead double agent Henry Greasley.

I
t was time to explain everything to his bride, whether he wanted to or not. Since the *Confiance* had left port, Hag didn't have any other guests staying at the inn, and she and her ever-loyal henchman had moved across the room to allow him to explain what he must. He should not have discounted Hag's

past and how she might react to Máira's unwitting participation in this mission. Yet he found it somewhat astonishing the past would stir any emotion other than mere annoyance in Hag.

Throughout the years of cold indifference, he hadn't suspected a moment of emotion until Hag looked into his eyes and said, *She's your wife.* In those three words he saw every tear she never allowed to drop, every cut to her heart she'd seared over with the heat of her anger. Until the day her husband died with a noose around his neck, Hag had been the most beautiful woman he had ever laid eyes upon. He just hadn't realized her grief still tore at her to this day. He'd truly believed she had moved past it.

Now, he realized the danger in allowing Hag to see a kindred spirit in his wife, because for however short their marriage would be, Máira deserved the truth. "The Earl of Astley needs my assistance here in France."

Máira gasped and covered her mouth with the same delicate hand she'd wrapped around his cock not an hour earlier. "Simon?" She asked.

His stomach flipped uncomfortably when she used the earl's Christian name, and he narrowed his eyes. "Yes. Do you know him?"

"Of course I do."

Of course she did. Everyone knew of the earl, but not everyone knew him well enough to use his Christian name. He waited for her to explain. When she gave him no more information, he found it difficult not to infuse animosity toward the man he was to rescue in his next question.

"How well do you know him?"

"He often dines with us when we are in town." Once again, her answer gave him less than he'd asked for. He waited for her to elaborate. Waited for his wife to say she knew the earl on a more intimate level. The muscles in his chest twitched with his desire to punch something or someone with Simon Clark's jaw. He didn't want to hear it, yet every ounce of the man he was told him that one look at Máira and the earl couldn't help but want more. Her lips. Her neck. Her décolletage...

Merde. He was usually good at interrogations, quietly waiting for a prisoner to fill in the blanks as he stared them down. He could use none of his interrogation techniques with her, and he found himself becoming increasingly more impatient.

His next question escaped through clenched teeth. "Why would an earl frequently break his fast with you and your sisters?"

Her adorable brow puckered in consternation, as if it was ridiculous for a husband to ask such a question. "He's Ross's best friend."

"I see." No. He didn't see at all. Did men of the *ton* often visit friends' homes first thing in the morning? If a gentleman was to eat his morning meal away from his home, wouldn't it be with his mistress? Not that Elias could afford to keep such a woman, but the earl certainly could. And of course, now he wondered how much he dared share about why the earl had been kidnapped in the first place. The last thing he needed was for the mission to become fodder for the Blair sisters to discuss with various guests over a meal.

"Elias. Please tell me what has happened to Simon." The imploring look in her beautiful blue eyes was enough to undo him.

"Astley was kidnapped and is being held for ransom by French authorities."

"No!" Her hushed denial of the truth as her fingers covered her mouth spoke volumes to how well she knew the earl.

He knew the earl by reputation alone—if one included having seen the caricatures in gossip rags of the earl's exploits with widows and women of questionable morals. Or of the images of the ladies of the *ton* dropping like a litany of flies at his feet as he walked through a ballroom. The Earl of Astley was a consummate rake and gambler. Until Elias had been given this assignment, he'd no idea Astley had any worth beyond his title.

It was even more obvious now that Astley was worth *more* to

Elias's wife, and that made him want to hit someone. He swallowed the anger he shouldn't feel and replied with the controlled command of a captain. "Yes, and I've been sent to recover him."

"But how will you rescue him from the French?" She looked around the room, seeing it for the first time as the foreign land at war with England. She eyed Hag and Tomás with even more uncertainty before saying, "It's not as if they will open their doors and say, 'Come, take your English comrade back to England.'"

He grabbed the drink Hag had poured. "By any means necessary." He downed the contents.

"What is that supposed to mean?"

He let the alcohol settle and replied, "It means I will bring the earl home to English soil regardless of the cost."

The spark in her eyes fluttered. The glow dimming like the stars in the morning light. "You mean you would stoop low enough as to marry a desperate debutante?"

He nodded his head, not letting the fingers around his glass inadvertently smash it to bits. There was enough broken glass on the floor, and he'd certainly done enough injury to her ego, if not her heart.

Her question was barely audible. "Why?"

He frowned. "Why what?"

"Why choose me as a means to an end? What made you choose me as part of your ruse?"

"Astley is a peer that I had been tasked to recover. To obtain information as to his whereabouts, I had to obtain some Scottish whisky. In order to obtain the whisky, I had to be married to a Scottish lady."

"And you chose me as your target."

He nodded, knowing he would hurt her all over again with his acknowledgment. He didn't say she'd captured his attention the moment he laid eyes on her. Everything about his growing feelings toward her were irrelevant.

"And you are...what? A mere knight tasked to recover him at

all costs—even if you destroy my reputation? My virtue? My sisters' chances at good marriages? How much am I to sacrifice in the name of your mission?" Her voice became shrill as a laugh which held no mirth, escaped her lips.

"I would not sacrifice you. I would not—"

"That's exactly what you did! I was forced upon a ship without my knowledge, nearly died as we sailed to God knows where in France. I nearly lost my virtue right there—" Her finger jutted out in the direction of a table in a corner near the door. "—in a tavern on the floor." A flicker of the horror she'd endured flashed in the depths of her eyes as she accused him of being the worst sort of man.

"That man died lying next to me. His blood stained my wedding gown...*my wedding gown*." Her voice broke, and he wanted to take her into his arms and comfort her. Apologize for all the pain she'd endured. He knew she wouldn't allow it. She would fight him. Bite him. Kick and scratch and do everything to him that he deserved for taking her from the comfort of her family. He looked away, too ashamed of what he'd inflicted upon an innocent.

"And yet, do you want to know the funny thing, dear Husband?"

No, he didn't, because he knew there was absolutely nothing funny about the pain he'd inflicted upon her.

"If you had asked me to do all of that to save Simon, I would not have hesitated. I would have stood at my family church in front of God and my loved ones and said, 'I do.' Swearing my reputation, my virtue, my life to save Simon, because he is a better man than you could possibly hope to become, a better person than I will ever be."

He did not flinch at her words despite the gaping hole she left in his chest. What she spoke was nothing but the truth—about him. He deserved her wrath and so much more. She, however, deserve none of her self-deprecation.

"I will get him back for you."

"What if you can't?"

"I will."

"How do you know you will?"

He ground his teeth. She could question his character, he had no qualms with that. His ability to complete his mission, however, was backed by a perfect record. Since the day he'd shown up at his uncle's doorstep with a letter from his mother, his uncle had questioned everything he had ever learned. He'd questioned his ability to saddle a damned horse, earn his commission in the navy, and eventually command his own ship, but Elias had proven his worth as a military man, if not a gentleman.

"Because I was tasked to do so," he bit out, with more irritation than he'd meant to show. What he didn't say was, *because you wish to have Astley back*.

"That doesn't mean you can do it. There are some situations you won't be able to overcome. What if he's in Bagne of Toulon?" She asked.

He looked at her in disbelief. Her beautiful, innocent, mistrusting face that he adored despite knowing he shouldn't. He had created her wariness of him and his abilities. Yet he couldn't understand how she had so little faith in him rescuing her precious earl. He had sent his ship into the worst squall he'd seen in a decade at sea to avoid the British warship that had somehow seen them leaving Dumfries in the middle of the night and had chased them relentlessly off the coast of Scotland until he'd done the one thing they would never do, enter a damned storm that would swallow a lesser ship commanded by a lesser man. He wasn't being arrogant. It was the damned truth. He'd had little doubt they'd survive.

Then he'd sent the *Maribelle* and his crew back into the same storm when the French had attempted to hunt them down as well. It was as if their mission had been reported to someone who did not want him to rescue her earl. Or perhaps her brother-in-law had discovered his duplicity and was attempting to stop him from stealing his sister. Either way, their short-day journey had taken multiple days, not hours and they had survived because of his ability to captain his ship in the worst of conditions. "Then I will rescue him from prison."

"No one escapes Bagne of Toulon."

He tamped down the growl threatening to surface as he chose to take another tact. "How do you know about Bagne of Toulon?"

"A member of the *émigré* army visited us at Caerlaverock and often spoke of the deplorable conditions at Toulon."

Good God, how many spies dined at Caerlaverock? Not counting himself, because the ladies had not known his occupation, but the earl and now this nameless *émigré*. Perhaps he was the source of their trouble after all. Trying to inflect as little emotion as possible he asked, "What's his name?"

Her brow rose as she ducked her head in a coquettish display that made him want to crush her delectable mouth with his own. Something he could never do again. "Why do you think it was a man?"

Focus on her question and not her mouth, he warned his over-eager libido.

"Because the *émigré* army wanted to restore the House of Bourbon to power, not establish women's rights."

"That doesn't mean there weren't members of the female aristocracy fighting with them."

He sighed. This conversation was getting them nowhere. "The name of the *émigré*, Máira. It could be vital to Astley's recovery."

She dropped any semblance of flirtation and gave up the name without another word. "Comte Mathieu Armand du Motier. He is cousin to the Marquis de Lafayette, Gilbert du Motier."

Good God. Did her family ever look into the lineage of nobility? He had worried over one of the sisters checking DeBrett's and finding his lie, but it turned out he wasn't the only man to hide behind a title while entertaining the Blair family. The Marquis de Lafayette, Gilbert du Motier, had no cousin. Mathieu Armand was as big an imposter as he was.

Damnation. He let out a beleaguered breath and told her the brutal and honest truth. "I regret to inform you Mathieu Armand du Motier is a fraud."

She laughed, a disbelieving sound that was not her normal joyous fare, until she saw the serious expression he leveled at her. Her face dropped. "You're joking."

He slowly shook his head. "I am not."

Her lips pursed and her eyes narrowed. "Yes, you are. I have known Mathieu Armand du Motier almost my entire life." When he did not waiver, she continued. "If you are not joking than you are sadly mistaken. The comte was business partners with my father. We lost contact with him after my father's death, but he has just recently come back into our lives."

That caught his interest. "How recently?"

Her anger turned to suspicion. "I don't see how this is relevant to rescuing Simon."

"Is the comte French?"

"Of course he's French. He fought in the *émigré* army. What else would he be? He barely escaped with his life in 1789. He came back to France several times and fought in the war. Each time he returned to Scotland injured and would recover with my family."

"You remember him recovering at Urquhart Castle, not Caerlaverock?"

She gave one curt nod as if she'd proven him wrong. "Yes. The same man who visited my family and was my father's business partner in the Highlands, began visiting us again last summer at my sister's home."

Could a man remain in one alias that long and never be detected?

"What was he doing while you and your sisters were living in destitution?"

"He searched for us, but was told the same thing Ross was told when he looked for us: we were sent to live with relatives. It was only when the comte saw the announcement of Iseabail's betrothal to Nash that he learned our location, and he sought us out imme-diately."

The man had not been living as Comte Mathieu Armand du Motier for the past ten years at least. How long he lived the lie before that, was still in question. By the frustrated look on Máira's face as she began to pace, he didn't think she would tolerate him questioning the comte's identity any further.

"The comte is a fraud." Hag spat out the truth in brutal fash-ion, her voice filled with recrimination and Elias groaned. The woman had the tact of a sailor using a canon.

Máira spun around, a gasp on her lips. She was just as shocked by Hag's blatant eavesdropping as he was, only Máira's surprise was wrapped in indignation. With her hands clenched in fists at her sides she accused, "That is a lie!"

"When a woman reacts blindly to a man's ruse, she is being as stupid as a deer in rut."

He had to give it to Hag, she knew how to shock and blatantly tell the truth in a manner no one could deny, including a well-born lady.

His wife sputtered for a moment. Took a deep breath and walked over to Hag and met her toe to toe. Hag quirked an amused brow but didn't take a step back. She'd never been one to back down for as long as Elias could remember.

"My father trusted him completely. That is enough for me."

"Your father was a fool."

The slap to Hag's cheek left a silence in the room no one seemed willing to break. Máira's chest heaved with each breath she took. Hag raised her hand to the quickly forming red hand imprint on her face and stared at Máira, her face blank of emotion. Elias eyed Hag and then Tomás, silently willing them both not to retali-ate. If they did, he wasn't sure how he would react. Tomás eyed him as well. They both knew Hag could hold her own against Máira. Neither knew if his wife had any skills in fighting.

Before he could step between the two women, Hag smiled and

said in her thick French accent, "It's about time you took a stance for yourself."

"I took a stance for my father. He was the best of men."

"I can only take your word for it, but I can tell you he was a fool when it came to his judgement of that scoundrel." Hag caught Máira's hand before she could land a second slap, the two women sizing each other up and Elias knew it was time to intervene before they began fighting in earnest.

He stepped in between them and bent down to look Máira in the eyes. "She has the tact of a whore selling her wares."

Hag laughed and Tomás growled but did nothing to keep him from continuing. "Let her explain why she said what she said. She obviously knows something we don't about the Comte."

Máira searched his eyes and reluctantly agreed. "Fine." She crossed her arms across her chest and Elias ignored the temptation she waved in front of him.

Damnation, the woman challenged his self-control.

She peered around him and asked Hag, "Why do you think my father was a poor judge of the Comte's character?"

"Because I know the Marquis de Lafayette. He has no cousin on his father's side."

Máira's brow furrowed, her eyes tracking back and forth as if she searched her memory for something to disprove Hag's statement. He was certain she wouldn't find anything. In his gut he'd known the Comte was a fraud the moment she mentioned him, and he wanted to take her in his arms and tell her Hag's knowledge did not change the man she knew her father to be. It only meant her father had been human. Everyone was capable of being duped, including Hag. That was why she was the woman she was today.

Except he couldn't tell her Hag's story. If he did, he would be pointing out the similarities Máira shared with the woman—both had been fooled by the men they married. He only hoped he had not created the same cynicism in Máira as Hag's husband had created in her.

Máira's eyes closed for a moment and when she reopened them, he saw her determination to move forward in the hardness of her gaze. She'd accepted what she couldn't change, how that admission changed her, remained to be seen.

"How will you break into a prison?"

He gave her the straightforward answer she deserved. "If I must pretend to be a guard, I will be a guard. I'm a very good actor." He got it from his mother.

"I see." Her mood dropped and he knew exactly what she was thinking. He had acted when he was with her. He supposed to a point it was true, but everything he'd felt while he was with Máira had been real. Every emotion, every desire. It had all been real. Especially the physical attraction. She brought out the best, and worst in him. He wanted to be a better man when he was with her, yet he also wanted to steal every moment and enjoy them to the fullest, even though he knew he would not be there for her in the future.

He ignored that pinch, which was turning into a clenched fist in his chest and continued. "Our Regent is depending upon me to bring the earl home. I will bring him home one way or the other."

The color drained from her face as Máira thought of the implication of his words. "You mean alive or...or dead?"

"Yes. I would prefer it if he were alive, but if he is dead, I will return his body to English soil."

Máira began pacing the tavern back and forth across the dark gloomy room. She stopped. "How will you find him?"

"Máira, I can't tell you everything."

"I could help."

"You can't. Not in this."

"But I—"

"Are you willing to sell your body?" She needed to understand what was at stake.

She hesitated and then lifted her chin. "If that's what it takes to save him—yes."

"Like hell," he ground out between his teeth as he walked to her and grabbed hold of her upper arms. He gazed down into her expressive eyes and wished they were upstairs in bed. He wished he were a different man, a gentleman she could truly love and that this was a real honeymoon trip. But he wasn't, this wasn't, and they didn't have the time to pretend it was anything but a deadly mission.

"I will not let you sacrifice your body and soul for a mission you did not undertake."

"Simon is a family friend," she argued.

For a moment he didn't care much for Astley if his wife was willing to sacrifice herself for the man. "Do you love him?"

She pulled back, but he refused to release her as she searched his face...for what, he didn't know.

"You're jealous," she accused, as if the thought popped into her head without her realizing it.

He laughed and pushed her away. "Don't be ridiculous."

"You are!" She grinned and he wanted to punch the wall.

Yes, he was jealous. He shouldn't be, but he was. No one had ever wanted to sacrifice their body for him, yet her willingness to do so for Astley—was unthinkable—unless she knew him intimately. Unless Astley was the one to show her how to handle a man's cock as she'd done upstairs.

Damnation. He needed to gain the upper hand once more. "My point being, unless you are willing to lie on your back and spread your legs, you cannot help."

"That's what you planned to do with me, is it not?"

"No! It was nothing like that."

She folded her arms across her chest once more, and he couldn't help but be drawn to the taut, thin fabric of her borrowed wrapper and shift pulling tightly across her perfect breasts and pert nipples. "Then explain to me how different it is, because I'd truly like to know."

He returned his gaze to hers and tried to stay focused. "I did not intend to bed you. You were to be returned to England yesterday morning on the *Confiance*."

"Oh."

"Yes, oh." He repeated. "I arranged for your transportation back to England with the captain, and my superior was to meet you at the docks on English soil. When you don't arrive, there will be hell to pay."

"I see." She rubbed her hand across her eyes, fatigue evident in her posture.

"You weren't supposed to be here in the first place," he continued. "You were supposed to be back at Caerlaverock."

"You planned on leaving without me?" The wounded sound to her voice made him want to puke.

"Yes."

"So why didn't you?"

He saw the hope in her eyes and vowed to extinguish it then and there. "I told you, the man I bought the Scotch from would only sell to a member of the *ton* who was wedded to a Scottish bride."

"That explains the wedding, not why I'm here."

"The smuggler wanted to see you, and then he made certain I left the docks with my bride in tow."

Suspicion began to cloud her face. "Why don't I remember any of this?"

He debated on lying once more. He was good at lying, but Máira deserved better than what he'd done. "I made certain you over-imbibed at our wedding supper."

"You what?" Shock and disbelief masked her anger—momentarily. Once she accepted that she hadn't just made bad choices, she would be furious.

"The seller demanded to see my Scottish bride before he would turn over the merchandise."

She snorted. "Let me get this straight. You met me, wooed me, married me, and then got me drunk to get a man to give you some Scotch?"

"He didn't *give* me anything. I bought it."

"Oh, forgive me for getting that one little detail wrong." Her cheeks were turning pink as her anger grew. "How did you get me there?"

"I carried you."

"Like a sack of potatoes?"

He nodded. It didn't matter how she pictured it, from her perspective he supposed her description was close enough.

"Why didn't you just leave me there?"

It was the hundred-pound question. "I didn't trust him."

She laughed, but there was no humor in the sound. "You didn't trust him? Are you certain that you're more trustworthy than he?"

He winced but remained silent as she began stalking the room once more, her feet pounding the floorboards as if she were a man twice her size with boots on, instead of her bare feet that were as tiny as he'd ever seen.

"How about Peter? Is he more trustworthy? After all, he did abandon me on land with no money and no direction except to go to The Happy Hag and seek out a woman who cold-bloodedly killed a man in front of me. Is she trustworthy?"

Her voice had risen to the point where he feared someone might hear what she was ranting on about. Yet still he kept his mouth closed.

"No," she laughed. "It seems I would have been better off with the smuggler in England—"

"Scotland," he corrected.

"Oh, yes. Forgive me. The Scots are less trustworthy than any of the Englishmen out there."

"That wasn't what I meant."

"Wasn't it?" She walked toward him, her bare feet slapping the floor once more as she approached.

"No," he said, as he looked down into her eyes that were as cold as any Scottish loch. She was half English and half Scot, but he suspected she identified more with her father's Highland ancestry than her mother's British blue blood.

"I would not lie to you about that."

"You would just lie about loving me?" Behind the anger freezing her blue eyes to ice, he saw the cracks of pain in the surface.

"I did not lie." Her breath hitched, but he continued so as not to give her false hope. "I told you I never wanted to marry before I met you. My feelings toward marriage have never changed. I don't wish to be married. Ever."

"You don't want children?"

He pictured little versions of Máira running across the meadow—the very place he'd asked Máira to marry him. If marriage were possible for a man like him, he would have chosen a woman such as her, but that was not in his future. He would not force her into making the same mistake his mother had made. No woman deserved that.

He shook his head. "No."

She searched his face once more. "You're lying. I saw it in your eyes. You want children just as much as anyone else, so why won't you let yourself?"

"I chose the life I plan to live. I will not subject a family to my choices."

"Isn't that your wife's choice to make?"

"Not when she didn't know what she was getting into when she married me, no. Máira, you are a wonderful woman—"

"Don't."

"Don't what?"

"Don't say if you could choose a wife, you would have chosen me."

"Even if it's true?"

"But it's not. From the moment we met, you had a plan in

117

place. Meet me, marry me, use me. How could that possibly involve you wanting to marry me, when you were scheming our marriage from the very start?"

"Because I grew to know the woman you are."

"Really? In the short time you've known me, you believe you could have fallen in love?"

"Didn't you?"

She shrank away with his cruel words. He hadn't meant for them to sound callous or diminishing, and yet that is exactly how it came out. He had in essence told her that her feelings couldn't be lasting. She felt infatuation, nothing more. It had never been love, nor would it ever be.

"You are cruel."

He nodded once in agreement.

"Is that why they chose you for this job."

"In part."

"Why else?"

It was the one question he couldn't answer. Wouldn't. It would put the only person he cared about in danger, and for that, he would hold his silence at any cost.

Hag's voice fractured the stillness like lightening splintering a deep stormy sky. "Because he's my son and he's a French citizen."

Nine

Hag,

My employer lost a shipment early last month headed for Le Conquet. It was supposed to be delivered to Leland Astier but never arrived. He fears the thieves are working with one of his clerks, Simone Ferdone, who disappeared last month as well. He received information from Simone's wife that he was traveling to Le Conquet, which made him believe Simone planned to steal the merchandise from there. If you see or hear of a shipment of 16 trunks of the best Empire silk to be made in the last 29 or 28 years, please contact me. I am staying at 312 Clarke Street. The recovery is worth 6600 francs which the 2 of us will split in 1/2. It may not be the fee you would prefer, but my employer is a merchant struggling to produce gowns for the peerage.

Your assistance is most welcome and appreciated,
Elias

—A numeric coded letter written to Hag in Le Conquet, France, April 1812—The numerals are the only indication of

*the decipher. "16 trunks" represents the 1st sentence, 6th word—
EARLY, "last 29 or 28 years" represents inverting 9th and 8th
words of the second sentence—ASTIER LELAND, "312 Clarke
Street" represents the 3rd sentence 12th word—Simone, and
'6600 francs" represents the 6th sentence 6th word—CLARKE.
The "2 of us will split in 1/2" represents the second sentence decipher words will be split in 1/2—ASTier-LEland=AST—LE.*

*From there Hag must decipher on her own the words:
EARLY AST-LE SIMONE CLARKE—Earl of Astley Simon
Clark is the missing shipment last seen in Le Conquet.*

She laughed. What else was there to do. She didn't believe
Hag was her husband's mother any more than Elias was her
legal husband—except according to him, he was, and
according to the looks on both of their faces, and their identical
deep, mossy-green eyes, Hag was indeed Elias's mother. Yet he'd
told her his mother was dead. Another lie mounting up on top of
the others. How could Hag be here in this tavern that wasn't fit for
a lady?

Holy demons. She'd been calling her mother-in-law *Hag*. Hag.
Surely that wasn't her real name, yet Máira had been insulting her
this entire time.

She curtseyed. What else was there to do when one has realized
how disparaging she'd been to her mother-in-law—to her face, no
less. Had she called Hag a cold-blooded killer to Elias? Oh, but
she had.

And she had slapped her.

There was a special place for women who insulted their
husband's mother. The woman who bore him, nursed him, and
made life worth living for him after his father had died. Elias had
spoken of that, but never deigned to tell her his mother's name was
Hag, despite referring to her as Hag since he'd entered the tavern.
Who would be so utterly rude to one's mother?

"You didn't think it pertinent to tell me of your mother's identity?"

"I haven't told anyone of her identity."

That gave her pause. "No one?"

Elias shook his head. "For her safety, I'd appreciate it if it didn't leave this room."

His mother laughed. "I'm the reason you're in this mess."

His smile was sad, sadder than she'd ever seen him, and it was as if in that moment she wasn't there with them. Mother and son bonded over a shared grief. "Father is the reason we are in this mess. You only did his bidding because you loved both of us."

Hag's eyes watered and Máira thought she was seeing another person. The woman she knew as Hag did not cry—she murdered people.

"I can't call you Hag."

Her mother-by-marriage blinked away her tears and cleared her throat. "You can, and you will."

"But—"

"It keeps both of you safe as well," Hag interrupted.

"Hag insists, and I find myself agreeing with her for the first time since she started going by the ridiculous name."

"I don't understand," she confessed. A week ago, when she'd said her vows, she had expected a quiet marriage in the country. Since then, she'd found herself drunk, kidnapped, transported to enemy territory, abandoned with nothing, married to a man she did not know, attacked by a stranger in a tavern, witness to that man's murder, and somehow beholden to the woman who committed the murder, who, it seemed, was actually her dead mother-in-law—now most certainly alive.

She nearly laughed. The *ton* had thought her childhood was full of scandal. Being the bastard to dead parents, who had lived as husband and wife until they died, hardly seemed like it was gossip-worthy compared to this. Her parents had believed they were legally married and had lived in the country while her father traveled to Edinburgh and Carlisle on a regular basis. Her mother had died giving birth to their sixth daughter, and her father had died of drink and a broken heart four years later. Debt had taken their home, and the girls had gone to live with their nursemaid until their mother's godfather, the Duke of Nithesdale, had taken Máira's oldest sister under his wing with plans to sponsor her. He ended up marrying her and making her a duchess on his deathbed. And then somehow, after giving birth to the duke's son, Iseabail had met another duke and married him.

Dukes were rare. One woman marrying two, an impossibility. The gossip had been understandable, but this? This would knock the *ton* on its ears—if she ever made it home.

"I think we should return home at once," she mused.

"I agree. Things have become far too complicated," Hag added.

"I would love to accommodate the two of you, but that is impossible," her husband interjected.

"Why?"

"The Earl of Astley? Remember?"

No, she actually had forgotten about him, which made her feel horrible. If it hadn't been for Simon, who knows what would have happened to her sister Caillen. He'd saved her life when she'd eloped to Gretna Green with her husband William, only to have William gunned down by highwaymen on their way back to London. It was Simon who came across them and saved Caillen from certain death. The highwaymen, however, had escaped, and Caillen had been recuperating at Simon's mother's house in the country for the past eight months.

It was horrendous of her to forget Simon's plight. "Of course. Let us be off. Simon needs our help."

Elias frowned. "Not our help. *My* help. You will return to the *Maribelle* immediately."

Máira stood up straight, thrusting her shoulders back and ignoring the way Elias's gaze strayed to her breasts. "I will not."

Elias, however, dismissed her objection. "Yes, you will. I will head out to find Astley on my own."

It was his mother who disagreed next. "No. You will not go alone."

Elias's brow puckered. "Fine. I'll take your henchman."

"Tomás is not a henchman. He works for me."

"He's your guard dog."

"A more loyal breed I've never found."

"Not even in Father?" Anger tinged his words, but Elias didn't back down.

"Especially not your father," Hag agreed.

Elias flinched but didn't argue.

"If Tomás disappeared there would be talk. I cannot allow him to go. Not now." Then she did the unexpected and nodded in Máira's direction. "She should go with you."

Elias spit out his answer before Máira could agree. "No."

"Yes," she and Hag said as one, and smiled at each other. God help him if they could actually agree.

"She could be useful," Hag said at the same time Máira said, "I can help."

"How can she possibly help?" Elias plopped down into a chair as if all the fight in him escaped. Then he closed his eyes and rubbed his forehead, his elbow resting on the table. He sighed and rolled his neck before looking at his mother.

"Traveling as a couple is better than traveling alone." Hag's argument made him stiffen further.

"We are at war. It is not safe—I can make faster time traveling alone." He rubbed the back of his neck as if it hurt, and Máira took over the massage. He stiffened at first, but then relaxed and melted into her touch. She tried not to think about how her hands were moving across his bare skin and every part of her was coming alive with the feel of his smooth, tight muscles flexing and relaxing underneath her touch.

She leaned into him, her nipples growing hard at the feel of his bare back against her front, and asked, "Do you know what Simon looks like?"

His muscles tensed under her fingers and his lips thinned into a straight line as she peered around his shoulder.

"That would be a resounding *no*." Hag responded, and Elias's eyes snapped in her direction with daggers in their depths. He was not happy with his mother. She, however, was grateful.

"Besides, how can I trust Peter?" she added. "He abandoned me on land without any money to my name."

"She could have ended up working on her back," his mother added.

Máira blushed, and she could have sworn she saw Elias launch those daggers of his in his mother's direction as he shrugged away from Máira's touch and stomped toward the door.

"Where are you going?" She asked.

"To the *Maribelle*. It's time I find out once and for all just exactly where Peter stands."

"Don't you think clothes might help?" Hag asked.

Elias stopped just short of the door and Máira covered her mouth, but a strangled giggle split the seams of her fingers.

"Are you telling me that now you magically have clothes for me, Hag?" His voice held back his temper remarkably well.

"As a matter of fact, I do. It seems my beloved husband was about the same height and weight as you are."

"I cannot take—"

Hag refused to accept his excuses. "I insist. He would have wanted it this way."

Elias didn't turn around but he nodded just the same. "Then I would be grateful and honored."

"Tomás?" Hag didn't need to yell—her ever-present shadow stood to face the three of them.

"Yes, Hag." There was no hesitation in the way he addressed Hag. It was as if he had accepted it a long time ago.

"If you could fetch my husband's clothes for Elias, I would appreciate it. He and his wife will be leaving at once."

"Of course, Hag." Tomás bowed and left the room as the three of them watched him go, with very different thoughts on their minds.

Ten

Elias—

I may have information that will lead you to your clerk. Bring plenty of Scotch, I am in need of more inventory.

—An unsigned letter delivered to Elias Allistair Drake, May, 1812, Carlisle, England, in the middle of nowhere

Prior to leaving the tavern Hag had pulled him aside and hugged him tight for the first time in a decade. It made him want to take her and Máira away from this place he had once viewed so happily.

He made it to the ship and back in record time, thanks to the help of Tomás. It had taken all his self-control to not beat the answers out of Peter while aboard ship, but his first mate had done exactly what Elias would have done in his shoes.

Cook had heard two men talking below deck but had not been able to identify them, and rather than take a chance, Cook notified Peter, and Peter had sent Máira to Hag, where Elias was supposed to be. Since Peter was uncertain if anyone else had been involved in the plot, he thought it best to get back to the ship posthaste and protect it. Elias couldn't blame him, especially after he saw the gash on Peter's head that he had suffered upon his return to the ship. His friend was in worse shape than he. Peter could not stand the light, nor could he even open his eyes. If Cook hadn't sewn up his skull and his gut, Peter might still be bleeding in his bed. His first mate was fighting for his life.

Jack and Billie had been intent on killing Peter after learning Máira was no longer aboard ship, and that was the last thing Peter could remember or communicate. Cook advised that Jack and Billie were the only two unaccounted for aboard ship, and the ship's jolly boat was missing. The men aboard the *Maribelle*, although happy to see him, were uneasy sitting in a French port. Elias put the second mate in charge until his return. Even though he had full confidence in his second mate, Elias decided Máira was safer at The Happy Hag.

Changing into a set of his own clothing and shoes that fit, he returned to the Happy Hag to find three French soldiers sitting at a table drinking ale and being less than polite to Hag. When one half her age pinched her arse, he'd nearly stormed inside. It had been Hag's open palm to the soldier's ear and the laughter of his two companions as he fell from his stool that had given him pause. Hag was used to men like that, he reminded himself.

His father would not have wanted this life for his wife, just as Elias didn't want it for his mother. Fate, however, did not allow her on English soil any more than it wanted him in French territories.

He quickly went around to the rear entrance and entered the tavern through the kitchen. The cook, a grizzled woman past the age of caring about life or the people around her, grunted upon his entry but didn't look up. She'd probably learned through the years that she was better off not knowing who came and went in Hag's establishment.

Elias peeked out to the tavern floor and captured the attention of an angry Tomás, who reluctantly left Hag.

"The soldiers arrived shortly after you left," Tomás whispered as he nodded toward the men. "I did not want to leave her alone, so I was not able to obtain a second horse."

Elias would have thought fate was once more dictating that he refuse to take Máira with him; the soldier's arrival, however, said otherwise.

"Will you leave your wife here?"

"No." That one word seemed to relieve a modicum of tension from Tomás's shoulders, and Elias had no doubt he was thinking one strong-headed woman was enough to protect. Two—insurmountable.

"My horse is ready in the stable. He is strong enough to carry you and your wife all the way to the Austrian Empire. Take good care of him, and I will watch over her." Both looked down the corridor toward his mother laughing with the soldiers as if she hadn't just left one of them deaf in one ear.

Footsteps behind them gave Elias pause until he saw Máira coming down the steps, wrapped in his mother's cloak with a determined look on her face.

"I don't think she would let you leave her even if you tried." Tomás said with a knowing smile.

"I believe you are correct."

When Máira reached them, he put a finger to his lips and ushered her toward the kitchen and out the back door. In the stables, he helped her onto the beautiful black Friesian stallion that stood at least sixteen hands at the withers.

Tomás may not have been able to acquire a second horse, but the one he'd given them was a thing of beauty. Between the horse and the woman, Elias was quite aware of the image they portrayed. The horse may be a draught horse, and the woman may be wearing simple clothing, but both held themselves with the breeding of the aristocracy. It was a look that could get them killed. Belatedly he realized his hand had caressed the length of her exposed leg of its own accord, and he yanked it back, waiting to feel the slap of her hand, only to look up and see her lips parted on a breathless sigh.

One way or another, the woman would be the death of him.

"My apologies," he said as he pulled himself up behind her. He nearly groaned when he found his cock nestled against the soft, round globes of her arse as they made their way out of the stable. He stayed to the snicket and avoided the main road for as long as possible, conscious of the way her arse rubbed up against him with every damned high step the horse took. Attempting to focus on anything but the sweet rub of her soft flesh against his cock was pure torture.

His torture was only made worse by Máira's bare legs being scandalously exposed as she sat astride the horse in front of him with her skirts bunching around her waist and thighs. He wanted to stroke her, caress the curve of her thighs all the way up to her apex. Instead, he struggled to keep his cock from grinding against her, his focus on their escape and not her delectable body, and her quiet—he failed miserably at the last.

"Where are we going?" She turned to whisper in his ear, effectively rubbing her breast against his left arm. Her hard nipple drawing his attention downward to where it rested against his jacket. It was the third time she'd ignored his instructions for silence. The third time he had to force his gaze back to the darkened road in front of them. It wasn't as if he could even see her breast against his arm, but in his mind's eye he saw her naked flesh brushing back and forth with the sway of the horse.

Each time he'd told her to hush, hoping she'd listen. She did not. He told her again. "You must keep quiet. We do not want to draw any attention to ourselves."

"I can't help you if I don't know the plan," she insisted.

"The *plan* is to keep quiet."

"You know the plan," she whispered.

"I made the plan," he whispered back. How had she manipulated him into breaking the silence over and over?

"If we're to be a team, you need to share your plan."

"We're not a team. I am on a mission and you are extra baggage." He winced as soon as the words left his lips.

She was silent—for far too long. He should be happy. Let his curt words maintain the silence required when skulking about the French countryside in the middle of a war. The sound of their horse's hooves hitting the packed earth should be welcome. Except for once, it was not.

He closed his eyes and shook his head. He had about as much finesse as a blunderbuss. "I didn't mean—"

"It's fine."

Bloody hell. Even the stupidest of men knew when a woman said things were fine, they were about as far from fine as English wine. "I'm sorry."

"It's fine," she repeated, and squirmed in her seat—rested her arse firmly against his cock.

Bloody fucking hell. He willed his body not to respond even more than it already had, but with her anger came a restlessness that was pure torture. She couldn't have aroused him more if she'd taken him in hand and lowered her lips to his tip.

Images of her head lowering to his cock earlier that night did nothing to help him gain control. The woman was a menace. "It's bloody-well not fine and we both know it!" He hissed through his teeth loud enough for the next town to hear.

"Shhhh!" Her head whipped back and forth, the long strands of her hair lashing his jaw, as if she expected men to jump out of the shadows, and once again he regretted his harsh words. He wrapped his arm around her waist, pulling her tightly against him before she fell from her seat.

Chances were there wasn't anyone out there. At least he hoped there wasn't. They were in-between towns, but they were at war, and more and more people who shouldn't be wandering around at night, were. Like him and his bride. He'd kept them to the outskirts of the past two towns, but as loud as he'd been...he could have been heard by anyone.

He left the roadway and they moved along in silence for what seemed to be an eternity. They wouldn't come across the next town until well after daylight. Máira broke the silence once more. "I just don't understand why you couldn't share our destination with me."

He'd have to explain it to her or she would never cease asking questions. "If we are captured, I cannot risk you giving out more information than you already know."

She gasped, as he knew she would. The affront was like a slap in the face, and he immediately explained, despite not wanting to. "They may torture you for the information. I can't afford for it to slip."

He heard her start to reply and then stop. She started again, and once more closed her lips without saying a word. Several minutes passed before she finally said, "I understand how important this is. Simon...Astley is much more valuable than I."

"He's not."

"He is, and I understand now why you wouldn't tell me."

She had it all wrong. It wasn't that Astley was more important, it was that Máira couldn't tell a lie if she were protecting the King Regent himself. She was transparent in her subterfuge, and *the French* would see her lie instantaneously. The war minister would do every nasty thing imaginable to her to get her to talk. Her closed lips would just mean that they would hurt her further. He wouldn't risk death by torture for her. What she didn't know, would save her life. "I won't risk you in that manner. To hell with Astley."

"You can't mean that." The disbelief was evident in her tone.

"I do."

"You can't. You were sent for him," she argued.

"Not everything between us has been a lie. Is it not true that we have always wanted one another?" He rubbed his cock against the sweet cheeks of her arse, his desire undeniable to both of them. How he longed to rub it through those plump, round globes.

Máira stiffened and he almost stopped, until she pushed back against him, tempting him further with her luscious form, and he couldn't resist rubbing the underneath side of her breast with his thumb. She had to know he couldn't fake his attraction to her. It had been there from their very first encounter, threatening his resolve to walk away from her in the end.

Wrapped in darkness, except for the distant glimmer of the setting moon peeking through the trees, Máira let out a small sigh, a sound so faint it would have been lost in the song of the crickets if he had not bent over to kiss her neck. Her back arched, her buttocks grinding against him as her chest strained for his touch.

"This has always been real," he whispered in her ear. For weeks he had longed to take her in hand, and somehow in this moment he could no longer control his desire for her. Something inside him snapped his restraint into pieces.

His lips trailed to the pulse point on her neck fluttering like a frightened bird trapped in a briar patch, except Máira was anything but trapped—she was free to soar. He ran his tongue across her jaw and loved the taste of her skin. Sweet and sultry, like a woman who prepares for loving and knows what a man likes. Máira had been the most innocent woman he'd ever known, and the need to torture her with ecstasy drove him beyond the boundaries he'd placed upon himself and their intimacies. He savored her taste, the smooth, silky feel of her flesh on the tip of his tongue. His fingers slowly traced the lace of her gown, and when she pushed her breast into his palm, he cupped it, squeezed it, and bit back the curse wanting to spill from his lips. She moaned into the night, her voice lower and more beautiful than any nightingale serenading its lover.

He nipped the tip of her ear as his fingers dipped into her gown. Máira gasped, the sound like the music of a siren to his cock, as it throbbed to the beat of his heart. His feet went rigid in the stirrups, and he ground against her, his body demanding more. More pleasure, more Máira. Her hips shifted as his thumb circled her nipple, taunting the flesh that seemed to glow in the night. He had to see more of her, and in an instant, he pulled down her gown, her corset and chemise—baring her full and beautiful lily-white breasts to the pale moonlight. Round and perfect in every way, they were too beautiful to not to be seen.

Elias had seen his fair share of breasts, small, large, some barely there, others large enough to fuck as a woman took him into her mouth. Dark nipples, pale nipples, he truly loved every breast he'd ever seen, but Máira's—her breasts were like none he'd gazed upon before. Plump and flawless, her ivory breasts in perfect contrast to the primrose delicate jewels of her nipples, which were on display for everyone to see, and no one but Elias was there to enjoy the view.

Máira's body was made for his, he knew it the first time he'd kissed her. It hadn't been her first kiss, but it had been the first kiss that made him wish for something more than just sex from a woman. With Máira, he had always been in danger. Danger of losing himself and becoming too selfish to care about his mission. For the first time in his life, a woman had meant more than just a night or two of pleasure, and he suddenly couldn't stop himself from seizing more.

Máira's arm slinked around the back of his head, her neck curving to offer herself to him—exactly what he needed. He dropped the reins, trusted the horse to continue the pace he had set and allowed his now free hand to pull up her skirts even further. The smooth curve of her thigh everything he had dreamed of, fantasized about. She was better than all the women he'd been with, combined and multiplied by a thousand. Ten thousand. Her murmurs and panting were about to make him explode in his trousers.

This wasn't real. It couldn't be. He had never been so completely out of control. They were on a horse, riding on a dangerous mission in the middle of the night in enemy territory, and all he could think about was touching her there...where his fingers skimmed on delicate skin and found her hot and...bloody hell, she was wet. Her skin like velvet, her sweet juices coating his fingers as he explored her folds, and she writhed in front of him inviting him to do more. Her nipples were as hard as the gems he knew them to be, precious, breathtaking, desired by anyone who caught sight of them, and when he found the matching bead of desire between her legs, she cried out in pleasure.

At that moment, a part of him regained his sanity. The open countryside gave way to woods and he searched the wooded area around them, his gaze scouring the terrain as he listened for any foreign sound, or the silenced melody of the night creatures that had become accustomed to their presence, as his hands continued to explore the treasures he held. Assured that no one lurked in the shadows of the woods, his hand left her breast momentarily to turn her head toward his as he devoured her mewling song of ecstasy with his lips. Thrusting his tongue in her mouth in tandem with the rhythm of his fingers delving into her delectable quim.

His only regret, not being able to feast on her petite mort, because she was close. So close her thighs quivered, her body strained, her breathing as erratic as his own heart, and he felt as if a spell had been cast upon them. As if nothing and no one could penetrate their unbridled ride of passion. Máira nibbled on his bottom lip, he sucked on hers, her soft, sweet mouth tasting of a heaven he'd never dreamed he'd reach.

His thumb circled her bud, going faster and faster, his middle finger stroking in and out of her tight, wet core. He added a second finger and she screamed into his kiss. Her fingers clenched his hair down to his scalp as her body convulsed, milking his fingers, clamping and pulsing, pulling him deeper into her core. He curved his fingers and found that spot to drive her further into oblivion. Máira's hips swiveled, her quim constricting tightly around his fingers as if she were choking the life out of him, except her pleasure was having the opposite effect. He'd never felt so alive, so aroused, and so in need of burying himself deeply inside the woman in his arms. She was so tight, if it had been his cock he would have expired from ecstasy.

When she finally grew silent, her breath rapid yet sated, a smile formed on her lips. Elias pulled at it with his teeth, wanting to consume every bit of this woman who tasted like joy and sunshine. She pulled back to gaze into his eyes, and despite the darkness, he could read the look of awe on her face as he pulled his fingers from her body and brought them to his lips. His own pleasure fell from his mouth in a raspy moan of delight. He never wanted to go without her scent on his body, her taste of bliss on his lips, the delectable *joie de vivre* that being with this woman brought to his life.

His senses returned. He had a mission to complete. A man to rescue.

Elias pulled his fingers from his mouth and smiled down on his temporary bride as he put her gown to rights, covering her titillating flesh from his view and he grabbed the reins once more. "Sleep. We have a long journey ahead of us and it will not be an easy one."

Máira smiled and snuggled into the crook of his shoulder. "That was wonderful. I never...I never knew it could be so...so...rapturous."

He reverently kissed the top of her head. "Neither did I, my sweet, neither did I."

Eleven

Hag,

I have a shipment of Scotch to sell for the right price. Expect delivery soon.

Elias

—A letter from a son in England to his mother in France, both wanting to protect the other from certain capture.

"*Ma chérie.* You must wake up."

She didn't want to wake. She'd had the most glorious dream of being in her husband's arms on horseback.

"The sun is up and I haven't been able to feel my left arm for the past couple hours. If we don't stop, I'm afraid I will drop you."

She snuggled in closer. Loving his scent, the feel of his bicep under her cheek. Who needed a downy pillow when strong arms were available?

She felt his lips brush her ear. "Máira, we are coming close to a village. We must make ourselves presentable."

Village. France. Danger. The warning was clear, and Máira awoke in an instant, sitting up straight in the saddle and giving her poor husband's arm a break from holding her weight. Except he really wasn't her husband, was he? In a fortnight this would all be a dream. A wonderful, enticing dream she would remember the rest of her life—alone.

"Why didn't you tell me sooner?" she asked, as she ran her fingers through her hair. For the love of everything she held holy, it was an utter disaster.

"You needed your rest."

"And what about you?"

"I am accustomed to going without sleep."

She looked over her shoulder, her face scrunched in irritation. Elias winked as he pulled the horse off the trail behind a particularly large patch of bracken, the vibrant colored fronds of the ferns and bushes tall enough to graze her thighs as Elias guided the horse forward.

"You couldn't have chosen a better place to stop."

"I have done this a time or two."

"Spy, you mean? You've come to France to spy—" A hand clamped down over her mouth. Her eyes darted around them, looking for the source of his fear, until she realized he was looking no further than her. Elias was scowling down at her with one arm wrapped tightly around her waist, the other still holding the reins and her head from moving.

"I am not a spy," he hissed in her ear.

She protested into his palm and his lips rolled in with irritation.

"My mother may have said that, but that is not what I do."

Again, she was forced to talk into his palm. She didn't mind his hand covering her mouth the moment he thought they were being watched, but that was currently not the case. She bit his palm.

"Ow! There was no cause for that," he complained while shaking out his hand.

"I didn't even break the skin."

"Because I pulled my hand away."

She rolled her eyes. "In spite of you pulling your hand away."

"He looked around the area once more and repeated his statement. "I am not a spy."

"Your mother said you were."

"I haven't been able to convince her otherwise."

"Then what are you?"

"A recovery agent."

"A recovery agent? What's that?"

"Someone who works for neither government, but rather a family."

"A family? Simon's family?"

"Precisely."

"They know he's been taken? How awful." She paused. "His sisters must be devastated, and his mother...I can't imagine how she's coping."

Elias reined in and dismounted, before he lifted her off the horse. He shook out his numb arm several times, which made her feel guilty for biting him. He was doing an honorable thing, and he was rescuing a family friend. She looked at his long strong fingers and images of what he'd done with those fingers came crashing into her thoughts as if someone had just charged through the shrubbery. She nearly fell to the ground as she stumbled backward, her legs feeling weak and numb from the ride.

Elias looked over at her. "Are you alright?"

"Of course." Except she wasn't. Her heart was racing and her body was much more awake than she had been two minutes ago.

His brow puckered as if he was trying to read her thoughts, to which she proceeded to clear her throat and turn ten shades of red. His forehead smoothed and that sultry grin he'd had the day they first met played with his lips.

"As much as I would love to revisit last night, we must get ourselves more presentable, instead of less." He winked again, and she wanted to sink down into the ground. She was proving that it wasn't just men who thought about compromising the opposite sex. She was thinking about all kinds of ways she could make him more presentable. Tearing his shirt from his body would absolutely be more enticing to every red-blooded female. And the way his pants hugged his thighs, well, *that* was presently looking delectably large as it strained against the front of his falls. But a fully naked Elias was a glorious specimen and she loved the way his masculine hair showcased every ripple of muscle and sinew on his powerful body.

Elias groaned. "You will be the death of me, *ma chérie*."

"You've gained an accent since we arrived in France and you use more French terms."

"I slipped once in England. Do you remember?"

She did. At the time it had been the most romantic moment of her life. *Will you be my wife, ma chérie?* Then he cleared his throat and laughed and told her it sounded much more romantic in his head to speak in French—after he'd said it, he didn't think it was appropriate. They were at war with France. She, however, had never heard of a more enchanting proposal in her entire life.

Except it was a lie.

"No, I'm sorry. I don't recall," she lied. She didn't want him to know how big a lie it actually was, so she turned away and began finger-combing her hair. She should have thought of how bad her hair would look.

"Take this." His hand appeared over her shoulder with his leather que dangling from his fingers.

"What will you use?" she asked, not daring to turn around.

"My hair will be fine down. We are in the countryside of France, not among the *ton* in England."

She took the strap of leather from his hand, being careful not to touch him. "Thank you."

"You're welcome."

They sounded like strangers. She cleared her throat. "I hear a brook over there. I'm going to go refresh myself."

"Very well." Was that hurt she heard in his voice?

No. She was hearing what she wished to hear. If she looked at him, she would undoubtedly see that he was rolling his shoulder or cleaning his shoes without a second thought to her response. Without looking back, Máira made her way through the bracken to where a small brook flowed leisurely across a path of stone. Heather adorned the opposite bank, making the scene appear completely serene and similar to some of the English countryside. How strange to see similarities in terrain, but a world of difference in the language and viewpoints of people. Although she imagined the French people didn't want war as much as the English soldiers she'd seen heading off to battle.

She knelt down at the water's edge and reached into the cool, refreshing water, her fingers skimming the surface as she closed her eyes. Birds harmonized, their song a thing of wonder from such small creatures with no keyboard to stroke. The stream splashed against the rocks, the symphony of nature playing for an audience of one as the leaves on the trees applauded in appreciation and the breeze whistled its praise. Máira felt as if she had never been in a more serene place in her entire life.

"Hand over your purse!" The demand in French, jumbled in her mind at first, but the dangerous tone translated the meaning of the words an instant later. The threat broke the tranquility of the moment, and her eyes flew open, expecting to see a gang of highwaymen leering at her with thought to do more than just rob her of her purse. Except the other side of the bank was empty. The tree line vacant. A shot echoed through the forest behind her. Her body flinched involuntarily and she searched her chest, certain to see a crimson blossom expanding across the front of her gown. Her hands felt around the front of her gown expecting the worst. Finding nothing. Her dress remained as it was, not clean, but not painted with blood either.

Máira reached under her skirt and grabbed the dirk strapped to her thigh as she looked around. Heated words between two men silenced the peace. Elias!

She tore through the woods in the direction of the fight as quietly as she could. Her heart leapt, and her feet followed. Over the dead tree and through the undergrowth she raced, unable to imagine the unfathomable even while her mind pictured her husband's white shirt stained red. Fronds whipped at her skin and tree branches slashed at her eyes. She brushed them aside as the sight before her made her blood burn. She couldn't allow it to boil. If it boiled, she would shake, and she would not shake.

Elias wrestled for his life with a bear of a man. Teeth flashing and paws batting, he caught Elias on the side of his head. It was a wonder he remained conscious. Elias tackled his opponent to the ground as a tall thin rail of a man stood over them—a pistol waving back and forth in his hand as each man fought for dominance on the ground in front of him.

Elias couldn't win. If he gained the upper hand on the ground, he would be shot in the back. If he lost on the ground, he would be shot in the head.

Recognizing his impending defeat, the large man rolled onto his back. His face bloodied from a constant barrage of Elias's fist, he grinned as he exposed Elias to the worst of fates—a bullet he would never see coming.

The thin man steadied his weapon and forged steel aimed at the broad muscled expanse of the man she loved. Máira didn't think. Winding her arm back, she let her blade fly. Steel soared through the air the razor-sharp tip pointing at its target, slicing through the air like the blade of a guillotine. The forest was eerily silent. Elias stopped grunting. His attacker ceased groaning and the trigger of pistol behind him—pulled. A heartbeat after her blade lodged in the shooter's neck, his eyes bulged, and he crumpled to the ground and Máira became what she swore she would never become. A murderer.

She didn't have time to think as the giant bellowed and Elias went flying. He landed with a thud before Máira could determine if the bullet had struck its mark on his back.

Then the beast was on his feet, blood pouring from his nose as if a spigot on a barrel of wine had been left to flow. Elias didn't look much the better, lying on the ground with one eye nearly swollen closed, his lower lip split in two different places. His shirt, loosened from his trousers, was torn down to his waist. She didn't mind the ruined shirt. The injuries, however, were a different matter altogether. Yet no blood spewed from any holes in his chest, and she had to believe the shot had gone wide of its target.

The huge Frenchman stalked Elias like the giant in the story about the beanstalk and she could have sworn she heard him repeat the stolen line from King Lear: *"Fee Fi Fo Fum! I smell the blood of an Englishman. Be he alive, or be he dead, I'll grind his bones to make my bread."*

Elias lifted his head, looked at the giant and then at her, before his head dropped back to the earth with a hollow thud. It was as if he'd raised the white flag the Frenchman did not recognize. Malevolence radiated off of him as he chose to end the brutality with nothing short of death. He snarled and reached for her Elias's shirt, lifting his limp body off the ground and into the air.

With no weapon, Máira did the only thing she could. She launched herself onto his back. With the man's height and breadth, that feat alone was difficult. Her efforts produced a growl low in the man's throat as he turned his head to see what he had failed to notice—her—and she suddenly questioned her own sanity. Perhaps it had been the tenacity and fierce determination she'd seen in her mother-in-law's eyes as she killed the man in the tavern that gave Máira strength.

It was in that moment she understood Hag. Máira had to be like her to save her husband from certain death, because the fight was out of him—

Until it wasn't.

From the ashes of certain death, Elias roared. His arm swung and his fist, wrapped around a huge rock she hadn't noticed before, slammed into the temple of the man who stood between them. The three of them landed in a tangled heap on the ground and Máira was thankful she landed on the top of the pile.

"Did you kill him?" she asked Elias between breaths.

"I think I did."

"You think?"

"He's not moving, is he?"

"Well, no, but that doesn't mean he's dead."

"His chest fails to rise."

"My sisters say I sleep as if I am dead. He could just be unconscious."

Elias blew out a long, heavy sigh. "Are you injured?"

She shook her head. "I don't think so, no. Are you?"

He quirked a brow. It happened to be the brow over his left eye that was currently red and swelling shut. It looked ghastly.

"Other than your face," she qualified.

Elias chuckled and pushed her hair away from her cheek. "My ribs feel as if a herd of sheep have trampled across them for the past week."

"That's awful," she said.

"Mmmm," he responded. "Could I ask a favor?"

"Of course. Anything."

"Could you kindly get off my chest so that I might breathe?"

"Good heavens, I'm sorry!" Máira scrambled off the top of him, feeling as stupid as a young girl seeing the first real man who'd struck her fancy. How was it possible Elias still rattled her so.

Pulling herself to rights, Máira attempted to help him up only to be turned away.

"I can do it."

"Of course you can," she replied, but she knew he couldn't. He was badly beaten from his head to his toes, and everywhere in between, the pain evident in his grimace. He staggered to his feet but she was there for him, under his arm and guiding him away from the carnage they had created.

Elias looked over at what she now recognized as the body of a French officer in the military, her knife in his neck. "Is that your work?" He asked.

She didn't want to look, but she supposed she had to face what she had done. "Yes."

The dead man's eyes were open, his jaw slack and his arms spread wide from his body. The pistol lay on the ground less than a foot away. It was hard to imagine the menace she had seen on his face moments earlier. His sheer determination to end Elias's life was an image she would never forget.

Elias stopped for a moment, placing his large body in-between her and the dead man, and looked down into her eyes. Even though one of his eyes was completely swollen shut, the other looked at her in a manner he had not done before. "Thank you."

Her eyes filled. Her hands began to shake. "For killing a man?" she croaked over the emotion tightening in her throat and looked away.

His hand raised to her chin and turned her head, forbidding her to look anywhere but into the depths of his mossy green gaze. The sincerity she saw was the same as she had witnessed on their wedding day. Solemn in nature, truth in volumes, as he wiped away tears she hadn't realized had fallen. "For saving my life." He kissed her forehead, and she wished he'd kissed her lips.

His large body swayed and she let her emotions fade into oblivion as she wrapped her arm around his waist once more to guide him to a fallen tree where he could sit and she could tend his wounds.

"We'll need his gun to see this through," Elias told her.

"You're expecting more trouble?"

"We are English citizens in France. I expect those two won't be our last battle."

"You are in no shape to battle."

"I've been in worse. I'm fine."

"You're not fine. You can barely stand."

"Enough, Máira. In an hour I'll be as good as new, and I will get you somewhere safe where you can wait until after I recover the earl."

She wanted to argue but knew better. Having five sisters taught her to recognize a losing battle. Robina, the youngest Blair sister, shared the same tranquil and friendly nature as Elias—docile and calm with a witty quirk of the brow—until she wasn't happy. Thoughts of Elias aboard the *Maribelle* crashed into her thoughts like the angry waves that had battered the ship. He'd been angry at her, but more importantly, he'd been angry at himself and nature for endangering her safety. It had been the same look he'd held when he'd killed the man mere moments ago. Every thought had been to protect her.

When in battle, he was a completely different creature. Initially, she'd believed she'd been duped; when she woke up to find this imposing man aboard the *Maribelle*, she should have recognized the duality of his nature. The autocratic figure in front of her was like Robina when she was told she must dress for an occasion and put on proper shoes. As a child, she'd resisted with every bit of her will. Robina had been of the mindset that a stiff upper lip wouldn't get her as far as a stiff uppercut of her fist. There had been several instances when their nursemaid had to hold Robbie still while Máira slipped a gown over her head and shoes onto her feet. Robbie's fist were weapons of mass destruction. They landed blows on any chin in the vicinity if she was in a mood, and then she would present herself in public as the ever-obedient, contrite little girl.

Like Robbie, Elias was congenial in polite society. A gentleman who would recover her package and grin a devilishly forward smile as if he knew her every thought when she'd stuttered a shy *thank you*.

Take the man out of the pomp and circumstances of their

courtship and put him into a mission to save another, however, and the docile man she'd known, rarely appeared. Yet somehow, she found she loved this strong, powerful, and utterly ruthless side of him more. He commanded respect without the obvious station of a gentleman dressed in his finest attire. Even off ship, most men stepped out of his path to avoid his raw masculinity.

But there was something else she liked even more when she was with Elias. She liked what she became while with him. She liked this new fierce side of her personality. She had done what she needed to do to save him. An intensity she'd never known she possessed came to life when she was in his company.

Still...now was not the time to poke the injured beast, because whether he realized it or not, Elias needed her to see his mission through.

Twelve

My Lord Duke,

Sir Elias Maximilien Allistair Drake is the captain of the *Maribelle*, with a healthy reputation as a ruthless privateer. The ship left English soil out of the port of Dumfries the morning after your sister's wedding. Sir Drake does fit the description of the man who married Miss Máira Blair, and he was last seen leaving port with an unconscious woman over his shoulder who was said to be his bride. He was en route to Le Conquet, France, with a hull full of Scotch.

I further learned that Sir Drake is the son of Thomas Jefferson Drake, a spy for the Crown, who married a French woman. Her identity is unknown, but Mr. Drake was murdered ten years ago by none other than Maximilien de Danton, a general for Napoleon. Rumor has it the general has been estranged from his daughter since then, and that his daughter, who is currently a widow, was married to an Englishman. I've been able to locate one sailor who swore the Englishman the French general's daughter married was none

other than Thomas Drake. The couple owned a pub in Le
Conquet, and the widow is currently the sole proprietor.

I will be leaving for Le Conquet, France, on the morrow,
and will advise you of my findings at the soonest date possible.

Your faithful servant,
Mr. Johnathan Payne

—*A letter from Bow Street Runner, Mr. Johnathan Payne,*
to Nashford Harding, the Duke of Ross, who hired him to locate
his sister-by-marriage, Miss Máira Blair.

M *on Dieu*, but he hurt. Nothing had gone right from the moment he'd said *"I do"* to this woman. She was a menace to the cause. A thorn in his side, wiggling deeper and deeper into his flesh until she pierced his very heart. He'd known he loved her for quite some time. He wasn't a complete fool.

Then again, maybe he was, because he'd thought he could ignore the tug of his emotions, the draw of her mind, body, and soul. Then she'd gone and saved him.

He hadn't seen her throw the knife, but he'd seen where it landed with deadly aim and precision. The act still baffled him, what lady of the *ton* knows how to throw a knife? For that matter, where had she kept the knife?

He found that thought sexy as hell. Máira Blair was not raised to be part of the dangerous life a wife of his would lead. Máira was gently raised to attend parties of the *ton*, take strolls in Hyde Park on the arm of her titled husband as their children ran around them giggling and laughing at the loving antics of their parents. Simply put, Máira deserved the love match he led her to believe she was getting.

She deserved more than a filthy, bloodied fool wearing a stolen French uniform. He rode with her on the front of magnificent beast that wasn't his, while trying to keep his cock in check under the caress of her sumptuous arse. *Mon Dieu*, she was going to drive him mad with lust.

The prickling of the stallion's ears brought his attention to their surroundings.

"Someone's coming," he whispered in Máira's ear, and pulled the horse off the path, deep into the forest. A few moments later, he heard the chatter of a man and woman. The worried tone of the woman's voice reached him before her the words in his native language.

"What if we didn't leave in time? What if the babe becomes sick?"

"He will be fine, Lizette. Do not worry," a man responded. Elias assumed he was her husband.

"How do you know? All those people looking for shelter could have brought the ague to our village. What if they contaminated the water?"

Her husband's voice softened. "Let's not bring trouble where we do not need it. You and the baby will be safe at your parents' house."

Elias could see the couple dressed in the attire of country peasants. They were younger than he and Máira, and the woman was holding a baby in her arms as it nursed on her breast.

"What about you?" she asked. "Who will keep *you* safe?"

The young man kissed his wife's hair as he wrapped an arm around her shoulder and looked down at the infant. "Your love will keep me safe. Would you like to stop and remind me of just how much you love me?" The young man's eyebrows waggled and his wife giggled. "You are insatiable. It hasn't been an hour since I showed you how much I adore your cock down my throat." She batted at her husband's hand as he attempted to bring hers to his crotch. "Besides, your son needs to eat."

Every nerve ending in Elias's body came alive. It was bad enough that he'd been forced to relive every move and counter move of the fight of his life in an effort to distract himself from the feminine form making his own cock want exactly what this woman was discussing. If he had to endure watching the act, he wouldn't be able to keep his body from showing Máira just exactly how much he desired her to repeat her performance. No woman had unmanned him the way she had, and his base needs were hammering against his restraint, challenging his will to keep it at bay.

"How about I show you exactly how much you mean to me as I eat that sweet cunny of yours."

Máira's breath hitched.

The young woman giggled and swatted at her husband. "Maybe when we stop for the night and your boy isn't making me feel like a milking cow."

"You could never be mistaken for a cow. The sweet Lord gave you curves to drive a man insane." He planted a kiss on her cheek and wrapped his arm under his wife's to help support the child in her arms. "Why don't we stop for the night."

Damn, if they stopped—

His wife's joking disappeared. "No, I fear if we rest so close to the village, we will expose our son to the ague that is destroying it. We must continue."

The smile the man gave her was indulgent, yet his own worry was evident. "As you wish, but I must insist on carrying that little man as soon as he is done eating."

The baby burped in her arms and drew the couple's attention back to him. Despite their circumstances, they appeared content. Something in that look pierced Elias's heart, making him realize everything he was giving up. Before Máira, no woman had made him want what this couple had, and yet he could picture her with a suckling babe at her breast as he held them both in his arms.

No. The job was his family. The men of his crew were his children in need of guidance. They were also his brothers-in-arms, despite the treachery of Billy and Jack. Most of his men, although sketchy when bringing a woman around, were dependable when trouble was at hand. As a man he didn't have to watch his back—his family had it.

Yet still...this couple had given him a glimpse of what he was missing.

Elias and Máira sat in silence long after the couple passed. When he was certain they were gone, he directed their horse out of the woods.

"What illness would drive them from their home?"

"I don't know." It was a lie. When Hag had held him tight for the first time in years right before they left, she'd whispered the name of a contact close to Mont Saint Michel who could guide them across the bay to the prison. A trustworthy man who would have a specific medal for him, and him alone. Then she'd warned about a fever sweeping across the countryside, driving people from their homes because the ague was killing the strongest of men.

The sun was high in the sky now, and by the sounds of her stomach growling, Máira was as hungry as he was. "We'll be stopping to eat soon."

Máira shook her head. "I'm fine."

He couldn't stop the rumble of laughter building in his chest. "You are not fine. Your stomach sounds like it wants to eat you from the inside out."

She let out a puff of air that pressed her breasts against his hand holding the reins. She was going to kill him. He was going to hell, and she would put him there.

"What I meant to say was, yes, I am hungry, but I'm fine. I've gone without food before."

Her confession made him pause, the humor of their conversation gone.

"You've gone without food? When?"

The serene smile on her face became brittle. Silence coated her like a coffin sealing the dead, her body saying what her lips would not.

Two minutes ago, he would not have expected her to be stiff

from her calves to the tilt of her head. As a man, he wanted to engulf her and protect her from whatever haunted her so. As her husband he wanted to make her forget, ease the tension from her body, but he wasn't really her husband, was he?

He approached the topic with the caution of a man approaching a wounded animal—not a man comforting his bride. "A rough winter in the country?"

She shook her head once, her movement just as succinct and stilted as it had been when he yelled at her on board the *Maribelle*. She obviously wasn't going to share, unless he did as well. He took a deep breath and exhaled before telling her about the worst night of his childhood.

"When I was fifteen, my best friend and I had too much to drink one night. I'd just lost my virginity to one of the barmaids, and I was bragging about my prowess with the ladies." He felt his lips turn up with the memory.

Not that he remembered what the barmaid looked like or what her name had been, but he did recall how he had finished before she achieved her *petite mort* and she had slapped his face for his error. It was a lesson well-learned. He'd given none of his partners since a reason to complain. It felt much better to leave a woman exhausted from multiples tiny deaths than to leave her hopping mad while he tried to pull on his britches and get out of her reach before she beat him to death. Still, like most young men, he'd felt indestructible.

Until soldiers appeared.

"We were sitting under this tree drinking and laughing, not paying attention to anything but our stories, and then suddenly we were surrounded by the fiercest soldiers I'd ever seen in my life. Before then we'd seen soldiers and sailors in Le Conquet. Even privateers were known to eat at The Happy Hag. We'd been in a few scrapes even, and had come out with little to no injury to our pride.

"But..."

She waited patiently for him to continue. If he wanted her to trust him, he must do the same with her.

"But those soldiers were the fiercest men we had ever encountered, and their leader was an imposing man. Tall and broad, he cut a fine figure in his uniform, yet he had the coldest eyes I had ever seen. Even now, I can't say as I've ever faced a more malevolent man. I had no doubt he would cut down anyone who got in his way. He was much different than the man who taught me to fish."

"Wait." She leaned to the side, and he felt her eyes searching his face for the answer to her unspoken question. "The man who taught you to fish?" she asked. "You knew the soldier you speak of?"

He nodded in response, still unable to look her in the eyes, but her compassion touched him even if her hands did not.

"He was *mon grand-père*."

"Your grandfather?" The incredulity in her voice matched his at fifteen.

There was no way the man on that giant horse had laughed and ruffled his hair. "I'd only met my mother's father a couple of times before that, but he wasn't the type of man you could soon forget."

"Why? What was so different about him?"

"For one, he's a general in Napoleon's army."

She shifted in the saddle so she could look at him more comfortably, but if he was going to make this confession, he needed to talk without establishing eye contact. Even now, the events that occurred after that meeting were difficult to fathom.

"And he was a bastard through and through. If he were still alive, I would kill him." The venom in his voice was unmistakable. He despised his grandfather with every fiber of his being.

Her next question was filled with caution. "I would like to know why...that is, if you would like to tell me. What did your grandfather do to cause such hatred?"

Telling the story, however, would only make it fester in his gut, but he'd gotten this far, he had to finish the story. If she didn't open up with her own painful memory after this, she never would.

"My grandfather didn't recognize me. I had grown two feet since the last time he'd laid eyes on me, and my body had filled out from the scraggly kid he'd tossed up in the air. I tried to tell him who I was, but he refused to listen. Instead, he backhanded me for my insubordination. We were boys of fifteen, playing at being men, and he felt we should be serving our country. He conscripted us on the spot."

She swallowed audibly but remained silent.

"Claude, my friend, resisted at first and received a rifle butt to the head. He lost consciousness and I wondered if he was dead. I changed into the uniform I was given, and when Claude came to, I helped him dress as well. I have never felt so helpless in all of my life. We were to walk behind them, but I argued that Claude could not walk, said that if they had not been so stupid and hit him, he could have. For my insubordination I was once again beaten, only this time *mon grand-père* couldn't be bothered with the act of knocking me into submission. He left that to his captain-of-arms, who proceeded to beat the hell out of me. That's when my father came out of nowhere. He beat the man and two others until three more joined the fight."

It was his turn to swallow audibly. The next part of his story he'd told only once before and that was to his mother, or rather Hag, the very last time he called her *Mother*. The very last time she had shown emotion. Since then, she had been almost as cold as her father—almost.

"They were able to subdue him when two more soldiers joined the fight. By this time, I had figured out my arm was broken, it was of no use to me. Claude was shaking his head, trying to see what was happening, but it was obvious he couldn't focus, let alone stand on his own.

"Then *he* spoke. He recognized my father, in fact he seemed happy to see him. For a moment, I thought the world that had turned upside-down would right itself again."

He felt her hand on his cheek, her touch tentative and gentle. It was only then that he realized a tear trailed down his face. It was the only one he'd shed for his father since that day. He let her wipe it away and gave her a grateful smile, meeting her gaze for the first time since he began to describe his nightmare.

"You don't have to tell me the rest if it's too painful."

"You need to know the type of men we are up against, because that general may be dead, but his successor is the man who has Astley."

Her eyes widened, the only sign of her understanding about the severity of the situation they faced.

"Your grandfather is dead?" She asked.

"Yes. When I was twenty, I received a letter in England from my mother, telling me he had died." He didn't tell her it was the only letter his mother wrote. He'd gotten past the pain she had caused.

"I'm sorry."

"Don't be. What he did that day changed my life forever." He took a deep breath and released it before continuing. "*Mon grand-père* said my father was the reason they were there. That he was a traitor to France, an embarrassment to his daughter and grandson, and my father would be hanged for his crimes."

She gasped. "No."

"Yes," he said, with no more emotion than if he'd admitted he was tired and wanted to sleep. "My grandfather judged my father guilty of treason, said he had been sending information to the British and that he would die for his crimes. My father didn't deny it. He asked the general not to hang him in front of his son. It was then that general looked at me and realized who I was. Then he laughed." Elias's chin tightened involuntarily. "He laughed and denied my father's request. I stood there and watched my father die...I watched the life drain out of his eyes and his body twitch as he swung from a tree."

Tears were streaming down Máira's cheeks, but he couldn't see them. All he could see was the vision of his father's feet swinging and hear the horrific sound of the soldiers laughing.

"He left me there with my father, said I must be the one to deliver the news to my mother. So, I climbed the tree to cut him down. It took me three times because I kept falling, and once I lost consciousness from the pain in my arm. When I finally got him down, I made a sling out of that damn military jacket they forced on me, and I...I used the rope that had taken my father's life to drag him back to Le Conquet. I reached the house just as the sun was rising in the most glorious burst of color I've ever seen.

"My mother wailed her grief when she saw me drop to my knees in front of the house. She'd been waiting up, knowing that something was seriously wrong when my father and I hadn't returned the previous night. She used her wrapper to cover my father's body and took me inside to tend to my arm, and the rope burns on my other hand and back. She listened to my recounting of the events with her eyes growing colder and colder with each word I uttered. By the time I finished telling her of what my grand-father had done, I no longer recognized the woman who raised me.

"In my grief and pain, I didn't know she had put laudanum in the tea she gave me to drink while I told her what happened. While I slept, she washed my father's body and buried him behind our home in her garden." He rubbed the back of his neck. "I have no idea how she did it, where she obtained the strength to dig his grave and bury a man so much larger than she, but she did. Then she put me on a ship the very next day bound for England with a letter to the War Office."

"The next day? But your arm..."

"*Mon grand-père* had told me he would come for me in one month, after my arm healed. She didn't want to take a chance I was still there."

"What happened to Claude?"

"I don't know. The soldiers tied him to a horse and took him. Over the years I thought about Claude from time to time. I even asked Hag if she had heard from him, but as far as the people of Le Conquer knew, Claude was as dead as my father."

He paused, then looked up at her. Tears were streaming down her cheeks and the look on her face he would never forget. "Claude's parents passed on believing their son to be dead, if not by the hands of the soldiers, then by the hands of war. I suppose we all died that day."

As far as he was concerned, his own *grand-père* died the moment he sentenced his father to death. He only wished he'd had the opportunity to return the favor to the bastard.

Thirteen

My dearest Simon,

I received word the brooch was destroyed. Regardless, I don't want you to face unnecessary perils. Please come home to me.

Your loving wife

—A coded letter to Simon Clark, Earl of Astley, secret agent of the Crown, from Sir Robert Williamson, War Office London, England. It never reached the earl because double agent Henry Greasley killed the messenger, a young man with a son to feed.

The town was deadly quiet. Nothing stirred. No cats, no dogs, no owls hooted in the night air. Even the tavern was empty of no-good men and whores trying to survive. Elias kept their horse to the shadows, watching every doorway, every rooftop, every nook and cranny that did not waver with movement.

One of his absconded pistols was hidden in the skirts of Máira's gown, ready to use on the first man to make a move, yet something told him no one in this village was a threat, at least not in the manner he was accustomed to facing. The conversation of the couple came back to him. Hag's warning of a deadly sickness made him want to turn back and forget his mission regardless of the cost to England and Astley. The silent woman wrapped in his arms was too precious to lose for a man who went on suicide missions for the Crown.

He felt as if he were on his own mission of murder, and the only victim would be his wife. *Mon Dieu*, if his plan of using her as a wife caused her death...

"Don't worry. I never get sick," she whispered in French, her accent a bit too stilted for his comfort.

Máira was in tune with his emotions. It was uncanny and unlike anyone else since his father's death. Even Hag no longer knew his heart the way she once had. He squeezed Máira's waist and spoke in his native tongue as well. "I'm going to hold you to those words. Now be a good wife and be quiet."

She gave a huge sigh, as if she found him impossible.

He nuzzled her hair and whispered in English in her ear. "Your French is atrocious."

She smacked his hand but did not argue. For now, for him she would be the obedient silent wife, later she might throttle him.

Elias found a stable where he would have to either rest their horse or talk the proprietor into trading the stallion for a fresher mount, an act of necessity that would cost him plenty with Tomás.

He relieved Máira of her pistol, shoved it into the back of his waistband and dismounted before lifting Máira to the ground. "Stay behind me."

He had already told her they would not speak in English again until they were safely aboard the *Maribelle*. He'd thought she would object, but she acquiesced without argument. Just as now, she stayed behind him as they entered the large stable with the stallion in tow.

"*Bonsoir!*" he called out to the quiet space in front of them.

The stable was lit. Someone had to be inside. No fool would leave lanterns burning in a veritable tinder box if someone wasn't there.

The snick of a musket being cocked behind him made him slowly turn, reaching behind him to wrap his arm around Máira to keep her close to his back as he turned to face the threat.

Looking down from the loft above the main door, stood a teenage boy with eyes wide as he held the weapon up against his jaw, the barrel aimed in their direction. If it weren't for the way the boy quivered, the muzzle would have been aimed at his chest.

"We mean you no harm. We are looking for a fresh horse."

The boy shook his head, his dark black hair spilling into his eyes. "We have none."

Elias smiled. "As you can see, I am from the imperial guard." He hoped the blood on the borrowed uniform did not show too much. "My horse is of good stock. He is more valuable to you than any of the nags you have."

The boy shook his head once more. "You need to leave. Everyone here is infected."

Elias nodded his head. "That's why we have come. We are on our way to Mont-Saint-Michel. My wife will tend the sick there. When I became ill, she did not, and she saved me. She is blessed by the Almighty. She can help the military men at Mont-Saint-Michel survive as well."

The shake of the boy's head made Elias want to stop him from talking before the words left his mouth. "They're dying like flies. Everyone is."

Well, shite. That was the last thing he wanted to hear. "Then it is important that we get there quickly."

"I told you, I have no horses."

Elias looked from stall to stall. Every stall appeared as empty as the boy said. "None? Why?"

"They were stolen by people trying to escape the illness."

"So why do you have the stable lit up as if you do have horses available?"

"To let my aunt know I am well."

"I don't understand?" None of it made sense.

"She is caring for her children. They are all sick. My uncle died, and that's when people stole their horses. My aunt asked that I come here and make sure nothing else was taken. She sent word of her husband's death to my parents, and they sent me to help, but when I arrived, the children were sick. She did not want me to go inside her house out of fear that I will get it as well."

A donkey brayed in the rear of the barn.

"You have a donkey?" The beast of burden would have to do. It would kill the stallion if they continued.

His question brought a bark of laughter from the boy that was hardly filled with joy. "Pierre cannot help you. He is nearly twice my age."

Elias winced. No, he could not take a chance with a stubborn old beast that may drop dead before they reached Mont-Saint-Michel. They would have to stop for the night and move on in the morning after their horse rested, but if things were as bad as the boy made them out to be, he wasn't about to leave his horse unattended here.

"We need to rest our horse."

"You are still sick?" The caution in the boy's question was understandable.

He lied. "No. It has been over a fortnight since I recovered."

The relief in the boy's eyes made him feel dirty for his deceit. "Very well. I'll tend him."

Elias held up his hand to stop the boy before he scurried down the ladder. "I will take care of him, but we will need a place to stay."

"The tavern—"

"I have no doubt the tavern keeper has fallen ill as well. The tavern was dark when we came into town. In fact, very few places had a light on. If I take my wife to the tavern, I have no doubt she will get caught up with caring for the people there and she will never leave. We must rest. She will have her hands full soon enough."

The boy began shaking his head as if he knew what Elias was going to ask before the words left his mouth.

"I have herbs that will help your aunt and her children." The soft voice behind him rose to the boy as Máira stepped out from behind him and pulled some purple flowers from a small satchel tied to the saddle. Damn her.

"You need to keep quiet," he hissed.

"The boy needs our help," she shot right back.

Bloody hell, her bleeding heart. He should have never mentioned her tending to the ill.

Feet hitting the ground behind him made him turn to face the boy, expecting the rifle to still be pointed at his chest. Instead, it was slung over the boy's back.

"You have an angel for a wife," the boy said as his eyes took in Máira's form with a little too much admiration.

He cleared his throat. "Eyes on the plants, *garçon*."

The boy's cheeks reddened and his chest puffed up at being called a boy. His wife slapped his arm for his trouble.

"Stop it," she scolded, and then turned to the boy. "Steep the leaves in their tea, it will calm their stomachs. Then you must feed them chicken soup, put these in the soup." She handed him a different plant from the satchel. "It will give them strength."

The boy nodded as he took the plants from Máira.

"Now go. The sooner you get these in their bellies, the better off they will be."

"*Merci Madame,* but what of my aunt's stable?"

The way the boy had watched Máira's mouth move, Elias wasn't certain if he was mesmerized by her delectable lips or if he was observing how her English tongue struggled with the words. He stepped between them before Máira could respond. "I understand your apprehension, but we will be here until you return in the morning. I will guard the stable." When the boy still shook his head, Elias continued. "I obviously have to protect my own horse if things are as bad as you say."

He softened his tone. "You look like you have not eaten in a week. If you do not stay strong, you will get sick as well. Go. Cook them a meal and eat heartily."

Once more the boy looked affronted. "I don't cook."

He tossed him some dried meat Hag had provided for their trip. "Every good soldier learns to cook. Boil this in water with some potatoes. Then get some sleep before you return. It will keep you healthy." Elias had no idea if what he said was true or not since no one had identified the illness.

The kid, however, seemed to take his advice to heart. Elias and his wife had survived the ague, there had to be something truthful about what he was saying. "Only one night?" The boy asked.

He and Maria nodded in unison. "One night," he said. "Then my horse will be rested and we will be on our way."

"Very well. Madame, you can sleep in the loft. The hay is clean and it is warmer up there."

"*Merci.* What is your name?"

Damn her obstinate tongue. He didn't give a damn what the boy's name was.

"Hubert, Madame. It is my father's name." The boy blushed once more.

Elias barely refrained from rolling his eyes.

"Hubert, we thank you for your hospitality." Máira bowed her head to the boy, and the boy's eyes darted to Elias. No lady would bow to a servant or someone in working class, he wanted to throttle her.

The boy's lips quirked in an uncomfortable smile and then he ran from the stable. No doubt ready to turn them over to the first soldier he saw.

He turned on his wife. "I told you to keep quiet."

"He needed my help."

"When did you pick those plants?"

"After I heard the couple talking about the townspeople being ill. When you were..."

He winced. When he was burying the bodies of the men they'd killed. He'd gruffly sent her back to the stream with their horse to see to the animal's needs.

He ran his hand through his hair. "He knows you're not French."

"No, he doesn't."

"He was watching your mouth."

"He was focused on my instructions."

Women. Did they not know the male mind? Not only had the teenager been focused on the way her tongue moved when she spoke, he noticed her curves. Hell, he'd have to be blind not to notice them. Hag's gown did little to hide the woman beneath, even if the gown was too big.

He turned toward their horse. "I better take care of the horse. You can clean up in the other stall."

"Elias..."

He froze mid-step but wasn't man enough to turn around and face her. When her hand touched his arm, he flinched, and she withdrew her touch.

"None of this is your fault."

A snort slid from his lips. Everything that she'd experienced was his fault.

"You only did what you had to do to save Astley." Her voice was soft and soothing, as if she spoke to a child.

He turned and grabbed her with so much force she stumbled back, but he was there, pressing her against the wall of the stable with a sneer on his face. The venom in his voice split the silence of the night. "Where is Astley, now? Is he safe? For all we know he died at the hands of the soldiers months ago, and if he did survive, who's to say the sickness hasn't already taken him, as it has so many others? Will you say it was worth it then, when he is dead?"

No, she would hate him for everything.

Her kindness did not disappear, despite his rough handling. "You will find him," she reassured. "You will return him to his family...one way or another."

He searched her eyes looking for her hatred. She should hate him with every fiber of her being, every other lady of the *ton* would want him hanging from a rope for what he had put her through. Yet in Máira's fathomless blue gaze, he only saw forgiveness, and then she reached up to caress his cheek, her soft skin in direct contrast to the coarse beard he now sported.

Mon Dieu. It was there burning brightly within her, it was in her touch, her voice...in the way her body pressed against his despite the distance he'd made certain to keep. This was more than just curiosity and lust, this was the reason a woman said *yes* to a man. He had convinced himself the emotion he saw in her eyes was the infatuation of a lady seeking a marriage of comfort and security, but he'd been wrong. It was something a great deal more.

It couldn't be. *They* couldn't be. Máira was everything he never wanted.

He released her and stalked the horse, who shied away from him the way Máira should, but didn't. "Get cleaned up and get some rest. We leave at first light."

Máira stood at the stall wall that separated them since he'd taken on the task of grooming their horse. She watched through a small hole as Elias cared for the stallion. The way he spoke to it, relaxing the horse with the smoky gravel of his voice as he whispered words she could not discern, only made her think of things he'd whispered to her in the heat of passion.

His touch was gentle and soothing, the exact opposite of what she would expect from large, sea-roughened hands, yet she knew exactly how tender that touch could be. Watching the way he cared for the animal as he wiped down its lathered neck and brushed its sweaty coat, had mesmerized her. It was as if the horse was being bathed in the luxurious care of his touch, and Máira was jealous—of a horse.

There should have been nothing erotic about what he was doing, but the way his body moved made a woman feel every last stroke. From the moment she met this man, her body responded to him, acknowledged his presence before she was even aware he entered a room. It was as if the very air she breathed became an intoxicant when he was present. She counted herself lucky to be able to watch the way the muscles of his back and arms had flared to life with each stroke of the brush, and his buttocks...

Dear Lord, he had a glorious backside. Tight and rounded, his trousers clung to his form as if they were a part of him. Like the flesh covering his bone, muscle, and sinew. She had watched his arse tighten and flex, imagined stroking him there, feeling the strength of his movements under her fingertips as their bodies became one. It had been torturous, and then when he'd finished and the stallion was grazing on grain, he'd removed his shirt to bathe!

She was supposed to be knee deep in her own ablution, but that was the trouble. While she washed the dirt away from her person in one stall, she had noticed the knot hole in the wood panel and Elias's masculine form move in the other. What red-blooded English or French woman wouldn't watch a display like that?

And so, she had watched him through the cracks. It was naughty and sinful, but oh, so delightful as her own hand brought the wet cloth down her arms, and across her torso. She had been transfixed when his own hand trailed across the dips and swells of the waves of muscle on his abdomen. None of the sketches in the books she had seen depicting the acts of sex had come close to displaying a male form like his. Looking at the books, she'd found the male body curious and interesting, not arousing. No wonder they didn't display the image of a man like Elias. Every man of the *ton* would think himself unworthy, every woman would be greatly disappointed in her husband if they came across one of those books in her husband's library and it contained one of Michelangelo's male models pleasuring a woman.

The barn had become almost too warm to bear. She had seen nude sculptures on her one trip to London, had been fascinated by the art and the reaction of the women to the art. She'd thought it odd how the ladies found the sculptures to represent commoners. They had made the sculptures seem vulgar when they exclaimed for all to hear, "No *gentleman* would ever look like that!"

No gentleman, indeed. Elias was more than a gentleman. He was her husband, and like the ladies of the *ton*, Máira could not stop looking at the muscled form created by God. What an awful existence she would have led had she never known a man such as Elias.

"Are you cold?"

She froze at the sound of his voice, then jumped back from the wall, her heart pounding. "No. I'm fine."

"Very well," he said, and Máira sighed with relief.

A shuffling sound, however, brought her attention back to Elias.

Máira bent over and watched once more through the cracks of the wood as her husband took off his shoes and then pulled his trousers down in one fell swoop. It wasn't the first time she'd seen his manhood, but it was the first time she had seen it in the light. Long and thick with veining traveling its length, Elias's cock was another aspect of the male anatomy she suspected to be uncommon.

There was no gratuitous slant that made him look ill-proportioned or false as the drawings in the books had been. Elias's manhood was just as long, if not longer than those depicted in the books her sister had shared. The difference was how well the power of his cock seemed to match the power of his body as he fisted its length and slowly stroked it up and down.

And so she watched him as she washed her breasts, her nipples distending with the desire to be touched. It was the first time she'd indulged in that craving only he had stirred. She caressed her flesh until she was nearly moaning with fantasies of what Elias would do to her if she were truly his bride.

She dreamed of Elias pulling her into his arms, reveling in the strength of his embrace as he enfolded her into his heat. There was no other place she'd rather be than in that stable with him, naked and unafraid of what tomorrow would bring.

Her body came alive. It sparked and tingled as if a fire were springing to life in her core as she watched the color of his green eyes darken to a color deeper than any forest in Scotland. They glittered with what she had come to recognize as his desire, as his hand stroked his shaft.

There was no denying it. She loved this man with her entire being. From their first meeting, she'd known he was the one. She'd set her sights on him just as much as he had her. He may not have wanted to marry her for the same reasons, but he had chosen her over her sisters. He'd chosen her over Mary Wimberly. She knew he had married her out of a pretext to save Simon, but the spark between them was real; it was lasting. It wouldn't go away if he was rescuing a strange duchess from the wilds of India. It wouldn't disappear if he were ploughing through the rough and tumbled plains of the Americas.

Elias Allistair Drake was her husband. He wasn't just a chapter in her life. He owned her, heart, body, and soul. Nothing could change that.

She didn't care what society thought. She didn't care that she was ruined, but if she was going to be ruined in the eyes of the *ton*, then she would make certain she was thoroughly ruined.

She may have been daring before, but this need to be his in the one way she was not, made her heart choose for her. If they lay together as man and wife, perhaps he wouldn't take back his name. Maybe she could remain his wife, even if he left her behind while he traveled the world, fulfilling his need to rescue abandoned souls. She had no doubt one way or the other, he would leave her on English soil and continue his work. That's where his heart lay, but if she could own his body for one glorious night...

Máira let her dress fall to the ground. Her drawers and shift soon followed. Then she asked, "Elias, could you help me?"

She waited for what seemed like a lifetime, but was probably mere seconds, and then she heard the hay crunch under his bare feet. She tracked that sound as he walked to the stall gate, and the iron creaked and groaned as he opened and closed one stall, then approached the one she occupied.

A lump formed in her throat, and she swallowed it down before the gate shielding her naked form from his eyes scraped open and he was there.

She had expected an expression of surprise on his face as he stopped to stare. That, however, wasn't what she saw as his gaze slowly perused her nakedness like a visual caress. He'd looked at her face that same way on so many occasions, but the intensity of this moment was almost too much to bear. She wanted to run to him, wrap her arms around him and have his hands skim across her body the same way his gaze did. Instead, she stood there, absorbing his admiration one step at a time as he circled her, the fresh hay crinkling under his weight.

Elias had buttoned the falls of his trousers, but his shoes were gone, his chest was bare, and his cock strained against the fabric of his trousers. He circled, admiring her body without touching her. She couldn't calm the thundering of her heart or the rapid rise and fall of her chest. She could feel color flood her chest, neck, and face. Not from embarrassment, as one would think of a virgin standing naked before her bridegroom. It was desire flowing through her body in a heated rush demanding to be quenched.

"Please," she whispered.

His eyes slowly rose to her face, and she couldn't stop her tongue from wetting suddenly parched lips. His nostrils flared, his hands curled into fists, yet still he held back. Not coming within her reach, and denying her of his touch.

"What do you want, Máira?" His words caressed the air around her as he continued his perusal, and she shivered with anticipation.

She looked over her shoulder, her gaze skimming down the length of his body and holding where she wanted him most. A growl rose from his chest as he continued to stalk around his prey, driving her dizzy with desire. Finally, he stopped in front of her, one finger lifting her chin so that her gaze would meet his.

"I need your words," he demanded. "Not your looks of desire."

She didn't hesitate. "I want you to fuck me."

He flinched with her base words, and for a moment, she thought she'd offended the gentleman within him. Until his thumbed brushed her bottom lip and forced her mouth open. "You want me to fuck this sweet mouth of yours?"

"Yes, and more."

"More?" He searched her face, looking for the truth.

"I want to be yours completely." She wished she could say more, be more for this man than what she was, and perhaps in time, she could be.

"What of our annulment?"

Despite knowing that would be how this affair ended, his words cut her heart as if he'd driven his dagger through her chest.

"You can still have your annulment. I will not try to stop it."

"And if you're with child?"

She searched his face, trying to determine if the deepening of his tone, of his voice was from fear or hope. "I understand there are ways to prevent it."

He nodded. "Is that what you wish?"

"Yes." Her response came out in a rush. She was lucky she didn't expose how she really felt by saying, *God, yes. Take me now. Please.*

"You won't be able to give your next husband your virtue."

"I don't care." She was giving it to the only husband she would ever love. "If I marry again, it will be a marriage of convenience, the same as this marriage is for you." Because she could never be drawn to distraction again by this raging desire coursing through her blood and her heart. It was forever lost to this man. "Besides, no man will expect me to be a virgin after crossing the ocean with you."

He froze, his thumb resting on her lip, and for a moment, she thought the truth of the matter had ruined any chance she had with him.

"Can you forgive me?" he asked.

"There is nothing to forgive. If you had been honest with me in the beginning, I would have married you and crossed the sea to save Simon."

She twirled her tongue around the calloused thumb on her lip, sucking it in as if it were his shaft. His nostrils flared, and she knew she'd succeeded in bringing him back to the matter at hand—her complete and utter ruination.

"Unbutton my falls," he ordered. Her heart nearly stopped with the joy of finally being his, and as she reached for the buttons on his trousers, her hands shook with anticipation.

"Are you afraid?" he asked.

"If you were anyone else, I would be. But with you, no, I'm not." She felt what her words did to his cock. It twitched, lengthened, hardened, and she loved she did that to him. Little bastard, Máira Blair made a man larger than life *come* to life. A smile played on her lips at the filthy words dancing through her thoughts.

"What's going through that devious little head of yours?"

She fisted him and loved the way the deep-green forest of his eyes blazed with the fire of desire. "I do this to you. Nothing could make a woman feel more powerful than to make a man want her."

He shook his head, denying what she did to him. "*Ma chérie,* my body can turn hard with the prospect of sex with any woman."

"I know what you're doing. You're trying to make me think

twice about what I am offering. Letting me know you'll be with someone else when I'm gone from your side. It doesn't matter though, because at this moment, you are mine. Not some widow's, or a tavern wench's, or even a lady of the French court. For tonight, Elias Allistair Drake, fake Earl of Dorset, you are my husband and I am your wife. Nothing and no one can change that."

She drew her hand down the length of him, stroking his cock the way she had seen him do to himself in the adjoining stall. "You can say what you want, but I know the truth of the matter. And the truth is, dear Husband, that no one makes you feel the way you do when you're with me." She reached up and kissed him before he could deny it.

As if unable to resist her anymore, Elias pushed her back against the stall, their bodies colliding with the wall in a soft thud. His lips devoured hers in a passion she had not thought possible. It was explosive and real, as unbridled as it was fierce, as he forced her hands above her head and assaulted her senses with the pure maleness of him. His knee separated her thighs, forcing her legs wide. His tongue speared through her lips as if to destroy her with the inferno of their passion. Yet if he had meant to scare her away, all he succeeded in doing was bringing her back to life as his sexual phoenix.

She bucked against his thigh, rubbing her clit against his form-fitting trousers she so adored. Elias leaned into her, holding her hands with one of his own rough, calloused ones, as his other hand sought her breast, kneading, plumping, pinching, driving her mad with longing. She moaned and nipped his lip in a wanton plea for more. More of what only Elias could give her as her body began to quiver with need.

The sounds of their passion filled the barren barn as if it were an opera house and they were on stage making the music of love. Except there was no audience, no orchestra, just her and her body being played by a maestro. He stroked the strings of her hunger, caressed the keys of her desire, and made her sing to the rafters in wanting as his lips traveled down her jawline to the pulse point in her neck. It beat wildly. Violently. Demanding to be heard.

The hunger of his open mouth kisses played her body in concert with his hands, his thigh, his beard that drove her to distraction, teasing and scraping her flesh as he reached her collarbone and she became incendiary.

Yet Elias was as lost in the inferno of lust as she was, as he took her breast into his mouth and growled, the vibration of his appetite traveled to her core where she was wet and wanting. Her blood on fire, pulsing at the spot between her legs where she needed more. More of him and him alone. She whimpered with frustration, unable to reach that pinnacle of her desire.

"Patience, *ma chérie*. I will take you there."

"Now. Please, Elias."

"Take hold of the hook above your head and don't let go. If you do, I will stop."

She panted in frustration, searched for the hook, and latched on, before demanding what she needed now more than ever. "Make me come."

Elias chuckled. "In due time, Wife."

Wife. She was his wife. Never had she heard a more beautiful word uttered by a man. He may be playing a role as her husband, but he could not deny that she was his wife. Not this night. She would be his, and he would be hers for the eternity of one night.

Elias nipped and licked, explored and conquered every inch of her body as he pulled off his trousers and went down on his knees in front of her. He breathed in her scent, his eyes falling closed for the briefest of moments. "There is nothing more erotic than the essence of you," he whispered before his tongue travel the distance from her opening to her clit and back.

Máira gasped. She may have read about this, dreamed about Elias kissing her there, but never had she imagined it would feel so wicked. Her back bowed, her breath hitched, and she became lost in the sensation of Elias worshiping her body with his own. The warmth of his breath, and pressure of his tongue as he licked and flicked and savored every inch of her. His thumb pressed against her clit, and her breath hitched once more in what sounded like a sob but was more shock than anything. He was there, his tongue piercing through her womanhood, stroking and fucking her the same way he had with his fingers. None of the books mentioned a man's tongue penetrating a woman—*there*.

Elias looked up at her, and never had she seen a more erotic image than this bulk of a man on his knees before her, pleasuring her, his own body rigid with need, while his eyes mirrored her rapture. The sounds escaping her lips, his groans vibrating through her core, all became lost to their shared ecstasy as her body tightened and she fell over a cliff of bliss, shattering into an explosion of paradise reached.

Her knees buckled, but he caught her. His arms under her buttocks, her core to his navel as he carried her over to the ladder as if he were going to throw her over his shoulder and ascend to the loft. "Elias," she panted. "I need you now. I need your cock the way you gave me your tongue."

A grin spread across his face. Sultry. Masculine. Arrogant. Everything she loved and needed from this man. His lips crushed hers. The scent and taste of her pleasure was more of an aphrodisiac than she could have imagined as he leaned her back against the ladder, then made sure her left foot was stable on the rung, but her right leg stayed wrapped over his forearm, opening her sex to him completely. Elias pulled away from her lips, his eyes traveling down the length of her body as if he were seeing her for the first time. The raw carnality of his gaze nearly made her come once more.

"Make me yours, Elias. Here. Now."

It was shameless and immoral, wicked to her very core, and she loved it more than she could say. Elias guided his cock to her entrance where he rubbed her wetness. She moaned as velvet hard tip of him separated her folds, teased her clit, and drove her mad with want. Her chest heaved, as they became transfixed by the way their bodies reacted to the other. Like a couple on the dance floor, moving and shifting, twitching and gliding, mirror images that looked nothing alike, but complimented the other in perfect harmony. As one they came together in a sensual meeting she never dreamed to experience. His thick, gorgeous length breaking through her barrier and filling her beyond. She gasped, her eyes widening, her legs quivering.

His jawed tightened as if he were in pain as well, and he froze. "Are you alright, *ma chérie*?"

"I think so," she whispered, because she wasn't quite certain.

"I can stop—"

She grabbed hold of both of his forearms before he could pull out of her body. "Don't you dare."

"Máira—"

"I want this. I want you. Every bit of you, Elias. Make me yours."

"I will make it quick."

"Don't rob me of the experience."

"But you're in pain."

"Pain, that won't last. Iseabail assured me the pain is but momentary."

"Are you certain?"

She touched his cheek, loving the look of concern on his face, and his desire to stop for her comfort, not his. "I have never been more certain than now."

Elias pushed forward, slowly, inch by inch. Filling her, stretching her, hitting every nerve she never knew existed, until he was completely seated and sweat broke out on his forehead. He moaned and something changed. It was as if his pleasure, brought her pleasure. The pain ebbed, and in its wake something wondrously tender.

"Are you alright?" he gritted out, his eyes closed, his restraint evident in the clipped tone of his words. She would have laughed if he wasn't so magnificent.

"I am more than alright," she breathed, and flexed her sheath around him.

His eyes flew open, searching her face for the pain that had abandoned her.

"Move, Husband." Her command brought a litany of curses to his lips before he crushed hers in a kiss she would remember for the rest of her life as he pulled his cock out slowly and entered her again. She whimpered against his mouth, savoring every moment, yet needing more. Wrapping her hands around his backside, she dug her nails into the firm flesh of his arse, loving the give and flex as she pushed and pulled on his body.

A guttural growl rose from his chest and he needed no more encouragement. He pumped in and out of her body, his speed and force demanding she release his buttocks with one hand and grab hold of the ladder rung. It was erotic and magical. His cock making her wonder where she began and he ended, yet it was him filling her completely. Stroking and grinding, he pushed her beyond pleasure to a point where darkness threatened. Her chest stopped rising. A scream perched on the edge of her release as tingling heat filled her feet, her calves, her thighs, and then she was there, screaming into the ecstasy of his kiss. Her quim gripping and pulsing around his cock, the friction of it all sending stars into her eyes.

Elias immediately followed her. His body bucking at a fierce, punishing pace. It was anything but torturous. He dragged out her pleasure, creating waves upon waves of ecstasy as the rasp of his roar sent shivers through her core, and he fell sated against her. His chest heaving, her name falling from his lips, "Máira."

It was indeed heaven.

Fourteen

Madame,

I remain Your Grace's most obedient servant and would like to offer my sincere apologies for the ruse in which I deliberately deceived you and Máira of my true identity. I hope the War Office has explained the situation to you prior to our return. My marriage to your sister was necessary and is legitimate. I will not, however, take advantage of my title as her husband, and will return her to her family post haste so that she may seek an annulment and put this unfortunate adventure in the past.

Please know that I hold your sister in the highest regard and will preserve her honor.

Your most humble servant,
Sir Elias Maximilien Allistair Drake

—A letter personally delivered to the Duchess of Ross at her home, Caerlaverock Castle in Dumfries, Scotland, by Sir Robert Williamson of the War Office. It was supposed to be delivered to the Duchess after the Earl of Astley was recovered and was on his way home; however, Sir Williamson arrived

with a black eye and the Duke of Ross at his side before word of the Earl's status was learned. The letter was delivered two days after the Drake marriage was consummated.

This was hell. Not heaven. Not purgatory, but pure unadulterated hell. Máira was sleeping in his arms on the saddle once more. The soft globes of her arse cradling his cock as her breast rubbed against his arm with each step their horse took toward Mont-Saint-Michel.

Memories of their night together stormed through his thoughts like an invading army and his defenses deserted him, leaving him to be tortured with his want to taste her, take her again and again...and again. He would never survive the suffering and torment of knowing what it was like to hold her in his arms and never experience it once more.

He would never make love—fuck her again. Hell, he should be flogged for the manner in which he had disposed of her maidenhead. Taking his virgin wife, who was gently-bred and raised to be a lady, in a stable against the ladder to the loft.

A scoff escaped his lips. He had no honor. He had been raised as a gentleman, maybe not by the standards of the *ton*, but his father had taught him to cherish women, and yet he had let his baser instincts control his actions just as they had when he was a teenager. He'd turned into an animal with the one woman who did not deserve to be treated as such.

He glanced down at his beautiful wife with the faint hint of a smile on her lips. She was probably dreaming of the Duke of Ross calling him out and putting a lead round in his chest.

Damnation.

He had sworn in a letter to her sister that Máira's honor would remain intact. Instead, he'd shredded it to bloody hell by fucking her like a tart in a tavern. He closed his eyes for a moment, yet the only thing that filled his thoughts were images of her, her lush, rounded breasts so pert and demanding of a man's attention, her soft body bending to his will, and the way her pink, tight quim felt on his tongue, his cock.

Máira stirred in his arms, and he quieted her. "Shhh, *ma chérie*. We don't have much farther to go." They had been traveling all day, and within the next couple of hours, they would arrive at the outskirts of Mont-Saint-Michel, where he would have to gauge the tide and determine when the best time to cross would be. He hoped low tide came in the middle of the night. The full moon was two days past, and the sea level would be high, the currents too strong for him to navigate. He had to cross at low tide.

He also worried about leaving Máira. Danger seemed to follow her, or him, or both of them everywhere they went. He wasn't quite sure which one of them was worse at attracting the pitfalls of peril. Either way, he brought her with him to keep her safe. Mont-Saint-Michel, however, wasn't safe for anyone. He knew that before leaving English soil. The coast of France along the English Channel was fraught with Napoleon's troops. It was the reason he used the port of Le Conquet.

That and Hag was in Le Conquet. Her connections were invaluable. She'd advised him to stop at the windmill of Moidrey, where he would find a monk to guide him across the bay which turned to mud during low tide. They'd experienced the need of a guide firsthand when he was a boy and had gone running across the muddy surface, only to sink in one of the many pockets of quicksand that appeared randomly across the expanse. He had screamed in panic, and his mother raced toward him. It was his father who had stopped her from becoming mired in the muck and him from sinking beyond his waist. He could not afford that type of mistake on this trip.

Once they were at the walls surrounding the abbey, Elias would have to scale the ramparts and make his way through the vendors and merchants of Mont-Saint-Michel before breaking into the church.

Rescuing Astley was up to him. After the fiasco with Máira

and his crew, he hadn't thought it wise to leave the *Maribelle* without Peter to watch over things. He would, however, leave Máira at the mill and return with Astley in tow. He just hoped he wasn't bringing back a corpse.

Máira stirred on his lap, and he groaned with the teasing touch of her body. He looked down to find her watching him. "You are a demon," he teased.

"A sexy demon?"

"I don't think I need to answer that."

She wiggled her arse and he couldn't resist thrusting his hips up into her welcoming body. He couldn't take her again. He'd made an oath—

Máira lifted her skirts, exposing the expanse of her legs and he knew he was going to hell.

"Máira—"

She turned on his lap so that she was facing him, her décolletage tempting him further as she reached between them and unbuttoned his falls with the speed of an experienced courtesan.

"Máira—" Her name on his lips sounded like a plea, a curse, a surrender to the pits of eternal damnation as his cock sprang loose from the constraints of his clothing and Máira lifted herself on top of the long, hard length of him and wrapped her legs around his waist.

"*Mon Dieu—*" he breathed, as she gasped and then froze. He had to be hurting her, yet every part of him wanted to buck up into her wet, sweet warmth as the horse continued its course through the forest. He reached up and cupped one of her breasts, the same breast that had been torturing him as it grazed up and down upon his arm. He squeezed and plumped her curves, pulling down the neckline to expose her creamy soft flesh to the night sky.

"I have wanted to do this since we got on this horse hours ago," he whispered into her ear as he trailed kisses down her neck until he reached her taut nipple and began suckling. Her scent was that of a meadow, and fresh spring, and he breathed it in as if he would never again inhale her essence. With his hand now free, he found the bead of bliss underneath her skirts eager for his touch. The noise Máira made was one of pure pleasure as she began moving on his cock in rhythm with the horse's stride.

"Fuck. I've never dreamed of taking a woman while on a horse. Certainly not when my mind should be focused on something as important as keeping us alive."

"I need this to live," she gasped. "The joining of our bodies is everything I want and desire."

"Then I am yours." He let Máira set the pace while he held them astride the stallion. Let her explore her sexual appetite— which just might kill him. His little wife was turning out to be so much more than he'd ever realized. She rode his shaft as if she were born to. Up and down, in and out, flexing and squeezing every goddamned inch of him as she mewled and panted and made him want to come without thinking of her release.

And then she was there, her warm, tight core pulsing around him as he took her lips in his to silence her scream in a passionate kiss he never wanted to end. He pushed up from the stirrups, meeting her downward thrusts with those of his own. Stars exploded in the sky, or perhaps it was just in his mind's eye, but they were there, brighter, more blinding, and more explosive than any fireworks released by Louis the XVI and Marie Antoinette. The only thing both events had in common was the impending doom and tragedy that would no doubt follow, at least to his heart.

But *mon Dieu*, as he pumped the last of his seed bursting from his body and deep into hers, all he could think was, *tu es à moi*.

You are mine, Máira. Now and forever.

Máira pulled back from his kiss, her chest heaving as her soft languid body relaxed into his. They were one. The way he wanted them to always be.

"How did you keep us on this horse?"

"I don't know," he breathed.

"That's twice you've given me pleasure while sitting astride this horse. The poor thing must feel used."

"I will get him a mare when this is over."

"I'm sure he will appreciate that." The coy smile on her lips transformed her into the siren she was meant to be.

Elias cleared his throat and lifted her from his cock. The greedy bastard was charging up to go again, but he couldn't risk it. As it was, he would have to ensure she wasn't pregnant before they filed for an annulment. "Máira—"

She pulled back allowing him enough space to close the falls of his trousers. "Don't, Elias. I know this means nothing. I will not hold on to you if I am with child."

"That wasn't—"

"It was the risk I was willing to take. If I somehow end up with child, I will find a solution." She leaned back and swung her body around as if she were one of acrobatic riders he'd seen in Covent Gardens, all the while pulling her skirts underneath her and her cloak over her head so that he could no longer see her beautiful face. She'd built a wall between them which angered him more than her words.

"What the hell does that mean?"

"It means I relinquish you from all paternal responsibilities."

He couldn't believe his ears. "And if I don't want to give up my rights as our child's father?"

She shook her head as if it were a moot point. "It doesn't matter. We both know this wasn't a real marriage."

"What in damnation are you talking about? I told you it was legal."

"You also told me you would not be bound to me. It's fine." She patted his hand on the reins as if she were appeasing a child. All he could think about was their child.

"We will be fine."

"You dismiss me as if I donated my seed to your cause and that is the end of my role in our child's life."

She shrugged in response.

He'd thought he would have to let her down easy, but that wasn't the case at all. In fact, if any heart was breaking...no. The pain in his chest was not from his heart.

He snapped his hand out of her reach and the horse complained for the first time, but he ignored it, too upset by the recent turn of the tide. "What if I *want* to be bound to my child?" He didn't say 'bound to her,' and if his comment caused her any personal duress, there were no signs of a blow to her heart. "My child will not be born a bastard," he spit out.

The laugh escaping her lips was brittle and false. "I will find a father for my child if need be."

A growl escaped his lips, shocking her and him. "He has a father."

It was her turn to bristle. "But *she* does not?"

A little girl. He'd never thought of having a daughter, a daughter like Máira, full of laughter and love he wouldn't experience.

Over his dead body.

"Of course I will be there for my daughter. A girl needs her father."

She didn't argue, and he knew his misstep immediately. She had been very young when her father died, even younger when her mother died birthing Máira's youngest sister. "Máira, I didn't mean—"

"It's nothing," she lied.

There was nothing he could say. He knew her pain more than most. He had lost his father as a teen and his mother when she sent him away to live with his uncle in England. It was all to keep him safe, but it didn't mean the loss of both his parents hadn't affected him. It had, profoundly.

They rode on in silence for the next couple hours. Both trapped in the losses of their past and now their future as well. But as the forest began to thin and the brine from the sea seeped into the air, Elias's senses alerted. They were close, which heightened the chances of running into more troops. He leaned forward to whisper in her ear and felt her body stiffen. How different it was from mere hours ago. "We are close. We must remain quiet."

She acknowledged him with a nod and nothing more. Nor did her body sink back against his. She stayed rigid and as far away as she could get. Twenty minutes later, he caught sight of the Mill of Moidrey, the blades turning in the wind as the forest gave way to the rolling hills near the coast. He avoided the cottages of the town and directed their horse to a copse of trees near the mill where he lifted Máira from the horse. "I need you to hide in the woods. I will be back when I know it is safe."

Her eyes widened as if she realized for the first time since they'd buried the bodies of the soldiers that the danger wasn't over. "Don't leave," she whispered.

"I'll be back. You'll be safe here."

She laughed a humorless laugh as if he'd said something ridiculous. "I'm not worried about me. We're better off if we fight together as a team."

"I will be better off knowing you are safe."

"What about me? Do you think I'm better off knowing you're in danger?"

"Do you care, Wife?" Could he dare to hope?

"Of course I care. I don't want you to die."

It wasn't exactly a profession of undying love. "I won't." Elias turned the horse in the direction of the mill, giving her no choice but to get lost in the trees or stand out in the middle of the field and put them both at risk. He heard her huff and watched over his shoulder as she disappeared into the darkness.

Mon Dieu. Their marriage seemed like a real marriage, considering how much work it was taking.

He turned and focused on the horizon for signs of trouble, for shadows moving toward Máira or himself.

Nothing. Not even a flicker of light from the cottages they'd already bypassed.

The wind caused the leaves and grasses to dance as the mill twirled round and round at a slow lazy pace. An eerie calm filled night as he slowly made his way up the hill.

Once he was at the top, he could see Mont-Saint-Michel in the distance. The lights giving it an ominous appearance with its stone walls, gothic buttresses, and the golden form of Saint Michel brandishing his sword at the moon from the top of the tallest spire. As a boy, his family had made the pilgrimage to Mont-Saint-Michel, but that was a very different time. The sacred abbey was now a prison of the worst sort.

Elias allowed his shoulders to slump and his head to bob up and down with the fatigue he longed to give in to while he approached the windmill as if he were a weary traveler hoping for shelter. Dismounting, he purposely stumbled and then tied the horse to a fence that kept stragglers from inadvertently walking into canvas blades. From a distance the wooden skeletons which allowed the sails to capture the force of the wind, were invisible. Up close, one realized how deadly those blades could be.

He looked up at the stone building sporting a thatched roof, one window on the second story and two wooden doors down below. He hoped it was a one-monk castle as Hag had said it would be. Using the side of his fist, he pounded on the door.

The door slowly creaked open, the light from a candle illuminating his face, not the mill-keeper's. "Who are you?"

It wasn't exactly the greeting of a holy man. Elias squinted into the light, unable to see the man beyond the flame. "Hag sent me."

"I know of no *hag*." The man drew out her name as if it was filthy and disgusting, then moved to close the door, the candlelight withdrawing inside.

Elias shoved his boot into the opening and said, "Aventine sent me for Father Charles." The door still slammed against his foot. He ground his teeth, but didn't remove his foot.

The glow of the candle felt warm against his face as once more the man lifted it to look into his eyes. He could feel the man study his features as the light shifted back and forth across his cheekbones. "Elias?"

"Yes, I am Elias, her son."

"You're a soldier?"

He hesitated. Knowing he had to put his trust in Hag's knowledge of this area and this man despite being over a day's ride away. "No."

"Yet you wear a uniform."

"Half a uniform."

"Does that make you half a soldier?"

Damnation. Was it not bad enough he'd argued with his wife over the existence of an imaginary child, and now a priest was going to split hairs over a bloody jacket and hat? A perilous quiet filled the air as he stared at the man beyond the candle. His fists clenched. His jaw tightened. It took everything he had to rein in his anger and frustration and not kick the damned door down. The priest must have sensed the danger in the air. His rising temper. One moment the door was pushing hard against his foot, and the next it swung open to expose the man in monk's robes looking up at him.

"You have grown into a big, fine man," the monk said, as he looked Elias over from his shoes to his messy hair sticking out from under his hat.

Elias's brow drew together. "We've met before?"

The monk laughed. "Of course we have. I am Father Charles. I was in charge of ensuring the pilgrims made it across to Mont-Saint-Michel safely. You were but a boy of seven or eight then, I believe."

Elias tried to remember the round cheeks, straggly gray hair, and shining grey eyes. He was average height, but his dark robes covered everything else, and nothing about this man brought a memory to mind.

"I'm sorry—"

The monk shook his head. "I could not wear my robes back then. I couldn't show my allegiance to the church over the King, nor could I show my allegiance to the King over the church. It was a difficult time."

"And now?" Elias knew the life of a priest in France was not an easy one. Supporters of the revolution had killed the refectory priests who remained loyal to the Pope, and supporters of the church had killed constitutional priests loyal to the King. Because of the political upheaval, most holy men and women had been arrested and deported or killed.

The man's smile was genuine. "We have a reprieve, since France is focused on outside forces."

"Even while Napoleon is holding the Pope captive?" Elias had heard of the Pope's kidnapping a few years prior. As far as he knew, Napoleon still held the leader of the Catholic church.

Father Charles response was hesitant. "He is a *guest* of our leader."

Elias nodded as he looked around the interior of the mill, which housed two silent millstones that were not moving in tandem with the sails of the windmill as he'd expected. Instead, they stood stationary on top of a larger stone covered in flour dust. He glanced at the monk.

"I don't make flour twenty-four hours a day. I live here. Can you imagine the noise I would have to sleep through?" The wheels of the sails groaned at that moment, emphasizing the constant noises of motion within the mill.

Elias nodded and continued his visual search of the interior as he casually walked the inside of the building to ensure no soldiers were lying in wait of an unsuspecting Englishman hellbent on rescuing an earl. Another stone hung through a hole to the second floor above them, the cogs of the turning mechanism visibly engaged to a sister wheel made of wood hanging above it. There were ropes and pulleys throughout the entire space and made captaining of a ship look easy.

The interior room was lined with bags of flour stacked against the walls, with a smaller room the size of servants' quarters bordering it. Peeking into the space, Elias observed two bunkbeds, and a hammock like the sleeping quarters aboard ship. The accommodations were small and tight, a place that would make most sailors feel right at home. Only one bed contained bedding that looked like he had awakened the man from his slumber. The other bed frame even lacked a mattress. A well-used trunk sat at the end of the bunkbeds, and a small washstand stood on the opposite side of the room. The room lacked personal touches beyond a bar of soap and a wash basin.

He looked back at the priest. "You work alone?"

"Yes. The farmers bring the grain, and I work the mill."

There was no fireplace for warmth or to cook by. He understood the desire to keep fire away from the grain, but wondered where the monk cooked or how he kept warm in the winter.

Steps leading to the second floor hugged the exterior wall. "What's on the second floor?"

"That is where the grain is brought in and sent down toward the stones."

Elias raised his brows and pointed toward the steps. "Do you mind?"

"Be my guest."

"I will be done shortly." Keeping an eye on the priest while he ascended the steps, Elias listened for additional creaks in the floorboards that might disclose the presence of another. The second floor of the mill contained the chute for the grain, along with numerous wooden wheels which made the mill functional as a one-man operation. He had no doubt the monk worked long, hard hours, and suspected the robes concealed more muscle than fat.

Finding nothing out of the ordinary, he returned to Father Charles. "Hag—Aventine said you would have a gift for her."

The priest paused and looked at him as if the man had no idea what Hag wanted. A warning skittered down his spine, and he slowly reached for the knife on his belt as the priest tapped his chin in contemplation. Elias took a half step back and removed his knife from his belt when the priest suddenly raised his hand in triumph. "Of course! I have been holding it for some time."

Without a misstep, Father Charles went into the small sleeping quarters and Elias followed. The priest glanced over his shoulder and Elias shrugged. "I need to ensure you're not getting a weapon."

"We all have our weaknesses, Elias. My guess is that yours is trusting others."

"Hazard of the job, Father." Until a month ago, the only weakness Elias had was his mother. Now there was another woman who could bring him to his knees much faster than Hag.

The priest pulled a box out of the trunk at the end of his bed, opened it, and dug around inside it, before finally pulling out a chain with a delicate medal attached.

Elias didn't need the medal. He just needed the priest to tell him who was on the medal. If he truly was Father Charles, the man Hag said he could trust to take him across to Mont-Saint-Michel, then he would have a medal of Saint Nicholas of Myra for him. "What saint is on the medal father?"

Father Charles held out the medal. "The patron saint of children. She said one day you would come back, and she wanted your child to have it."

Elias pointed the knife at the priest. "That's not the answer I was looking for. Who are you really and what have you done to Father Charles?"

The man pulled his chin back and looked confused, a bead of sweat trickling down his forehead. Holding his hands out to the side with his palms open, he played the part of innocent well. "I don't understand."

"That is not what Aventine said you would give me."

"Of course it is. Saint Nicholas of Myra. She accidently left it at Mont-Saint-Michel when you came as a family. I wrote to her and told her and she told me to hang on to it when you came back with your own child on pilgrimage."

"I'm not on pilgrimage."

"Of course not. No one goes on pilgrimage to Mont-Saint-Michel anymore. It is a prison, but she wrote me last week and said you were coming and would need my assistance. What else could I possibly have to give you?"

Elias hardened himself to do what he had to do and firmed the grip on his knife. "You tell me, Father, or you will die before your next breath."

"I don't understand. This is all I have for you."

Elias took a step toward the priest.

The priest put his hands up as if to stop Elias's attack with his bare hands. "Saint Nicholas is the patron saint of children, brewers, archers, sailors, merchants, repentant thieves."

Elias froze. "Did you say 'sailors'?"

Father Charles swallowed visibly. "Yes, Saint Nicolas of Myra is the patron saint of sailors."

Elias' shoulders dropped. "Bloody hell, why didn't you say that first?"

"Because Aventine bought it for her child, not a sailor."

"Aventine told me the medal was the patron saint of sailors."

"Your lack of knowledge of your religion nearly cost me my life."

"I've had very little reason to believe in your religion, Father."

"I suggest you start."

Elias turned around and walked out of the room. *Sacré bleu!* He'd nearly killed a man of God because of Hag's cryptic instructions.

"This is yours," Father Charles said, as he scurried up behind him.

"Keep it." He didn't want the bloody thing.

"Your mother bought it for her son. Maybe you should keep it for yours."

Elias froze. His child. He could have a child. Twice now, he'd lost his head and hadn't taken any precautions to keep Máira safe. He turned around and looked at the priest who was holding out the chain with the medal of Saint Nichoas of Myra attached.

Patron saint of sailors and children.

He took the medal and pocketed it as he shrugged. "Can't hurt." He cleared his throat and changed the subject. "When can you take me to Mont-Saint-Michel."

"Are you going after the earl?"

"Why do you ask?"

""Rumor has it that a certain English earl is to hang in three days. I can only assume that is your purpose of visiting the abbey."

"Hang?" *Mon Dieu*. That was not part of the equation. "And you're willing to help?"

"Your mother knows where my loyalties lie, otherwise she would not have sent you to me. Of course I will help."

"It could get messy."

The priest looked at the knife on his belt. "Messier than nearly losing my life?"

"Yes."

Father Charles sighed. "If it is to save a life, I must assist."

"And if it means you must take a life?"

"I will not."

Elias nodded; he understood the priest's limitations. "I also need to house someone here while we're gone."

That gave the priest pause. "Who?"

"My wife."

"Your wife? You brought your wife here on a mission that could get you killed? Get us all killed?"

Elias sighed. "It was the lesser of two evils."

Father Charles scoffed. "This is no place for a woman."

"It's the safest place for her."

"I disagree."

"I don't." The female response caused them both to jump.

Elias was the first to recover, even as his eyes drank in the delectable dishevelment of her hair and her rumpled gown, both reminding him of the passion they shared a few hours earlier. "Do you ever listen?"

"I heard your conversation, if that's what you're asking." Máira closed the door to the mill and locked it behind her.

The priest frowned. "I'm pretty sure I locked that."

Máira shrugged. "You did."

The priest looked at Elias with a knowing look. "Now I know why you brought her."

Except that wasn't why he brought her. If his wife had a hidden talent for breaking into places she wasn't supposed to be, it was news to him. "No." He shook his head. "No." He nearly growled. "She's not coming with us." He turned toward his wife. "Where did you obtain tools to unlock the door? You had nothing while aboard ship, otherwise you would have broken out of your cabin."

"When you went to confront Peter, I obtained them from Hag." She wore the smug expression of a devious woman, and he could picture the look on his mother's face when she gave her the tools. Damnation.

"Her skills would be most useful." The priest interjected.

Máira beamed. "See. You could use a woman like me on your team."

"This is not a team." His voice turned into a growl.

"What would you call it?"

"A one-man operation!"

That made the priest laugh...when he finally stopped and caught his breath, he laughed again. To make matters worse, Máira joined him. It was as if the two of them had planned to change his tactics from the very start.

"She is not going." He insisted.

The monk sobered. "We need her. My contact inside Mont-Saint-Michel is no longer available."

"Why not?" Elias demanded. "The man can just make himself available. I don't give a damn if he suddenly thinks there's too much risk involved. I'll pay him double, that will change his tune."

"He died." Father Charles made the sign of the cross, and Elias felt obligated to show that much respect for the man whose honor he'd just impugned.

"I'm sorry," he said.

"Unfortunately, he is not the only one on the island who has become ill. Many of the guards are ill, along with the shopkeepers, but it can work in our favor. Many of the outposts are vacant, and with someone who knows how to bypass locked doors, our task just got easier."

"What about the ransom? Why has Napoleon decided to hang the earl?"

"Hang? They're going to hang Simon?" Máira's face drained of color.

"We will get to him before they do." Elias assured, as he reached out and squeezed her hand.

"The Minister of War would like to make an example out of the earl who came here to spy. He's also received word that his own spy was executed by the English," Father Charles explained.

"Who was that?"

"Lord Greasley."

"He wasn't executed. He was killed on French soil. In The Happy Hag to be exact, by a French woman." Elias took off his stolen tricorn hat and ran his fingers through his hair. Why did everything circle back to Hag?

Father Charles nodded in sympathetic understanding. "That explains it."

"Explains what?" Máira asked. She looked as confused by the events unfolding as he felt.

"Why the Minister of War said his spy was killed by the English."

Except it didn't explain anything. "Why would he say that?"

The priest searched his face as if he realized for the first time Elias was missing a crucial piece to the story. His expression dropped. "She hasn't told you."

It wasn't a question, but Elias felt as if it was. "Who hasn't told me what?"

The priest made the sign of the cross once more and turned away. "We need to prepare, otherwise we won't rescue him in time."

"Now?" Máira asked.

"Now," Father Charles confirmed.

Elias was tired of secrets. Tired of attempting to figure out another person's thoughts. He'd been doing it too long, and after doing it with Máira, he had no patience for games. He grabbed the priest by the arm and confirmed his suspicions about the man's mettle. "We're not going anywhere until I understand all the cogs to this story, Father Charles. Who should have told me something she did not?" It really could have been every woman he'd ever met, he suspected, however, that it was his mother.

Father Charles huffed and closed his eyes as if he did not want to see Elias's expression. "Your mother."

"My mother?"

It wasn't really a question, but the priest answered it anyway. "Yes."

He didn't want to ask the next question, but lives were at stake —Astley's and most importantly, Máira's. "What has Hag neglected to tell me?"

Father Charles closed his eyes and scrunched up his face like he'd swallowed something bitter.

Elias stepped closer to the man, crowding him, his own anger and frustration boiling to the surface as he bumped the priest's chest with his own. "Out with it."

"The Minister of War is your grandfather," Father Charles said it so fast, it took a moment for the words to penetrate Elias's anger.

Máira gasped.

Elias looked between her and the priest.

"*Mon grand père?*" It wasn't possible. Hag had said both her parents were dead. The only grandfather he'd ever known had been a general, but he'd died while Elias was in England. He trusted her word to the point where he had not even looked for the man to kill him. "That's not possible," he insisted, but the look on the priest's face told him it was. "Why did she tell me her parents were dead?"

The priest shrugged. It was Máira who filled in the answers that made the most sense. "Her parents probably disowned her when she married an Englishman. The same thing happened to my mother when she married a Scotsman in trade. It's all in their hatred of bloodlines."

"No," he said, slowly shaking his head. The feelings of betrayal washing back over him after years of dormancy as he remembered his father pleading with *mon grand père* to take Elias away before the general killed him.

"That's not it." He dared to expose his pain to Máira as he looked into her deep blue eyes for an anchor to ground him as he explained. "It's because I swore to her that I would kill him." The hatred he'd felt for the man years ago returned with each word he uttered. When she reached for him with tears welling in her eyes, he knew she felt the waves of grief washing over him, threatening to drown him. He should have grabbed hold of the lifeline she offered. But he couldn't. He'd taken an oath, and as captain, he was going down with the ship he'd sworn allegiance to years ago. He would not, however, take her with him. He didn't see the pain his rebuff caused her as he turned toward the door. He was too caught up in his thoughts of revenge against the brutal French military man who still lived.

"I made a promise to my dead father as we fell from that tree together. I vowed the bastard who killed him would die by my hand. I made it once more to my grieving mother as she cried over his body. And it's a vow I mean to keep."

Fifteen

Dearest Iseabail,

I am told that you have been advised of the circumstances surrounding my marriage, but what you cannot possibly know is that my feelings for my husband have only grown. I would not change one moment I have spent getting to know this incredible man who owns my heart completely. I will not seek an annulment as he has suggested. If our union is to be dissolved, it will be done by him, not me.

Do not think that I have been absconded or abused in any manner. On the contrary, my husband has treated me with caring consideration. Beyond love, no woman could ask for more. Our honeymoon has taken on the greatest meaning a person could hope for. Do not fret, I am well and I will see you upon my return.

Your loving sister,
Máira

—A letter written to the Duchess of Ross, from her younger sister Máira Blair Collins, or Lady Drake. The letter was never

sent by the young bride, however. Hag found it and sent it to the
Duchess. It arrived one day after the letter from Elias.

Despite Elias's desire to immediately storm the abbey and rescue Astley, the tide had not cooperated. They'd discussed the plan over and over until Máira had made him stop. Father Charles was dead on his feet, and so was she. He relented and was somehow able to sleep the rest of the night on the bed next to her, while the priest slept in the hammock he'd moved to the second floor of the mill.

The entire next day was spent preparing. Father Charles had introduced them to intricate maps of the island he'd created in preparation for the rescue. Although Hag had not told the priest about the rescue, Father Charles had anticipated it, as there was no other reason for Elias to want to visit the prison.

The abbey was surrounded by battlements all along the Mont Saint Michel Bay. To the west, craggy cliffs rose up to a less guarded wall that was hidden from the main outlook, Gabriel's Tower. There was also a small stone chapel, dedicated to the priest who was directed by the archangel Saint Michel to build the church. Elias had wanted to enter the abbey through the staircase leading up the mountainside from the Chapel of Saint Aubert, but Father Charles rejected that immediately.

"I do not know what is happening at the Chapel of Saint Aubert, but whatever it is, it has become heavily fortified in the past several weeks. We would be caught before we arrived."

This had caused another argument about Máira's participation, but Father Charles had stood his ground. "Their presence makes our need of her ability to break into places that much more important. She will cut down our exposure and the noise of you muscling through every gate and door."

Elias scowled, but in the end, agreed when they were ready to leave as the cloud cover disguised the sunset, and the tide began to ebb. Dressed in borrowed clothes from Father Charles she'd spent the day altering to the best of her ability, Máira secured her hair with twine and hid it under a farmer's hat the priest had in his barn. Father Charles had a fairly small foot, but she'd stuffed the shoes with remnants from her altered clothing into the toes to help with the fit.

Then she gathered supplies for injuries Simon may have incurred at the hands of the French and stuffed them in her satchel. Elias and the priest carried bags over their shoulders full of weaponry chosen because it was silent but deadly. Why a priest would have such a collection, Máira didn't know and she didn't ask. Elias, however, had been rather pleased.

Elias led the way as they traveled across the hills to the Couesnon River with Father Charles in the rear. From there, they followed the cold waterway to the Bay of Mont Saint Michel. Their pace was uncomfortable, but necessary to take advantage of as much low tide as possible.

As they reached the bay, they removed their shoes and the men stuffed them in their bags. Walking across the mud and muck of the bay at low tide felt as if the earth would swallow her whole if she stood in one place too long. Yet when the voices of the guards on the ramparts of the abbey carried to them on the wind, they were forced to stop. Máira wiggled her toes, and panic nearly overtook her as she began to sink.

"Don't wiggle, you're making it worse," Father Charles scolded, his voice barely audible over the breeze. "The more you wiggle, the more you sink and the more you sink, the more you get stuck."

Elias turned to look at her, his shock and the whites of his eyes flashing in the moonlight as he quickly took in how far she'd sunk in the muck.

She whimpered.

"Do not move." The priest hissed.

Her eyes shot to the Abbey. *Please let them leave. Please let them leave.* She could no longer hear the wind over the sound of her heart in her ears and her labored breathing. She shivered, her entire body shaking despite the warm breeze, as she watched one guard disappear inside a door.

Move damn you! The guard ignored her silent scream as he slowly ambled toward the end of the rampart. She didn't think it was possible for a grown man to walk so slowly, and when he finally turned the corner, she looked pleadingly at her husband.

Elias was at her side instantaneously, forgetting all about the guards. "Easy, *ma chérie*."

"Get me out." She sounded like a child to her own ears, but she was buried to her knees.

"Take my hand," he instructed as he reached out for her. Máira had his hand before he finished the sentence.

Father Charles began giving instructions on how to escape the clutches of her silt grave. "Hang onto your husband."

As if she would let go.

"Now rock one foot back and forth in a slow steady fashion."

Slow and steady did not win the race. She yanked furiously at her foot.

"You must listen," the priest insisted.

"Listen to him, *ma chérie*. He knows this land."

"This is not land," she argued, but did as she was told. Elias pulled on her arm as her first foot loosened the tiniest bit with a slurping of the mud. Every bit of space she created, the mud attempted to fill.

"This is why you insisted we go barefoot." The realization slipped from her lips with a sob.

"Yes," the priest admitted. She wanted to hit him. He should have warned her how bad the crossing would be, but then she would have never insisted on coming. She would have sat in the mill and waited, never knowing if or when Elias was coming back, just like her father. She was damned if she went with him and damned if she didn't.

"You're doing wonderful, *ma chérie*." Elias was down on his knees now, his trousers absorbing all the brine and mud that seemed to cover her from toe to head. He leaned forward and kissed her, a quick and intimate gesture that made her want to climb out of the mud and jump on top of him.

"When you get one foot free, kneel on it." The priest instructed. "Then rock your other leg."

She did as she was told and felt the earth begin to release its hold just the slightest bit. A sob of joy escaped her lips and Elias smiled down on her as he began reciting a French poem in a soft, gentle rasp that soothed her from the inside out.

> "La vie est une fleur,
> l'amour en est le miel.
> C'est la colombe unie
> à l'aigle dans le ciel,
>
> C'est la grâce tremblante
> à la force appuyée,
> C'est ta main dans ma main
> doucement oubliée."

With one leg free, and her second one well on its way, she asked, "Can you translate it into English?" She was afraid she was missing some of its meaning. She prayed she'd understood every word.

> *"Life is a flower*
> *Love is its honey.*
> *It is the dove united*
> *with the eagle in the sky,*
>
> *It is trembling grace*
> *With sustained force,*
> *It's your hand in my hand*

gently forgotten."

And she had.

As if fate intervened, the earth released her foot just as he finished and she was standing, folded in her husband's embrace as he whispered in her ear. "You are fine, *ma chérie*. Everything is fine."

"Who is the author of such beautiful prose?" She asked.

"A young French poet you've probably never heard of named Victor Hugo."

With her cheek held snugly against his chest, she smiled and relaxed her breathing as Elias stroked her hair with such a light, gentle touch, with the care one would only give to someone he treasured.

Victor Hugo was foreign to her, but the words were so heart-felt...and yet sorrowful. She never wanted to step out of her husband's arms, because once she did, she wasn't sure her delicate hold on her emotions wouldn't shatter into pieces. They stood there in silence as she hugged him tight, until finally Father Charles cleared his throat and Elias set them apart.

"We are going back." With his mind made up, Elias turned toward shore with her hand tucked in his. It was Máira who was forced to let go. She would never forget the feel of her hand in his when she seemed doomed to be swallowed by the underbelly of hell. She had no doubt anyone crossing this bay at low tide would feel as if they were on holy ground when they reach the solid rock foundation of Mont-Saint-Michel.

At any other time, with any other person, the experience would have sent her into a complete panic. The bogs of Scotland had been aggrandized into her psyche since childhood. The last thing she had ever wanted to do, was get lost in the bogs...again... and here, in a strange country, for one brief moment, she'd thought she was living her nightmare once more. The difference, however, had been Elias. He'd come to her, held her hand while he soothed her with a beautiful French poem she'd never heard before, and her childhood nightmare was lost on the tide.

He had saved her from her fears, and now she would force him to face his.

"We have come to find Simon. I will not leave without him."

Elias froze. "You've been through enough."

"Simon has been through more."

"I can come back for Astley when you are safe."

"Your grandfather is going to hang him." It was a low blow, but he had to see reason.

"I won't let that happen."

Father Charles joined the conversation. "If we do not move tonight, I am afraid it will be too late."

"I will not risk Máira."

"You already have." It was the worst thing she could have said to him. She knew it before the words left her mouth, but they had come this far, she would not let her fears destroy their hopes of saving Simon. She continued before Elias had a chance to argue further, allowing a nonchalance she didn't feel to fill her voice. "Besides, Simon is the one."

It was as if the hand he'd caressed reached up and slapped him across the cheek. Palm striking unsuspecting flesh with a resounding crack. His response was nothing but a whisper. A plea for her not to answer the question he asked. "What one?"

She glanced at the priest, not wanting him to hear what she was about to say. Luckily, Father Charles had proceeded some distance toward the abbey, allowing them space to argue quietly. "He's the one I will marry if I find out I'm pregnant."

Elias growled as he stalked forward, his chest brushing hers— he forced her to hold her ground and look up into his angry eyes. "It's a little hard for him to do that if he's dead."

She shook her head. "He's not dead."

"How do you know that? His body could be decaying in the same mud which tried to swallow you whole." There was no tenderness in his voice now, and despite all his claims that he could not be her husband, he was acting like an extremely jealous one. Her heart wanted to rejoice, because he did care. But if she melted, gave in to the love she felt, Elias would do what he needed to do to keep her safe and take her from the abbey without securing Simon. Yet in the end he would leave her anyway. She had to do whatever it took to save Simon. They were his only chance at survival. Her heart was secondary.

And she was going to hurt Elias in the worst possible manner with what she said next. "I've known Simon for a couple years. We've always had a...a connection." Elias looked as if he might break a tooth the way his jaw ground through her words, but she coldly continued to drive her dagger through the wall of his emotions and into his heart. "Before you, I'd always dreamed of becoming the Countess of Astley."

She winced when he raised his hand to run muddy fingers through his hair. He turned away from her, took two steps, and turned around with such speed she didn't see how he got so close to lean down and look directly in her eyes as he said, "*If* you are with child, we will remain married."

Hope for a different future began to lift the corners of her mouth.

"In name only," he ground out before her smile could fully form. "No earl will raise my son." He spat the words out as if the title left a bitter taste on his tongue, then grabbed her hand once more. Only this time he was not caressing the back of her knuckles like a lover, but squeezing her fingers like a prison vise, and Máira had a vision of what the future held—something altogether different from her dreams. He marched her past the priest without another word.

Father Charles looked at them expectantly, but neither offered an explanation, and so the holy man fell into step behind her as they made their way to the abbey at twice the speed they had been walking before.

Her altered trousers, now covered in mud, chafed uncomfortably. There was a time when she would have focused on her discomfort, the rubbing and scraping of the wet leather against her skin. Instead, she repeated the poem over and over in her head, wondering what tomorrow would bring. Would she ever see that tender side of Elias again? Or had she driven her dagger too deep, twisted it too hard, for his eyes to ever light up with passion for her once more?

They reached the ramparts of Mont Saint Michel in what seemed like minutes but was more likely just shy of an hour. Built on top of the craggy cliffs, the abbey's battlements reached high in the sky, blocking any light from the now cloud-covered moon. She couldn't see any torches burning on the wall, nor could she hear any more voices carrying across the bay. The void of light and silence of the night felt wrong, heavy and overbearing as if a cumbersome cloak weighed them down. Father Charles had warned Elias about scaling the walls at this location, saying it would be difficult due to the area being heavily patrolled.

Yet no patrol was in sight, and she worried the guards had seen them when she became stuck in the mire. Or the words she'd flung at Elias had alerted them to intruders and allowed them to prepare for a battle. Would the guards put a bullet through her husband's chest because she had given away their location? Her heart raced at the thought of her words being the cause of his death.

Father Charles and Elias, however, were in their element. The priest took the lead as they melded with the shadows like specters preparing to seep through the walls. They were making their way past the main tower Father Charles had called *Tour Gabriel*. It was a small, enclosed turret designed to provide protection to those watching the shoreline. Father Charles skirted the jagged rocks of the isle as they headed toward the Chapelle Saint Aubert. He stopped suddenly and Máira ran into the back of him, her breath coming in small pants from the pace they'd kept and her own trampled heart.

The small chapel appeared to stand on a small peninsula all by itself, unprotected by the walls and ramparts which protected the town and abbey of Mont Saint Michel. The faint light of a candelabrum flickered in the night through the one window of the chapel. It was there, at the top of the steps, that two guards watched over the expanse of sand leading to the shore. Elias backed up, pushing her with him, as they retraced their steps until they were hidden from the guards' view.

Elias addressed his comment to Máira. "Once we're inside, I need you to watch the tide. If it reaches the chapel, we won't be able to cross and will have to find a place to hide here until the next low tide."

She acknowledged his instruction with a nod and Elias began studying the cliffs. Despite being so close to the chapel and the tower, from the spot they were standing, only shrubs and trees growing out of the rock could be seen as they looked east and west. To Máira, the terrain looked impossible to climb. Elias and Father Charles, however, had prepared for the impassable.

"We will need to put our shoes on for the rest of our journey. Try to get your feet as clean as possible," Father Charles instructed her. Máira sat on the edge of a rock and began wiping off her feet. The mud extended up to the roll of her pants at her knees, but she only concentrated on her feet and ankles.

"Let me help you," Elias said, as he knelt in front of her and removed his shirt. She should look the other way for modesty's sake. They were traveling with a priest, but she could not stop looking at this man who had begun to mean more to her than she'd ever imagined possible. He wiped between her toes with care, making sure every bit of dirt and grime was removed.

"Give me your shoe."

She did as he said, unable to do anything but watch as he worked.

"Thank you," she whispered, as he finished and put his dirty shirt back on his body without a second thought. He bent over, and for a moment, she thought he was going to kiss the top of her head, until he stopped and turned away to put on his own shoes. Father Charles already had his shoes on and was taking a rope and hook out of the bag he carried.

Elias took the rope and motioned for her to step back as he let one end drop at his feet and checked it for tangles. He stood on the end of the rope and grasped the other end a couple feet away from the dangerous looking three-pronged hook. Once again motioned for her to step back and began swinging the hook in a circle before hurling it upward. The rope turned into a blur as it sailed through the air toward his target—the only large tree rooted in the side of the cliff.

She flinched as the prongs smacked against the wood, the leaves rustling before it snagged hold. Elias yanked on the rope to ensure it was secure. Clearly this was not his first use of the hook, and a shiver ran down her spine as she imagined him throwing it over the edge of an enemy ship.

Elias caught her movement and moved closer to her. "*Ma chérie,* if this is too much, we can go back."

Stiffening her spine she whispered, "I'm fine." The feel of his breath on her neck making her think of much more dangerous skills Elias possessed. "It's just the breeze." It was a lie, he knew and she knew it. It was the middle of July and hardly cold. "You go first, Father. You're more familiar with the abbey than we are, and that will allow me to assist my wife."

"Of course." The priest pulled himself up as if he were walking perpendicular to the wall. Hand over hand, he made the task look as easy as if he were walking across a bridge.

Elias then handed the rope to Máira. "Do you think you can do it?"

Máira looked at her husband, her brow cocking in challenge. "Do you think I can't?"

"Very few women could."

"You've climbed that many mountains with that many women?"

She didn't have to see he rolled his eyes to know he did it...she knew him. "I'll be right behind you if you start to lose your grip. Just let me know before you do, otherwise, we'll both fall to our deaths."

Just the thought of that was enough to give her pause. This was not a game, or a challenge to conquer. There was more at stake than her ego. "I may need your assistance," she admitted.

"I will be here."

For now.

Those words not spoken reverberated in the space between them. This was temporary, not the forever she wanted from this man. She wanted to laugh, to cry, to wail to the heavens about the injustices of giving her this man only to have him walk away from her. It was not better to have loved and lost. She would always love him, and he would always be lost to her.

She turned away without another word. Emotionally, she was on her own. And she was determined not to lean on him physically. Her first attempt ended in failure as she slipped to her knees, the rugged rock digging into her flesh through the muddy trousers.

"Bloody hell," she fumed, and she batted Elias's hand away as he attempted to help her to stand. She wanted to stomp her foot in frustration. Instead, she tried again. Her foot slipped once more, but she gained her balance and pulled herself up, gaining momentum with every step as her confidence grew.

She could do this. She was the one who hung the ropes in the trees for their youngest sister's swing, the one who jumped up and swung on the rafters in the barn just out of reach of little Robina to make the youngest Blair sister know what it was like to have someone strong and athletic in the family. All because their youngest sister not only missed out on what it was like to have a mother, but a father as well. Someone had to fill that role and Máira had been determined that Robina would experience all the physical joys of childhood she had, because Robina had missed out on the emotional joys of being loved by two adoring parents.

Granted it had been a few years since she had worn men's trousers and played the role of her father, but she still carried that same Blair determination and she would not fail now. Not while her husband and Simon were depending on her to be more than just a woman who could pour tea for the *ton*.

Suddenly a hand reached out in front of her. Her heart hitched until she realized it was Father Charles reaching for her hand. She clasped his surprisingly strong grip, and he pulled her to the top of the wall next to him. She swung her leg over and jumped down to the narrow walkway and raised her gaze to another wall between them and the abbey.

She'd never make it. As it was, it took all her mettle not to bend at the waist and rest her palms on her knees to catch her breath. Her chest rose and fell in tandem with her heartbeat. Thump, thump, thump, thump. She closed her eyes and took a deep long breath through her nose and then exhaled through her mouth.

She inhaled again and lips brushed against her neck, the warmth of his breath tickling her senses further as Elias whispered, "You are magnificent." He was gone before she had time to blush. She knew she wasn't magnificent, but the idea that he thought her so, or that he would encourage her with such words, was enough to make her confidence soar.

Elias grabbed her hand and pulled her back in the direction of the Tour Gabriel, until they reached a corner in the wall. All three of them leaned against the wall and squatted down. It seemed she was the only one who had trouble catching her breath, but it wasn't from exertion now. The anticipation of danger was far worse than facing danger. Her hands tingled. Her fingers stiffened, and with the rough cold stone at her back, she realized just how warm she was in the cool night air.

Elias put his hand on her knee and caught her attention. He took a deep breath through his nose and released it out through his mouth while indicating the movement with his hand. She nodded. He turned to Father Charles on his other side. Their conversation took place with hand motions only, and she was surprised at how much she understood. Elias would climb over first, Father Charles would help her, and then he would follow. Elias stood first and was climbing the wall before she even realized he wasn't using the rope. Instead, he used his bare hands, searching for a handhold no deeper than his fingertips and using the corner of the structure like a spider with its legs on opposite walls. She hadn't realized until that moment why he'd chosen the darkened spot as she gazed up in wonder at his strength. Even Father Charles seemed in awe as he made the sign of the cross and watched Elias as closely as she did.

Soon, she could no longer make out his form. His dark silhouette gone without a trace. It was as if the night sky erased his existence.

If he fell, she wouldn't see him. Silence followed. Then more silence until the rope dropped between them and she nearly jumped out of her shoes. They both let out an audible sigh of relief, and Father Charles grabbed it, yanked on it two or three times.

"You will use it the same as before. The incline is steeper, so it will be a bit harder," Father Charles whispered. "Hold on tightly to the rope. Your husband will be pulling you upward."

She acknowledged the priest's instructions and got in position to climb, when Father Charles tugged on the rope once more in a kind of silent conversation with Elias as she began climbing the wall. Suddenly she was climbing at twice the speed as she had earlier. It was if she were scaling the wall like a squirrel. No hesitation, no hiccups, and all the confidence in the world that everything would be fine. Within moments her husband's strong hand grasped hers and pulled her up on top of the wall where he knelt.

She hugged him tightly, clinging to him and taking in his raw masculine scent as she tucked her head into the crook of his neck.

He'd never smelled better than at that moment.

He waited for her to settle her nerves, seeming to understand her, and then he pulled her arms from the back of his neck.

He gestured for her to lie flat on the open walkway at the top of the wall. It was about five feet wide, and if she looked down, she thought she just might fall into the inky depths of darkness. She gladly followed his instructions, hugging the stone as she slowed her breathing once more.

Elias turned his attention to Father Charles, and she watched as he pulled hand over hand, the rope piling up in front of her until Father Charles was at the edge of the wall, his leg hitching over the top as he lay on his stomach. He lay there for a moment and Elias put his hand on his shoulder in question. The priest's one finger rose telling Elias everything he needed to know. Her husband, however, was a man of action. He didn't have a minute to wait. He gathered their rope and stuffed it in his bag, all the while watching the Tower of Gabriel and the chapel for any sign they had been detected. Then he leaned over and whispered in the priest's ear before he silently disappeared over the opposite side of the wall.

Her breath hitched. She had expected him to climb down and descend faster than Father Charles or her; instead, he had put one hand on the edge of the wall and jumped into oblivion.

She couldn't see him standing, crouching, or lying in a heap of broken bones.

A tap on her shoulder alerted her to Father Charles, who was holding a rope out for her to take, and she knew she was supposed to follow Elias. After taking the rope, she scurried down the wall, and before she knew it, strong hands were gripping her backside, molding around her curves with the familiarity of her husband.

Elias.

Her body sighed in relief as his lips brushed her ear, his warm breath soothing her rampant nerves. "I've got you, *mo ghaol.*"

His voice was so soft she swore it was her imagination as he guided her into a corner, the damp stone her only guide in the pitch-black night. Just as she began to feel a semblance of ease, he was crowding her, backing into her as he squeezed her thigh twice.

Something was wrong.

The rope dangled over the edge of the wall, swaying in the breeze.

The rope! She could *see* the rope and the walls!

Elias squeezed her leg again in warning. She could see the upper portion of the walls and the glimmer of a light flickering up and down as the person holding it moved in their direction.

A muttered curse bounced off the wall, and a soldier's footfalls picked up pace. Elias threw something that bounced off the walls and the soldier's light took a sudden change of direction, no longer headed toward them, but away as the soldier followed the noise. Then Elias was gone. Moving with the speed and grace of a born warrior as he tracked the soldier and disappeared around a bend.

Father Charles was there instantaneously, coming down the wall with the same speed as Elias. He hit the ground with a thud, his legs giving out as he sprawled on the ground in front of her. She bent to help him to his feet. Around the corner, glass crashed against stone and the soldier's light extinguished. A man grunted. The sound of punches landing created visions of flesh hitting flesh, blow after blow. Máira pushed past the priest and ran for the corner that was hiding everything from her view. She came up short as light from the nearby chapel illuminated the scene. A soldier missing one ear, his face battle scarred, his body toned and strong, wielded a sword toward Elias who was down on one knee. Her breath caught in her chest, threatening to strangle her as her husband rose up and gutted the man with a vicious blade she hadn't known he possessed.

The sword dropped to the stone and Elias withdrew his knife from the man's stomach as the soldier slumped to the ground. Something passed between them that was akin to hatred, under-standing, forgiveness, as if both men recognized the battle was not personal, but life and death were. Father Charles moved past her to the side of the dying man, and for a moment, the soldier's eyes met the priest's with one last look of knowing death was near on his craggy face. He nodded and Father Charles began administering the sacrament of the sick and dying. His voice became lost to the wind as she witnessed the oil he removed from his pocket and the sign of the cross he made on the man's forehead before the soldier's face and body went lax forever.

After a moment of silence, Elias picked up a pistol from where he had been fighting the soldier and shoved it in the waistband of his trousers. The elements of the battle that she had not seen were suddenly all too clear. Elias had disarmed the soldier before he could get a shot off, and the thought of how close she had come to losing him, sent a shiver through her body.

How many more would she experience before they were safe?

Elias turned back to Father Charles and lifted the large soldier by his shoulders while Father Charles lifted the man's feet. Not knowing what else to do, she picked up the bottle of oil Father Charles left behind and stuck it in her satchel, while the two men brought the man's body to the corner and propped him against the wall as if he were sleeping.

Elias then removed the man's jacket and slipped it on as they walked away. "Lucky for me, he was a dragoon. This jacket is cut high enough that there is little blood on it. The bad news is that he was a dragoon, which means there may be more here."

"At the top of this set of stairs is the gate to the courtyard of the abbey," Father Charles explained. "Máira will have to pick that lock. Once inside, you can follow along the wall of shrubbery on the left, where you will come to another set of stairs. That stairwell will lead you to the back entrance to the altar of the abbey."

She felt rather than saw Elias stiffen. "Where will you be?"

"I must go find someone else."

Sixteen

Father Charles,

I have received word that Napoleon has moved Cardinal Jean-Frédéric Linguet, and Pope Pius VII to Mont-Saint-Michel. If this is true, then you are to secure their freedom by any means possible. I charge you with the duty of bringing His Holy Eminence home.

Cardinal Cattaneo
Reims, France

—A letter to Father Charles at Moidrey Mill, France, from Cardinal Andre Cattaneo, who along with the Pope refused to denounce Napoleon's first marriage and give legitimacy to his second marriage to Marie Louise. Pope Pius VII and Cardinal Linguet were kidnapped from Rome by Napoleon's men, and have been in forced French exile since 1809.

The priest's words stopped them in their tracks.

"What?" He asked.

"I am needed at the Chapel of Saint Aubert," the priest told him.

"Who is at the chapel?" He asked.

"A special guest of Napoleon himself."

Elias swore under his breath. He should have known Hag had ulterior motives. She didn't like political intrigue. Since his father's death, she had been all about coin. She refused to embrace her French heritage, but she was barely tolerant of his English ancestry as well. If anything, she held them both in contempt. She wanted nothing to do with the war, or either side. Yet there was one man she would manipulate her only son to rescue.

"Who?" Máira asked, but Elias knew the priest would not answer. He answered for him.

"The Pope."

"The Pope?" She choked on the words. "The bloody Pope?"

He shook his head in disgust.

The priest frowned and made the sign of the cross.

"Are you telling me the Pope is here?" She asked.

Elias put his hand over her lips. "Shhhh."

Máira swatted him. "Don't *shhh* me!" Despite the lowering of her voice, she was clearly irate. "We're supposed to be rescuing a family friend, and he's being held in the same prison as the Pope?"

"And Cardinal Linguet, but they're not being held together," the priest clarified.

"They're on the same bloody island being held by the same bloody Frenchman."

The priest was in obvious discomfort dealing with a woman mad enough to shoot them and let the scavengers pick their bones. He was glad he hadn't given the soldier's gun to her when he decided to take some of the blame for this debacle. "That's why Hag sent us."

"Because of the Pope?" Her voice was blanketed with disbelief.

He nodded but didn't turn to look at her. "She is devout."

"Jesus, Mary, and Joseph," she muttered.

At any other time, her debauched language would be laughable, and he prayed they'd be able to laugh about it after making it through the dire situation they faced. "You're beginning to sound like one of my crew."

"I'm beginning to feel like one of them."

"If we're through discussing—"

"We're not through," Máira hissed. She pushed forward, but Elias held her back before she hit the holy man. She batted at him ineffectually and asked, "How are we supposed to get Simon off this island without you?"

"I will meet you here in one hour."

"And if you don't?"

The priest shrugged. "Then you'll have to make it back across by yourself. Remember, the tide will start coming in at three o'clock. You need to be over the wall before then."

Before she could argue further, Elias agreed. "We'll be here. Make sure you are as well."

The priest nodded. "That is the plan." He turned and walked away in the same direction the dead soldier had come from.

"If the Pope is here..." Her voice trailed off.

"We are as good as dead if he finds him before we find the earl." Elias confirmed. There was no reason to lie to her. "Let's find Astley and get the hell off this island while we still breathe."

He took her hand and led her up the stairs. They climbed for what seemed like forever. Blind corner after blind corner, he felt her fretting over what they would face. His jaw set with determination, he took each turn as if the damn dragons of hell awaited him.

Each turn, however, was empty except for the inevitable locked gate he had to allow Máira to conquer. He couldn't help the sense of pride he had in her when she magically opened each one. If he'd had time to admire her skill, he would have loved to watch her nimble fingers at work. As it was, he stood guard, watching her back, and then once he heard the lock click free, he shoved her behind him as they moved on to the next. Each time he prepared to slay an attacking guard on the opposite side of the door, it was eerily vacant. Where were the guards?

Máira bent to work her magic on the fourth lock, but instead of hearing the click of the lock, her soft curse caught his attention. He glanced behind him just as she looked up, frustration evident in her furrowed brow.

"I bumbled it," she admitted, as her eyes refused to meet his. "I'm sorry."

"Try again," he encouraged. "You can do it."

"You don't understand. I broke my tool in the lock. There's no way to open it without brute force." Her voice quivered.

Elias looked up at the wall. The odds were slim for the two of them not to be seen if they climbed up this particular wall this close to where the prisoners were being held. He was going to have to hide her somewhere and come back for her. Yet he didn't relish leaving her behind. "I'm going to climb the wall—"

"No," she answered before he finished his sentence as she shook her head and clutched the front of his coat in her hands. "You can't."

"It's what I do, Máira. I need to rescue the earl."

"Then you'll have to pull me over with you."

He shook his head. "I can't use the grappling hook here. I need to climb the wall and we don't know what awaits us on the other side."

"Nor do we know what awaits me if I stay here."

Every word she uttered nearly gutted him. He should've never taken her along. He sighed in defeat. "Fine. I go first and I'll drop you the rope if all is clear."

Her feminine smile of satisfaction made him want to show her just exactly who was in charge, but that would have to wait. "Remember how I showed you how to wrap the rope around you?"

"Yes."

"Good." A moment passed between them as he looked down into her eyes. He kissed her forehead, his warm lips meeting her cool skin. He didn't dare kiss her lips because despite the danger, or maybe because of the danger, he wanted more. He always would.

Elias draped his bag over his head and one shoulder and leapt up the wall. As quickly as possible, he climbed. One foothold for every pull of his hands. Ignoring the bite of stone across his skin, he gambled with the impossible footholds and momentum that wouldn't last if he didn't keep moving. He climbed and climbed till his fingers grasped the top ledge, where he paused to listen for any sound of movement on the other side.

The edge crumbled, his grip loosened, debris showered down over him, and he scrambled and clawed at the top of the wall with both hands. His grip slipping, the sound of Máira's gasp reached his ears as he nearly fell at her feet.

Desperately he dug his fingers into what suddenly felt like grass, weeds, and soil. He pulled with both hands, finding a bit of purchase in the wet, muddy ground. He could not fail. He *would* not fail.

Fighting the crumbling stone at his feet, the ground giving under his grip, every muscle strained with each inch he gained. Finally breaching the top, where he saw no nearby threat, he threw one elbow over and waited. Listened for a step, a stone, a bristle of leaves, or an intake of breath. He breathed in the scent of the ocean air, trying to detect body odor or the smell of a soldier's cheroot.

Once again, nothing. The night was as peaceful as if he were at the helm of his ship.

Nothing was that bloody tranquil.

He swung his second forearm over the edge, pulled himself up, and rolled to his feet in the grass. What he had not expected was to be at ground level looking at the abbey garden, filled with overgrown shrubbery reaching for the night sky.

Five pillars marked the opening to the grassy knoll he'd unwittingly breached. Silently he crept to the closest entrance of the garden where he hid amongst the shadows.

He waited.

The untroubled air held nothing but a wordless warning of danger to come.

Silently he made his way through the open corridors surrounding overgrown rose and boxwood bushes. He found no torches lighting the paths, and with the moon hidden behind dark clouds, the entire place appeared abandoned.

He made his way around the perimeter and quickly found the door to the abbey—locked. He cursed. How could Máira possibly open it after breaking her tool off in the last gate? Yet he had no choice. He couldn't leave her unprotected any longer, and he couldn't enter the abbey without her unless he made a hell of a racket kicking it in with his boot.

He returned to the edge of the wall, lay down in the wet grass, and looked over the edge.

"Thank God," she whispered, and reached up to take the rope.

Digging in his bag, he pulled out the grappling hook and rope, and dropped the rope end. He felt her tug, and pulled her up the wall, her small frame climbing the expanse as if she had been doing it her entire life. With one last heave, he pulled her over the edge, and she fell on top of him, her body forcing him onto his back in the tattered grass.

The two of them stood, and he took her hand in his as they crossed into the long open-air corridor. They hugged the wall as they advanced, their backs grazing across the ancient stone walls. He stopped a few pillars away from the door to the back of the abbey.

He leaned so close his lips almost touched her cheek and whispered, "The door is locked. Do you have any tools left?"

She nodded. He brought her up to the door and with his back to her, he stood guard.

Whispered curses befitting a sailor sounded at his back. He turned and gripped her arm, shaking his head for her to be quiet. A moment later the lock snicked free, and he turned around and grasped her arm again, pulling her close enough to whisper into her ear, "Stay at my back. Grasp the back of my shirt. I want you close enough to feel you there."

Her hand bunched a handful of his shirt under his stolen jacket and he cautiously made his way into the darkened interior of the abbey. It was not the altar.

Damnation. He'd chosen the wrong door. Going over the maps in his head, he oriented himself and prayed he didn't make another mistake, because once again, no sconces were lit. They entered the darkened room with Máira sticking close as he'd instructed. He reached up to feel sconces as they passed and found them cold and burnt down to nub. The candles had not been replaced. Something was going on at Mont Saint Michel that made the hairs on the back of his neck stand tall.

A moan reverberated off the stone walls, and he froze, the sound eerily like that of the dead coming back to life.

"Simon," she whispered.

He turned and covered her mouth with his hand while holding the back of her head with his other. He shook his head and waited a heartbeat, and another. With his lips at her ear he whispered, "If there is a prisoner close, a guard may be closer. At the other end of this room is the chaplaincy. Father Charles said the guards sleep there."

She nodded and pulled his hand away. Once again, they proceeded with caution until a squeak was accompanied by another moan. They waited in silence. Another loud squeak echoed down through the second stairwell from above them.

The stairs curved in a steep, narrow spiral, making him concentrate on what was in front of him instead of the woman clinging to his shirt. Pitch black turned to a shade lighter as the flickering glow from a torch began to filter from up above. Gradually the light became brighter, making him want to curse it and thank the heavens for the visibility it lent at the same time.

At the bottom of the stairs, he paused and looked down a long hallway banked with connecting arches that created individual temples to every saint ever canonized. Iron bars blocked off the sections of the hallway that had once held small alcoves for worship. It was ironically fitting to see bars where worship should occur, since the country had been at war with the Church, and the Church had been at war with the country as long as he could remember. Each seemed to want to hold the other accountable for sins they both committed.

Nearby moaning broke the silence once more, until someone yelled in a very unchristian manner for the person in misery to be quiet.

"Are these the prisoners?" She whispered.

He nodded, hoping to keep her silent.

"Do you think Simon is here?" She started to walk past him.

He glared at her, grabbing hold of her arm to both silence her and keep her where she was.

She started to argue and he pulled her back into the shadows, pushed her against the wall and trapped her there with his body, his forearms resting on the stone wall on each side of her head. He felt her breath hitch, saw her teeth pull at her bottom lip, and sensed her awareness of him as a man, just as his own body recognized the soft feminine curves being hidden by men's attire. *Mon Dieu*, but she did things to him. He leaned in, his lips brushing her ear as she shivered from his effect.

"There are more prisoners here, any of which might do anything to be freed. They will give us away in a heartbeat if given the chance to save themselves."

She froze as she understood the danger. Even the most desperate, desolate prisoner being held in this building could pose a threat to their survival, and they couldn't risk one of them tipping off a guard to a stranger's presence for the mere reward of a meal.

He'd heard the stories of prisoners-of-war too desperate to care about anything but survival.

"You will act as my prisoner, going forward. Do as I say. Understand?"

She nodded in agreement. He indulged in the briefest of kisses, uncertain of their future in the midst of this danger.

He pulled away, then placed one more upon her lips before stepping back and taking her hand as he headed toward the opening to the cloister. There he pushed her in front of him, grabbed her by the scruff of her collar and proceeded forward.

The first three cells were full of inmates sleeping on the floor, huddled away from their cellmates as if they were claiming a small place in the depressing cell as their own. The fourth held a man who was sitting up against the wall, staring out at them, a cough rattling his lungs as they passed. Despite the living, breathing person sitting before them, it was obvious from the flat sheen of his eyes, the man had given up on life, as his blank gaze barely tracked their progress before closing—possibly for good.

Elias gave Máira a shake, just to remind her not to get caught up in the stories of these men. The abbey may have been known as the *City of Books*, housing the scribes before printing presses were invented, but currently it looked as if it were the *City of Sorrow*.

"This is not a place of worship." The English words slipped from Máira's mouth as if the conditions had shocked her so much, they could not be contained.

"Not for English dogs caught spying," Elias responded in angry French, and gave her a small push for show. If he had not been holding onto her shirt collar, he had no doubt his shove would have sent her sprawling onto the filthy floor in front of him as she stumbled and turned to glare.

A young boy of seven or eight came scurrying down the hall out of nowhere. Elias stopped, pulling Máira back with him, away from the torch, away from being seen in any recognizable manner.

The boy stood in full view in front of them, the light glistening off his dirty brown hair.

"*Que désirez-vous, Monsieur?*" He asked.

Blast it. Another hiccup in his plan. The child could be an asset or he could be their downfall, depending on how well he hid Máira's identity as a woman, and how believably she portrayed a British spy.

"You can bring the two of us food. We've been traveling for two days without so much as a spoonful of millet or turnips," Máira responded, the deepening of her voice in the French language too sultry to be that of a man's.

The boy frowned, either surprised a prisoner would answer for a guard, or he was trying to figure out just exactly *what* she was. Her comment left Elias no choice but to shake her even harder by the scruff of her collar.

"You can help by taking me to the cell of the British earl. This one's to be held with him and ensure he is in good health until the ransom is received." He gave an uncaring laugh that made even Máira shrink back from him. "Apparently this lad was supposed to meet the earl to transfer information to the British army. One way or another, I'll get that information out of the earl." Elias nodded down the hall as if directing the boy to lead the way.

The boy hesitated. Uncertainty flitting across his face.

"Do as he says, lad, or it will only get worse for all of us." Máira's French was stilted this time as she stumbled over words she'd previously used flawlessly.

The boy turned on his heel and was on his way, glancing back over his shoulder to see if they followed. Elias released her collar and pushed Máira as gently as he dared. She stumbled, but righted herself quickly, glared at him over her shoulder once more, and followed the boy as if she were doing as she pleased. If they had been children, he would have pulled her hair; as it was, he simply growled and prayed the boy didn't notice her lack of concern for him as her captor. As they headed for another hallway leading toward the refectory, he dearly hoped the boy was taking them to Astley and not a guard or guard station.

Only a moment later loud noises ahead of them signaled that something was wrong. There was too much commotion inside the dining hall the boy was leading them toward at a hurried pace. If the room had been divided into cells as Father Charles had described, there would not be this much noise or movement.

"Máira," he whispered. He reached for her, but missed as she hurried in a manner no man ever would, to keep up with the boy. At a time when everything was not what it should be, he and Máira should be sticking to the shadows and avoiding the busy areas—not heading directly into the middle of the very full dining hall—the busiest place they'd encountered thus far. Whether the boy was double-crossing them or the priest had, Elias wasn't certain, but the boy was leading them into what could only be a trap.

"Máira!" he hissed, but she deafly passed through the large arched doorway and into the refectory where she stopped dead in her tracks. With one hand on his pistol and the other on the sheath of his knife, he entered the large hall with the authority of a guard and found the place was indeed the exact opposite of where the priest had said prisoners were being held.

The hall had been turned into a makeshift hospital filled with soldiers and guards, men so ill they could barely move. They were feebly lying on the tables and the floor.

It was a scene of horror and sorrow. Grown men reduced to helpless animals, unable to care for themselves or each other. A few women moved from man to man, but they, too, looked as if they were the walking sick, haunted by what they did and failed to do. If he weren't mistaken, there were several dead bodies lying around, already passed on to the heavens with or without the salvation offered by the priest, who was bent over one guard in the middle of the room.

With most of the guards ill, his job just got much easier. But whatever illness plagued these men, it was surely in the fetid air. He pulled his shirt over his mouth and nose. Then reached for hers.

"Cover your mouth and nose," he ordered, so that she might focus on him. Her gaze traveled up one end of the great room and down the other, taking in the desperate and the dying and the dead. He put his hand on her shoulder and pulled her shirt up over her nose. "We must go."

Her eyes had grown large, her argument there on the tip of her lips as she shook her head back and forth in dismay. She would not leave the sick and dying, not without him pushing her to do so.

"You cannot help them."

Her silence said everything. She wanted to help. She couldn't.

"Astley needs you. Your family needs you. I need you. Focus on that."

He took her wrist and pulled her along as he ducked into the narrow doorway the boy had disappeared through.

In the dim light, the child stood waiting for them in front of an oak door almost as thick as the exterior entries, his big brown eyes glued to where Elias held Máira's delicate wrist. Elias looked down to where the boy's eyes were glued. Contrast between man and woman as blatant as if they stood naked. He dropped her hand as quickly as if she scalded him, but not before the boy noticed the contrast between Máira's creamy smooth, soft skin and his bronzed roughened hand.

"Vous voulez bien l'aider, mademoiselle?"

"Oi." Máira responded with an earnest nod to the boy's question.

Merde. She was going to get them killed with her equally sincere response that she was a young miss who would help the man closeted behind that door. Her admission left Elias looking around them. Sounds from another room came from his right and he stepped forward to look inside. It was a kitchen of sorts, with exhausted, stressed women who were cooking soups, cutting vegetables, and boiling cloths and medicinals.

Elias stepped back.

The boy pushed open the heavy door that led to what had once been a meat larder, but now contained a pallet on the floor, where a man lay still and silent. Elias grabbed at the boy, but the boy batted at his hand and ran to the unkempt prisoner, who appeared too sick, injured, or possibly dead to do anything but lie with his back to the door. A tattered blanket covered a large frame that held little more than skin and bone.

Elias removed his knife from his belt and approached with caution as the boy shook at the man's shoulder in a futile attempt to wake him. Elias gently moved the desperate boy aside. The man was well over six feet tall, but his frame had been reduced to frailty. His dark hair, long and unkempt. Months of growth covered hollowed cheeks and sunken eyes rimmed with dark circles. The entire effect gave the man the look of a skull covered in skin and hair.

He rolled the man onto his back and watched his arms flop toward the floor with no resistance. It was Máira who spoke first, as she bent over the unconscious earl, lying half dead.

"Simon! I'm here. It's Máira." She pulled his hand into hers. "Caillen's sister."

"She's a horrible spy." The boy commented in broken English.

Elias bit his lip, wanting to agree, yet knowing he couldn't.

Reverting to his native French, the boy said, "I thought you were a soldier, but now I see you're not. Are you here to take him away?"

Elias studied the boy. Dirty clothes hung on his filthy body. He was malnourished with deep sorrow etched in his face. His expression bled the tears his dry eyes did not. A child his age shouldn't know that amount of grief. And there was concern—for Astley.

He bent down and let the truth be known, despite the risk of it coming back to bite him in the arse. "I'm here to take him home. She's helping."

"She's going to get you caught."

He shook his head and pointed to the woman in full-blown healer mode. Despite how shaken Máira had been at the ghastly sight of so many in need, she was in complete control of her emotions now, as she dug in her pouch and began pulling out herbs along with a flask and a small stone mortar and pestle to grind up her concoctions. He had no idea where she had obtained them.

"She was taken off-guard by how many people are suffering. She has a soft heart. Now she has a purpose that will drive her to do what needs to be done."

The boy still viewed her skeptically, so he continued. "If it weren't for her, we would have never made it this far. What's your name?"

"Sébastien," the boy said with a lift of his chin. The pride he felt in his name evident.

"Well then, Sébastien. It looks as though I will need your assistance as well. Can I rely upon you?" He held out his hand, waiting to see if the boy would grasp it, or leave him no choice but to lock him up while they escaped.

Sébastien's little hand got lost in his. So young, so frail with skin roughened by hardship—the boy's grip a mere pinch of his palm. His eyes, however, did not waver. They held the strength and conviction of a survivor as he proclaimed, "On my father's grave, I swear the earl will not suffer his fate at the hands of the soldiers."

Elias did a little swearing himself at that moment. He silently vowed the boy would never know the earl's fate, because the chances of Astley surviving were worse than their chances of escaping. He looked at his pocket watch. Half-past two in the morning. They were already late to beat the tide and he had no idea how to get his wife and the earl off this damned island.

Seventeen

Dearest Aunt and Uncle—

I am scared. Father is dead. The man protecting me is very ill. I think he will die. The soldiers watch...waiting for him to falter. He is the only reason I still breathe. They say I must pay a fine or forfeit my life. Please help.

Your loving nephew,
Sébastien

—A letter from the son of a spy killed by double agent Henry Greasley. The letter was sent from a cell in Mont Saint Michel, where the eight-year-old boy watched over the Earl of Astley. Greasley would have killed Sébastien had Astley not stopped him by surrendering himself. A monk delivered the letter to the boy's aunt and uncle, who burned it upon receiving it, too frightened for their own children to risk saving their orphaned nephew.

Máira looked up from Simon's unconscious body. "He's got a broken arm, fingers, possibly some ribs. He has head and facial injuries and more that I cannot discover without him being conscious."

"They beat him daily, until they all began to get sick."

Máira winced at the boy's words, wondering what he had witnessed but continued, "He is also gravely ill."

"I've been sneaking him what the women in the kitchen have been giving the soldiers, but he can't keep it down."

Máira studied the expression on the boy's face. "You have done a wonderful job of caring for him. I suspect he would not be alive if it weren't for your care." She dug in her bag and took out a small sample of the herbs and root she had collected along the river. "Give this to the women. Tell them these herbs are from Dinan—"

"Marseille," Elias interrupted. "We were in Marseille when you collected those."

The intensity of his gaze told her not to argue. He did not want the boy or anyone else to know where they had been, so despite not knowing if the flowers grew in Marseille or not, she agreed. "Of course, my mistake. It...it was Marseille. How silly of me. The innkeeper's wife asked us to check on her family in Dinan, but we never made it."

The boy shook his head and looked at Elias. "She is a terrible spy."

Elias winked at the boy. "Sébastien, go show the women what to look for and where to get it. The innkeeper's wife in Marseille said to mix it in wine and give it to the sick. But then come back here. We will need your help getting out of here."

The boy nodded and took off with her mixture of herbs and plants that would hopefully help heal the sick.

"You're helping the men who did this to Astley," he informed her.

"Not all of them are guilty."

"Not all of them are innocent."

"We will never know which ones did this to Simon. I do know I cannot leave without offering a bit of aid, but I did not mix the herbs with wine. I mixed them with water from the river."

"We don't know if the water supply on the island isn't the problem."

She agreed and then turned back to Astley. "How do you suggest we get him out of here?"

"Since he can't walk, I'll carry him."

"But his ribs—if they're broken it could kill him."

He nodded in agreement as he stood watch at the door for any soldiers coming their way. "And if I don't carry him, he will most definitely die. I didn't come here to recover his body. I came to give the man a fighting chance at survival. Wrap his mid-section as best as possible. When the boy returns, we leave."

She knew he was right. At most, she would give Simon a thirty percent chance of living.

Sébastien returned a few minutes later, his mood anxious as his gaze darted back at the door.

"What's wrong?" Elias asked.

"There are new soldiers coming to get the earl."

"When?"

"I don't know. I overheard the women talking, but then the cook saw me and slapped me for eavesdropping. I told her I was just waiting for them to finish talking, but I don't think she believed me. I told her one of the monks gave me the herbs to heal the sick and after a bit of grumbling, she told me to go collect the plants."

Elias frowned. "When did she expect you to return?"

"She wanted me to get a couple guards from Chapel Saint Aubert. That is where the healthy guards are staying. I'm to return at the next low tide."

Máira breathed a sigh of relief. That would give them several hours before the boy was expected to return. They could drop him off at the mill, provided Father Charles made it back—

"Bloody hell." Elias cursed, not even sparing a look at the boy. "The damn fool is going into a den of angry men."

"Who?" The boy asked.

"Never—"

Máira gasped. "Father Charles was headed to the chapel."

Elias threw his hands in the air. "Stop talking."

Sébastien shook his head. "A terrible spy."

Máira looked at the two of them and then directed her argument to Elias. "You're the one who said the fool was headed toward a den of angry men."

"You're the one who gave away the identity of your accomplice," Sébastien interjected as if she'd been arguing with him. Which she certainly was not going to do. He was a child.

Elias raised his right hand, palm in the air as if he were serving the boy's words on a platter. She stuck her tongue out at the two of them and turned to gather her satchel and supplies. A giggle sounded behind her, the joyous noise as strange as sunshine in the dark gloom of the diseased prison.

"He's ready," she told Elias, who closed the door and then moved over and sat down on the floor next to Simon. With Simon's good arm draped over one shoulder, Elias leaned over and pulled the earl up across his back, lifting one of the earl's legs over his other shoulder. Elias pushed to his feet and held Simon as if the earl was a cape covering his shoulders. She expected Simon to cry out in pain or at least moan, but nothing fell from his lips.

Sébastien looked out the door and then opened it. Elias followed with Máira picking up the rear, watching Simon for any sign of pain. They moved swiftly and entered the refectory and Sébastien went to the right, not toward the cloister where they'd entered. She watched the room, her nerves on edge as she waited for someone to yell, "Stop, they're escaping!" No one even glanced their way.

A raspy cough drew her attention to a soldier sitting up against the wall. His finger was raised in their direction...pointing. His mouth was open as if he was desperately attempting to raise the alarm, but the cough racking his body refused to allow him respite. She paused and leaned over the man, but before she could utter a word, the soldier grabbed her by the front of her shirt. Her hat tipped, her hair threatening to tumble out for all to see.

As if sensing she was not following him, Elias stopped and turned around slowly with the earl hanging like a limp rag doll on his back. His expression was as cold as she had ever seen it and she was afraid he would kill the soldier where he sat.

Máira took control and said in a loud voice, her tone turning scratchy as she attempted to deepen her words to sound like a young boy on the cusp of manhood. "The English scum died. He's going to burn the body so he can't have a proper burial." Her French was flawless.

The soldier looked at the unconscious earl, his eyes squinting to clear his unfocused gaze. A small lift of the corner of his mouth signified he believed her lie, before his coughing consumed him, his odorous breath worse than the air around them. He released her shirt and bent over in desperation to catch his breath. Too involved in his own fight for breath, the soldier paid no heed to their departure.

Sébastien waited for them at a doorway, then held it open for them to pass into the fresh night air.

"Where are we going?" she asked, as she quietly closed the door behind them.

"A different route." Elias gave her no hint of where or why they weren't returning the way they came.

"But—"

He stopped, turned around and glared at her. His left hand held the earl's wrist and ankle together, his knuckles white with the strain. Then she saw the pistol in his right hand, not directed at her, but ready to face any threat with deadly force.

He had been ready to shoot the man in the refectory...for her, he had been willing to risk his rescue mission, himself, the boy—

everything. She understood the anger radiating off him and the death glare that said, *don't push me*.

She nodded, and he turned back toward Sébastien as they made their way along an exterior covered walkway on the north side of the abbey. The sea breeze struck her in the face, fresh, briny, the weather cooler than it had been when they arrived. Clouds still covered the sky, making the full moon completely invisible. The motion of the tide hitting the rocks below made her pulse quicken.

They were late. Their pace increased, each one of them aware of what the crashing waves meant. They reached the opposite end of the abbey, and at the corner of the cloister, Sébastien turned toward the sea, and crossed the open piazza that ran almost the entire length of the north side. He stopped when he reached the wall. A heavy iron gate barred them from exiting. She quickly moved forward and bent down to look at the lock mechanism. It was similar to the lock that had broken her tool. It was also in similar condition, if not worse.

Her satchel clinked as she set it down, and she suddenly remembered the bottle of holy oil she'd picked up off the ground and shoved in her bag when the Elias and the priest were carrying the dead soldier's body. She pulled it out and stared at it for a moment, wondering if she was damning them to hell. She shrugged. They were damned if she didn't.

She popped the cork from the bottle with her teeth and dribbled the oil slowly into the lock and then on the end of her tool. Inserting the pick into the lock, she wiggled back and forth. She pulled it back out and poured more oil on the tip. Poking and turning until she found the right position and felt the mechanism tightening around it. Slowing she pushed, but still, it wouldn't budge. She pulled out the pick and ran her fingers down the length of it, afraid she would find a stress fracture.

"You know how to tease a man," Elias said from directly behind her.

She met his gaze over her shoulder, and for one blessed

moment she swore she saw love in its depths. Then he winked and she remembered the mission. The mission that started with a wink and a dropped package. That wink had stolen her heart the very first day they'd met, and she suddenly realized the fissure wasn't in her tool, but it would be in her heart when this was over.

"You can do it. I have faith in you."

He did. She looked at Simon who was on the ground leaning against the wall to her right while Sébastien stroked the hair from his face. She steeled her heart and refused to let it break. Simon was the reason they were here. It may not have been her mission in the beginning, but it was now. She would get him home.

She nodded and refocused on her task. She thrust the tool in the lock and turned, attacking the lock with as much force as she dared, and just as she suspected the tool would break, the lock snapped open, iron slamming against iron. It would have been loud inside the abbey, out here at the sea wall, the noise was drowned out by breaking waves as the door creaked open.

Elias turned toward Sébastien his voice low and steady. "This is where we must part, Sébastien. I cannot take you across the bay. Tell the women you could not make it across before the tide came in."

She stepped in front of him. "What? We can't leave him behind! That soldier saw him with us," she whispered.

"That man will be dead before dawn," Elias countered.

"I want to go with the earl." Sébastien pleaded. "He needs me."

Elias bent down and met the boy's pleading stare. "I cannot help you across the bay. The sea will be too rough."

Tears filled the boy's gaze as he looked at the earl, and Máira's heart nearly broke. He had lost his father, and God only knew the circumstances with his mother. The earl owned this boy's heart.

"I can take him."

Elias's jaw tightened. "You will barely be able to make it across the bay yourself."

"I can swim," she insisted, as Sébastien looked on pleadingly with big, round eyes.

"This is not a Scottish loch. This bay has some of the most dangerous currents known. We will be lucky if the three of us make it across."

"The boy comes, or I stay." The three of them turned to look at the man who had brought them to this holy place that was more hell than heaven. Simon's soft, shaky voice held his conviction as he looked at Sébastien. The effort to lift his head seeming to take every bit of the strength he owned. The boy hugged Simon, who gifted him with the briefest of smiles from within his scraggly beard.

"We won't leave him behind," Máira assured him.

"He is French. They will not hurt him," Elias argued as the muscle in his jaw ticked.

"His father...was French." Simon's voice was but a whisper. "And he betrayed his country."

"The boy did not," Elias argued.

"I have an aunt and uncle who promised my father they would take me in if anything happened to him," Sébastien interjected, hope evident on his face.

"His father...was caught with a letter..." Astley's voice faltered. It was taking every ounce of his strength to argue with Elias. His last statement also took all his fight away. His gaze slowly traveled to Sébastien, and what Máira saw in his eyes was unmistakable. Guilt racked his soul, but the fondness for the boy was his saving grace. "Your aunt and uncle can't take the risk, Sébastien." The earl's words were hard to hear, even harder to deliver for Simon.

"He could stay with Father Charles," Máira suggested.

"No." That one word held more passion than Simon had yet to demonstrate. "He returns home with us." His eyes closed for the briefest of moments before staring Elias down. "I will not leave him to die or to be raised by strangers."

A single nod from Elias was all it took to calm him and send

Simon into a deep sleep. It was as if the earl had used every drop of fight he had within him to argue for Sébastien. Máira bent down and checked his breathing, then she reached into her bag and pulled out her flask. She had a bit more of the elixir. If he could take a bit more now, it would help him and give him strength for their journey.

"Won't his stomach reject that?" Sébastien asked.

"No, it will soothe it and help him consume soup when we arrive at—"

"After we cross the bay," Elias cut her off before she could say where they were going.

Sébastien grinned. "You are a bad spy."

Elias squatted down in front of Astley. His irritation and resistance gone, once the decision to take Sébastien with them had been made. "Help me get Astley on my back before you blurt out any more of our plans." He winked at Sébastien, who grinned in return as they turned toward the steps.

"Stop! Identify yourself!"

They froze at the French command to stop. None of them had seen the large burly guard approaching them with a pistol in his hand. He held it across his chest with the barrel pointed in the air as if he were on a casual midnight stroll. His navy-colored uniform blended amongst the shadows, but as he walked toward them across the piazza, a scabbard holding his long-curved saber slung low across his left hip. It clinked against his leg, the golden braids of his uniform glistened across an imposing barrel chest.

Máira swallowed hard. This man was dangerous. Leather lined the inside of his pant legs, identifying him as one of Napoleon's reputed hussars who feared nothing and didn't plan to live past the age of thirty—an age he'd well surpassed.

Máira wanted to curse the bloody island where they stood.

The man's tall fur hat with more gold braiding and a thick frond stood nearly a foot off the top of his head. He didn't need the ridiculous hat to make him appear large. The closer he got, the more obvious the inches he had on Elias became. She'd never seen a man of his stature in her entire life.

Elias remained silent, yet with the man's demand to know who they were, was a question only Elias could answer. For two boys to respond instead of a soldier would be completely out of place. Elias stood rigid and tall, looking absolutely magnificent as he turned toward the new obstacle to their escape. The corner of the soldier's lip rose along with the corner of his long mustache, as if he suddenly relished the challenge in her husband's stance. He pointed his pistol in the middle of Elias's chest, and Máira was certain the man would shoot him with the least provocation. His actions might make one think he was afraid of Elias, except for the unabashed joy written all over his face at the prospect of killing.

If the soldier felt a drop of fear, she could not see it. Nor could she see one in her husband's hardened gaze.

She wanted to smack him for putting on such a display, but then he spoke in that beautiful French dialect she'd adored.

"My name is Elias Maximilien Allistair Drake, and I am here on a mission for my grandfather."

Máira blinked. Elias *Maximilien* Allistair Drake? Just days ago, he'd said his name was Elias *Allistair* Drake.

He lied. Again.

The soldier laughed and jutted his pistol in her direction and then Sébastien's. She pulled the boy behind her and focused on translating his French in her head. "With two boys? And what is that on your shoulders? Drop it."

Elias stood tall, scowling at the soldier who didn't care to be ignored. The soldier cocked his pistol.

Elias dropped the earl like a sack of grain. His feet hit first and then his upper body. The blanket that had covered him, somehow unfurled about his body, obscuring what was underneath. Simon groaned, and Sébastien immediately followed it with a curse a boy his age shouldn't know and hopped around as if Elias had dropped the earl on his toes. *"Mon Dieu!"* he cursed.

The boy was a good spy.

"Do you not recognize my name?" Elias asked, completely unfazed by what was happening behind him as he took on the air of nobility. Was he French nobility? Did that carry any weight in France anymore? Or would they want to chop off his head?

The soldier's head cocked slightly, as if he were contemplating Elias's self-importance. In the soldier's silence, Elias clarified his identity for *all* of them. "Elias Maximilien Allistair Drake, the grandson of the Minister of War for France. My grandfather is also Chief of Staff to Napoleon Bonaparte. Would you like to verify my identity with Napoleon himself? He is my godfather, after all."

Her heart stuttered. The soldier's grin faltered and his gaze strayed to the blanket on the ground when Simon moaned.

That was all it took. Elias charged. His large body slamming into the soldier's. The two collided in a bundle of arms, legs, and weapons, their bodies coming together in a blur. The pistol discharged, the sound rolling across the piazza to reverberate off the arched walkway.

"Move!" Sébastien's young voice held a desperation she had not heard before. The boy stood behind her with Elias's large pistol swaying in his grip.

"Sébastien, put the gun down," she ordered, and held her hands out to him, hoping the motion of her palms down pressing to the ground would calm the boy. His brow drew downward as he bit his lip. His eyes were wild, his movements jerky. He appeared too stunned to grasp what was happening around him as the fight raged on at her back. Elias was fighting for their lives with a soldier who was larger, more seasoned, and less affected by killing.

"He's the war minister's grandson! It's a trap, he will kill the earl! Move!" Sébastien waved the pistol and she was almost certain he'd not had a chance to load it—but Elias had.

"He's not the enemy, Sébastien."

Sébastien moved to the side, his view of Elias clear, the pistol in his hand aimed at her husband's back.

"No!" She swung at the gun, knocking it from Sébastien's hands. The gun hit the gate and bounced down the steps toward the sea. Sébastien didn't hesitate, he ran for the fight and jumped on Elias's back. Desperate to stop the carnage, she entered the fray as fists swung and heads collided. Elias tried desperately to protect her and Sébastien—the soldier did not. A fist struck her shoulder, and pain radiated through her body as she staggered backward. She reached for her knife ready to kill another Frenchman for the man she loved.

Elias cursed. "Máira, get him out of here!" The hussar's fist hit Elias in the nose sending blood everywhere.

"Bastard," he gritted out, and tackled the man to the ground.

She ran forward and put her knife to the man's neck, the blade firmly held against his flesh.

Everyone froze.

But it wasn't because of the threat her knife delivered. It was the much larger blade extending in-between the faces of the two men on the ground and biting into skin. On *her* neck. The blade pricked, and the hussar on the ground with her knife to his neck smiled. Máira slowly tilted her head back to look up at this new threat to her life and their escape.

Additional gold braiding and red ribbons, along with bear fur on the man's jacket marked his higher rank, but the gold belt for his scabbard and his bizarrely baggy red trousers screamed that the rules of standard issue uniform did not apply to this man. He was a hussar of great import. He led soldiers, and he held everything in the balance as he stood over them with his long, curled mustache pointing toward the sky and twitching with his grin.

"Despite all her machinations, it seems fate has insisted I meet my lover's son after all." With every word the new hussar seemed to mock them, but his words were meant for Elias and they hit with great force.

"Bloody fucking hell," he muttered.

Eighteen

My Lord Duke,

I have located the tavern where Lady Máira was last seen. The Happy Hag is indeed run by a woman who only goes by the name of Hag. She is a hard woman, who seems to be under a great deal of duress at the moment. I am told this is not her usual demeanor, which I can only deduce has something to do with the recent visit of an English privateer and a lady with dubious knowledge of the French language.

I regret to inform you that the Englishman was killed, and my source says he was a spy for Maximilien de Danton, the Minister of War for France. His name, however, was unknown and Hag would not speak of it. She, in fact, threw me out of her establishment with the aid of her righthand man, a man of little words but a great deal of brawn and loyalty to his proprietress.

The lady disappeared from the establishment with the privateer. It remains unclear if this was Mr. Drake's first mate, or a member of the crew from another ship docked that day named the Confiance. That ship is known to help French citi-

*zens in need of asylum. The Confiance should have arrived at
Pembroke Dock by the time you receive this missive. I have
dispatched a colleague to determine if Miss Máira returned on
that voyage. I am hopeful that she has indeed returned and is
currently under your protection.*

*I have also learned that Alexandre Baptiste Reynard Beau-
mont, Comte Legrand, and Napoleon's Hussar General and
leader of the Hellish Brigade, is on his way to execute the Earl of
Astley. Hag was desperate to keep Legrand from leaving, and
did everything in her power to keep him in Le Conquet. As I
await more news on Miss Máira, I will attempt to learn about
the earl.*

Your faithful servant,
Mr. Johnathan Payne

*—A letter from Bow Street Runner, Mr. Johnathan Payne,
hired to locate Máira Blair, to Nashford Harding, Duke
of Ross*

E lias glared at the man who dared to threaten his wife. The
Circassian shashka blade causing blood to leak from her
neck was almost as famous as the hussar who held it. The
saber was known for its ability to cut a man in two with its finely
made steel. The slightly curved blade was as long as any saber, but
the craftsmanship surpassed anything most of the Continent had
ever seen. More deadly than Elias had ever seen, until now.

"It seems I'm at a disadvantage. You know who I am, but I
have yet to make your acquaintance." Despite the politeness of his
words, his tone held all of the anger he felt for the man holding the
shashka to Máira's delicate neck.

The hussar laughed, his voice full of the joy he was known to
display in battle. "Ahhh, your mother has not shared the identity
of the man who inhabits her bed. I must thank her for her
discretion."

"There have been many men who've shared my mother's bed after my father died." It was a lie. Only one man had. The general of the hussars, the leader of the infamous Hellish Brigade. Hag may not have shared this man's identity, but Tomás had. This man was dangerous, and he worked for Napoleon alongside his grandfather.

"From my understanding, your father was murdered by your grandfather for being a spy."

Máira gasped, but Elias didn't flinch. He'd moved beyond the pain his grandfather had inflicted.

"Forgive me. That was rude of me to bring up such a painful memory. I am Alexandre Baptiste Reynard Beaumont, Comte Legrand. At your service."

Elias nodded but showed no recognition of the beloved hero of France. Only Murat and Napoleon himself were more popular than this general, who loved women like he loved his liquor—in quantity. Hag was lucky she hadn't acquired the pox.

"Remove the blade from my wife's neck, Legrand." Elias could taste the blood on his lips. It was his own, but the rage inside him demanded he taste another's. Specifically—the blood of his mother's lover. He had warned Hag about playing with that particular fire.

"Not before your lovely wife removes her knife from *le capitaine's* flesh. It seems to be drawing blood. Or is that her blood. It's hard to tell at this angle."

"Sébastien, go back to our baggage." The saber resting against Máira's skin cut into her flesh with every word. Each causing another drip of blood to drop as she spoke. Yet despite the obvious pain the saber caused, she did not flinch in the least as she looked at the boy hanging onto Elias's back like a monkey.

"But—"

"Do as she says," Elias ground out, in as vicious a tone as he had ever used on another living soul. "Do you not see the blood dripping down her neck?"

The boy was gone in an instant, scrambling off his back.

"If you would be so kind as to remove your person off my hussar, I would be ever so grateful."

"Only if your saber follows my withdrawal. If it does not, she will cut through his neck as if it were a holiday feast until she reaches the bone of his spine." He willed her to show no fear, and in that moment, it was as if she read his thought, for as he concentrated on her, she lifted her defiant gaze up to the man who threatened her life.

"My husband is correct. I have always wanted to carve a pig." She turned her sneer on the man beneath him and for the first time, he saw uncertainty in the hussar's eyes. Every hussar had a certain death wish to die in battle, but to die at the hands of a beautiful young woman as small as Máira, well...that was not the death of honour any soldier had envisioned for himself.

The man lording his power over all of them laughed, his face full of joy at the scene before him. He was an oddity Elias wasn't certain he could trust. He winked at Máira as if this was just a joke between friends, and with a slight bow of his head said, "I believe your husband and I have struck an accord, madame."

"Not quite," Elias interjected. "I want your word, as a gentleman, that no one will harm her or the boy."

Once more the man bowed his head, but like the first time, his eyes never left Elias. "On my honour, monsieur."

"Now, we have an accord." Elias slowly sat up, his hands still gripping the hussar's jacket, then he pushed to his feet and released it as the saber left Máira's neck to rest on his own. He backed away slowly, not wanting to give the hussar on the ground room to turn the tables on Máira.

"Máira, remove your knife." He hoped his voice sounded calm and rational and revealed none of the pleading his gaze relayed to her.

Máira stepped away, her hair falling from under her cap to cascade down her shoulders and hide the blood that marred her pale skin. Before she could get clear of the hussar, however, he grabbed her ankle and pulled her foot out from underneath her. Elias moved in her direction, but the shashka bit into his neck, stilling him to his spot, to watch in horror as his wife's body fell backward, her head hitting the stone piazza with a thickening whack that made his stomach roll and his anger burn. Máira's knife flew from her grasp and clattered across the piazza.

The hussar was on her instantly. Straddling her with his trunk-sized legs and holding her arms with his knees on her biceps. He laughed in her dazed face as she shook her head to clear the fog.

"Do not move," Legrand growled, his blade dug into Elias's neck, then disappeared as it whistled through the darkness with a speed faster than imaginable. The shashka returned to Elias's neck before he could surge forward. Máira gagged, his heart stopped, the hussar on ground froze, then his head dropped to the ground, a wet slap before it rolled away. Máira pushed the man's body from her own and was up off the ground in an instant. She wobbled. She didn't scream. Didn't drop in a fit of hysterics. She did nothing but sway and blink rapidly at Legrand, as Elias released the breath he didn't know he'd held.

Mon Dieu, but she was magnificent. He wasn't sure Hag could show as much ice in her veins at such a horrific sight. The sound of retching occurred behind him and Elias remembered Sébastien standing a mere fifteen feet away.

"My apologies to your wife and son, but Oudinot had always struggled with the concept of honour. I promised you, your wife would not be hurt. I keep my word." His sincerity was genuine, Elias was certain. However, he still had an escape that must be executed before the tide rose any further and left them stranded in the exact same cell from which they had freed the earl.

"I appreciate your gesture, but the fact remains, your word was broken and for that I must call you out, Legrand."

Legrand laughed, his bloody blade rocking against Elias's throat. "You think that a gesture? To kill one of my finest hussars?"

He shrugged, ignoring the bite of the blade. "I think you believe it as well. Both of our honours yearn for satisfaction. Me—I demand it. My wife just experienced something no lady should."

"The *ladies* of France experienced far worse."

"True, but we both know she is not French, and she has never treated the masses the way the French aristocracy has."

Legrand's grin grew, his laughter building as he swept his saber out and away from Elias with an elegant flourish. He bowed once more before addressing Máira. "Madame, your husband has challenged me to a duel. I would appreciate it if you would remove my hussar's saber and give it to him, so that we may see this unpleasantness to an end."

"No." Máira's voice still held ice, but was now somewhat brittle, the edges cracking.

Legrand quirked a brow. "No?"

"No. I will not let you kill my husband."

Elias took a step in her direction, but Legrand's saber pointed in his direction. Damn the man. He addressed his wife in a strong, yet calm tone, attempting to install as much iron in her backbone as possible. "Máira, he will not kill me. Have a little bit of faith in your husband. Please, my dear, get the saber. Focus on the task, not the body."

Her lip trembled and he feared she would collapse. Yet once again, she steeled herself to the task at hand and retrieved the saber without hesitation. He smiled at her as she pressed it into his palm. The weapon was not the caliber of Legrand's, but Elias was certain that despite his battered face, broken nose, and sore knuckles, he could and would defeat Legrand. He had way too much on the line not to—especially the woman standing in front of him.

He touched her face and gently kissed her precious lips. He would kiss her again, of that he was certain. Before Máira, he had never wanted a wife. Never desired to stay in one place, but for her, he would do anything and everything.

"A man should always have one final goodbye with his wife."

Legrand's words were meant to unravel, and for his wife, they did. Máira turned on him like a mother bear he had once seen protecting its cub. Elias grabbed her and kissed her hard. When he pulled away, he let his forehead rest upon hers. "Trust me in this. I will handle him. Go to Sébastien and the earl. When the fighting begins, head down the stairs. You'll have to drag the earl, just keep his head from hitting."

Máira clung to the lapels of his jacket. "No, I won't leave you."

"Máira, please. More soldiers will come. Trust me. I will join you." He brushed his lips against hers and pushed her toward Sébastien without another glance. He had work to do. He had to have faith in her ability to make the decision to save herself, Sébastien, and Astley. If he died, he would die knowing he gave her a chance, but if he was the victor, no army could stop him from joining her.

"You have your mother's confidence. It's most appealing in a woman, is it not?" Legrand goated.

Elias refused to take the bait but instead waited for him to make the first move, and with a grin Legrand lunged. Elias shed the attack, blades clanging with impact as Legrand's edge slid down his own. He immediately sloped to the left and parried, but Legrand was a true swordsman and deflected his blow with ease. Back and forth they fought, each deflecting blows, a test to their strength and stamina. Sweat poured down his brow and Elias swiped at it with his sleeve. Legrand was ten years his senior, but the man was a seasoned soldier who loved the fight more than the victory.

Looking for an advantage, Elias retreated toward the abbey wall, taking advantage of the shadows to hide his expression. Legrand lunged, the tip of his blade slicing across Elias's chest and scoring a point Elias could not afford to give. His borrowed jacket split. His shirt ripped. And his flesh tore.

He gritted through the burn as the wetness seeped into his clothing. Before he could launch an attack of his own, a long pipe swiped down upon Legrand's arm, striking his wrist and wiping the grin from the general's face.

Bone shattered with a deafening crack, the pipe struck the stone with its downward follow through. Legrand's shashka clattered to the ground, his wrist shattered, his hand hanging down as if the only thing keeping it attached to his body was the casing of flesh.

Elias dropped and twisted around toward this new threat, wondering if it had missed its mark, or if Máira had ignored his instructions. The last person in the world he'd expected to see stood in front of him—his mother.

Hag stepped in front of him, raised her pipe again, but held it up in a defensive posture. He tried to push her aside, but she was having none of it despite her small stature. He had seen his mother fight, knew she could handle her own, but the men she confronted were normally her own size. Anyone larger faced Tomás and he was not there.

He tried reasoning with her. "Mother, step aside."

"He will not raise his saber to me."

"It's not a saber," Elias and Legrand replied as one.

He could hear the eye roll in his mother's tone. "Leave it to men to argue while they're both standing there injured."

He stepped to the side of his mother and looked at the man standing before them, holding his arm and hand close to his chest.

"You once told me not to come between you and your son, and now you've attacked me...with my own weapon." Legrand grinned as if the pain he was experiencing was nothing new.

His mother twirled the pipe in her hand. "I did. I now understand why you sometimes choose to ride into battle with this pipe in your hand."

"I give it to you with my blessing," Legrand bowed slightly.

Ignoring his gesture, she asked, "Why did you come here?"

"Your barmaid, Louise, spoke of an English woman traveling with a very attractive pirate, bound for Mont-Saint-Michel. I followed my hunch that your persuasive seduction wasn't because of my charms, but to delay me from doing my duty."

His mother snorted. "You went through my things, found the letter, and then followed my son here."

"I swear on my honour, I did not know of any letter, nor did I know he was your son until he identified himself as the grandson of *Maximilien de Danton*. You know I am a man of my word, I killed my own hussar for not honouring it to your son's wife."

His mother nodded as if she would not question it.

"Yet you must understand that I cannot let him help the Earl of Astley escape."

His mother shrugged as if what Elias had been doing was inconsequential. "All I see is a mother and son on pilgrimage to a holy place. A place the emperor has desecrated with the blood of holy men."

Legrand shrugged, his attention no longer on him, and Elias felt as if he were interrupting something very intimate.

Legrand's expression sobered. "Your father will be out for blood."

"He is a blood-thirsty man. The only time he was not, was when Elias was but a child."

"You are not safe in France. He will hang you for treason."

His mother shook her head as if she was not guilty of any crimes. "I have only helped people caught in the middle of this miserable war."

"I will take her back to England with me," Elias interjected.

His mother bristled and looked at him as if his head was addled. "They will hang me in England as the daughter of the France's Minister of War. Your uncle said as much. That's why I did not go with you."

"Bastard." Elias swore. "This entire time he led me to believe you chose France over me."

"That is why…" Something in Hag's voice broke. "You never answered my letters."

"I never received any letters from you until after I came back to France on business." Elias hadn't realized how devious his uncle had been. There were many of the French nobility who had escaped France with their heads intact, his mother could have traveled to England among them after his father was killed.

"If your uncle wasn't dead, I would kill him."

"You'd have to wait until after I did."

"She must go this time," Legrand said, his entreaty spoken in a soft, but firm tone.

Elias agreed. "I will not leave her behind even if I have to truss her up and carry her kicking and screaming aboard my ship." His mother was going home with him, and Hag would disappear, never to be seen on French soil again.

All three turned at the sound of footsteps racing toward the piazza. Elias pointed his saber in the direction of the new threat, his mother stepped up beside him, wielding her pipe, and Legrand dipped back into the shadows as if he were a hidden weapon—broken wrist and all.

A figure stopped at the top of the steps and bent over. His chest heaving, his breath labored. He looked up, startled to see someone standing in front of him.

"Elias. Thank the Lord. We must hurry." The priest eyed his mother and swallowed an audible gulp of air. "Is your wife..."

"Charles," Elias said, purposely dropping his religious honorific. "This is Hag. Did you find what you were looking for?"

Father Charles shook his head, still eyeing his mother who refused to acknowledge their relationship. "He's not here, but there is someone else I must evacuate."

Legrand stepped forward, and Father Charles took a step backward, clearly shocked by Legrand's presence and that he'd been purposely hiding in the shadows. Elias could see the monk's suspicions rise as his gaze darted between the three of them.

"That stodgy old man attempting to get the upper hand is an acquaintance of Hag's."

Legrand moved closer, nodding his head in the monk's direction, the night sky lighting up as the cloud cover began to disappear. Legrand's broken wrist would make a lesser man drop to his knees with pain, yet Legrand acted as if he was staunching an annoying cut that would not stop bleeding. "You planned on taking Cardinal Linguet as well?" He asked.

Elias shrugged. "I didn't. It was a holy order or something."

Legrand looked at Father Charles who stood silently watching their exchange.

"And the Pope?" Legrand asked. "If he had been here, would you have attempted to rescue him as well?"

"I guess we'll never know the answer to that, since he's not here," Elias replied.

Legrand laughed as if he would have relished such a challenge. Elias waited to see what he would say about the cardinal's escape. A nobleman and a cardinal in one event were a bit too much for any of Napoleon's men to accept.

His mother stepped in front of Elias, her back to him as she whispered something to Legrand he could not hear. Legrand watched her speak, his expression giving away something far more intimate between the two of them than what either had displayed up to that point.

"I wouldn't want to come between a holy man and a higher power. Go before I change my mind," Legrand said, his eyes never leaving her face.

"I have a boat down near the chapel," Father Charles whispered. "He's waiting there."

Elias could have hugged the man. It was a much better option with the tide well on its way into the bay.

"You're going to steal my boat?"

Elias cringed inwardly. He truly hoped the boat wasn't the tipping point for this man of war, who was giving more sway than he probably had in his entire career.

Legrand huffed out a breath before acquiescing. "Fine. Take my boat."

Elias didn't hesitate. "Can you handle the boat by yourself and meet us at the bottom of these steps?"

Father Charles nodded. "The Fountain of Saint Aubert. I'll be there." He disappeared the same way he'd come, his steps much quieter this time.

Elias turned to his mother and put his hand on her arm. His voice gentle as said, "We need to go."

"I would like to speak to your mother for a moment—in private." It wasn't a request, more like the order of a man who was used to having his instructions followed without hesitation.

Elias bristled. If Legrand changed his mind and held his mother hostage...no, he would not leave her. Not now when things were finally leaning in their direction. "I will grant you some privacy, but you will not be alone with her." When Legrand began to argue, Elias cut him off. "As you said, the War Minister will be after blood, and you work for him."

Legrand laughed. "I work for Napoleon, and no other, but I understand your concern. Take my shashka as my guarantee. You can leave it at The Happy Hag."

Elias nodded but didn't relent. He picked up the shashka and moved ten feet away, within striking distance.

"I'm sorry about your wrist," his mother said, the wince in her tone evident.

"It is nothing I didn't deserve. I will miss you, Aventine."

"We were good together," his mother replied, and Elias really wished he could give them privacy.

"Perhaps, after the war—"

His mother laughed. "There will always be a war for you. You do not know how to do anything but battle."

"And love."

Mon Dieu, he didn't want to hear this.

"You deserve a better life, *mon bijou*. Go to England, see your grandchildren grow and be happy."

His mother said something Elias didn't understand, and he was grateful for that small gift.

Legrand's voice suddenly grew husky. "My heart belongs to you. My blood to the emperor. My life to honour."

"Goodbye, Alexandre." His mother's voice shook with an emotion Elias had not heard since his father died.

"Au revoir, *mon amour*."

As silence fell, Elias glanced in their direction and saw his mother kiss Legrand tenderly before she laid the pipe down at his feet and joined Elias. He caught her wiping tears from her face as she took one last look at her lover and exited through the gate.

"I lied when I said my mother had been with many men since my father's death. There was never any other man—only you." Elias confessed.

"I know."

Nineteen

Monsieur Berthier,

I regret to inform you that the Earl of Astley died at Mont Saint Michel from an ague that has struck the island and neighboring towns.

As to your concerns about England using your grandson and daughter in a plot to rescue the earl, they are unfounded cruel rumors. Your daughter and grandson have not been seen for several weeks, and it is believed he convinced her to return to England with him as he has settled down with a wife.

I apologize for my messy handwriting. I broke my wrist during a night with the locals who were overwhelmingly excited to celebrate our recent victories in the East. I will be staying on at Mont Saint Michel to convalesce. I will advise when my hussars and I are once again available for campaign.

Regards,
Alexandre Baptiste Reynard Beaumont, Comte Legrand

—A letter written one week after the earl's escape from the abbey at Mont Saint Michel, from the General of the Hussars,

*Alexandre Baptiste Reynard Beaumont, to the Minister of
War for France, Maximilien de Danton*

"Uhhh." Astley groaned as his feet bounced on the steps.

"I'm sorry, Simon. I don't mean to cause you pain. I must hurry so that I may return and help Elias."

"Wh—what are you…you doing…here?" His voice barely audible over the crashing waves.

Máira worried about the dangerous surf. She didn't want to think about how she would make it without Elias. It wasn't possible. Physically, mentally, emotionally. He had become the center of her world. When they'd wed, she'd dreamed she would be happy and content. Yet nothing about this experience had been happy, and somehow, she felt joy with him. In his presence, her heart blossomed in a manner beyond her comprehension.

Astley groaned once more as she took two more steps down toward the water's edge.

"It's a long story, I can't begin to explain at the moment. On our voyage home, I will explain everything."

A grunt was his only reply, and she prayed he did not lose consciousness once more. He had only awoken after his feet had struck their twentieth step. Máira struggled with the weight of his body. Sweat dripped down the center of her back despite the cool night breeze.

She slipped into French to talk to the boy. "How much farther, Sébastien?" she asked as the boy tried to carry Astley's feet with little success.

"I'm not certain. It looks like there is a tower below."

A tower? That could only be bad news. Had the priest unknowingly steered them toward more guards? "Do you know where these steps lead?"

Sébastien grunted from exertion. "I'm not sure. I heard something about the fountain of Saint Aubert."

Máira looked up and caught sight of people descending the steps. "Sébastien!" She hissed. "We must hide." She lifted her chin in the direction of the forms following them and turned toward the edge of the steps. Farther down to her right, the wall appeared to be crumbling, if they were lucky, she could pull Simon through. If she couldn't...

Desperately she searched for another option and then caught a glimpse of a roofline down at the water's edge. A large tower loomed in the distance holding unknown dangers. She had to get Simon over the wall, and quickly.

"I'm sorry, Simon. This is going to hurt, but I need you to keep quiet," she whispered.

A barely audible grunt acknowledged her apology.

"Sébastien, run ahead to the hole in the wall. Go!"

"But what about—"

"Go!"

Sébastien didn't hesitate. He set the earl's feet on the ground and ran for the break in the wall. For the first time in her life, she was giving orders as if she were a leader of something important. Granted, her audience was a man hanging onto life by a thread and an eight-year-old boy, but in her experience the male species didn't listen to anyone who wore skirts.

Máira increased her pace, her chest heaving with every heavy step. When she finally reached the crumbled spot on the wall, she was thankful to find it at chest height. A large man would hurdle it with little effort...Simon would no doubt do just that if he were healthy. As it was, he was little to no help as she leaned his back against the wall.

"Can you stand?" She asked between gulps of air.

"Yes."

She released him for a moment and he swayed. Then with a low guttural groan, he forced his body to comply as he braced himself with the palm of his good arm, his broken pinky sticking up in the air as if it were a vine sprouting out from the rock. Máira cringed at the sight, before climbing the wall and finding Sébastien on a narrow ledge on the other side.

"Ballocks," she swore, as she gazed down at the steep incline. The rocks would not be easy to maneuver. She leaned back over and whispered, "This will hurt, Simon, but we have no choice. We must hurry."

Máira squatted on top of the wall and braced her feet on the sides, testing the stability of both before she reached down and grabbed Simon under his arms. "I need you to use your feet and push yourself up."

"Máira, leave."

His order caught her off-guard. "Hell no. Bloody hell *no*." She grappled with his arms.

"Leave. I am more burden...than I'm...worth."

"I said 'use your feet,' or this is going to hurt like hell. One. Two. Three." She lifted under his arms and smiled when he finally gave into her command. Her legs shook, the muscles in her arms burned, and Simon's feet slipped time and time again as he snarled his pain, his left foot doing little to nothing to help him push. When his backside was finally even with the top, she leaned back and forced him onto the top of the wall, his weight counterbalancing her own. "Don't move." Her grip slipped.

"Do not try to kick me again, Astley," a male voice cautioned right before Elias appeared on the wall next to her as if he'd scaled the wall in one step.

"Bloody hell...it's about blasted time. It's damned...embarrassing...having your wee wife...drag my...pathetic...arse..." Astley's diatribe seemed to use the last of his energy, for as he uttered his final word, his body sagged against her, going completely slack.

Elias grabbed her as she began to fall with Simon's weight forcing her backward, his strong arms steadying her and Simon all at once.

"I've got you," he whispered in her ear, and she sank into his touch, relief nearly engulfing her. "My mother is here. She can help you stabilize Astley while I hop down to take him on the other side."

"What? Hag is here?" She looked up into the shadowed face of the woman she admired and feared.

"Yes, I am." Her tone was flat and brusque, the opposite of Máira's, until she said, "It seems you should start calling me by my Christian name, Aventine."

"Only if you call me Máira."

"And who is this?" Aventine asked.

"Mother, I'd like you to meet Sébastien."

Aventine bent down to the boy's height and held out her hand as if waiting for Sébastien to greet her like a lady, despite the trousers and men's shirt she wore. Sébastien looked toward Elias, tentatively gripped her fingers, and awkwardly bowed over Aventine's hand. Aventine gave the boy a brief smile.

Between the four of them, Simon was off the wall and draped over Elias's shoulders in a matter of minutes. "It's going to get easier from here."

Máira placed her hand on his chest. His heartbeat strongly under her hand, proof that he was not a dream. He turned to go, and her hand came away with blood smeared upon her palm. "Elias!"

He turned and saw her upturned hand. "Apologies, *ma chérie*. It is nothing but a scratch."

"A scratch doesn't bleed like this." Her comment went on deaf ears as he led the way down to the water's edge.

Despite their steep descent, going down at the tower was easier for everyone, except Elias. They traversed the rough terrain to a small inlet on the side of the tower that Sébastien had said contained the Fountain of Saint Aubert, and found Father Charles waiting for them with another man inside a small boat.

Elias swore under his breath.

"What's wrong?" she asked, but only got a shake of his head in reply.

When they got closer to the water, she understood. Accompanying Father Charles in a small pleasure boat was another holy man, who appeared to be of higher rank, if his manner and dress were any indication. He sat at the helm wrapped in a ruby-red *cappa magna* robe with a train long enough to fill more than half the boat.

"With all due respect, Your Eminence, the robe must go." Elias's voice brokered no other options.

The cardinal's posture stiffened, his voice full of authority. "It will not. You will make two trips across the bay."

"I will be making one. With or without you."

The silence that fell over them was deafening. Sea water lashed at the little boat as Father Charles jumped out to hold it steady. Sébastien's head turned back and forth between the two formidable men starring each other down. Aventine stepped forward and reached out her hand. Máira wasn't certain if it was meant to help the cardinal out of the boat or take his robes.

"Father Charles, I order you to take me to safety."

Everyone looked at the priest who was stuck in the middle of a losing battle as Máira grabbed the opposite side of the boat.

Father Charles shook his head. "I—I cannot take this boat across the bay alone. Tonight, the tide is beyond my strength."

Máira didn't believe the priest to be lying. The tide was indeed treacherous as white caps swirled in an eerie pattern around the island, some crashing into the rocks, others being swallowed by their own force.

"Either take off the robes or step out of the boat. If you don't, I will throw you out of the boat, Cardinal."

The cardinal stared down his thin nose at Elias, and Aventine snapped her extended hand with impatience. For a moment, Máira thought the cardinal would step out of the boat, until he tore his ceremonial robe from his body, and began folding it as if he planned to keep it.

"Mother," Elias said, his voice tinged with anger.

It was all that was necessary. Aventine place one foot in the middle of the boat, grabbed the robe and hopped off once more, the robe dragging in the water behind her.

"How dare—"

"A man of God would not value a piece of cloth more than a human life, would he?" Aventine asked, but the cardinal turned his head away, his nose so high in the air, Máira suspected the angels could see it.

"I need that cut in long strips." Elias said, and the cardinal gasped as he made the sign of the cross. Father Charles closed his eyes and sighed, while Sébastien watched on with his mouth dropped open and his eyes as big as the full moon peeking out from the clouds.

Aventine pulled a knife from her boot and cut the train from the robe and then cut it into long strips with Sébastien's help. When they were finished, Aventine rolled the rest of the robe into a ball, jumped up, and stuffed the entire garment into a drainage vent off the stone tower, effectively preventing the ruby red cloth from alerting any guards who might look over the ramparts.

"Get in the boat, Mother."

"I can hang—"

"Get. In. The. Boat."

Aventine bristled almost as much as the cardinal had.

"You can't swim. You are a liability outside the boat. Inside, you can care for Astley and Sébastien."

Elias turned to her. "You said you were a good swimmer."

"I am."

"Have you ever gone up against a current like this?"

She couldn't lie. Other than the open ocean, she had never seen waves such as these. Even the loch in the dead of winter didn't reach this level of hidden brutality. "No, but I swam the loch all the time. This water feels like bath water in comparison. I can do it."

Elias grinned and then addressed the cardinal. "Your

Eminence, I need you in the front of the boat with the boy." The cardinal's only movement was the firm press of his lips into a thin line. Her husband wasn't fazed. "Unless you would like to do the rowing."

The cardinal moved without argument, his displeasure evident in his stiff posture as he made his way forward.

Elias watched the ramparts for signs of their discovery while Aventine helped Sébastien into the stern, and proceeded to the bow, where she made herself ready to cradle Simon against her body. Elias waded into the thrashing waves, pulled Simon from his shoulders and laid him between his mother's legs. The cardinal shot a glance over his shoulder, his disapproval evident.

Father Charles whispered, "A light just appeared on the rampart. We must go."

Elias held the boat for Father Charles to get inside. "Are you certain you can handle this?" he asked her.

"Yes." No. The summer air might be warm enough, but the water wasn't the temperature of a bath and the waves were crashing against her legs as if they wanted to eat her alive. She wasn't certain at all about her swimming skills in the treacherous dark waters, but she would not be the cause of their failure.

"Tie this to your waist, the other end will be tied to mine." She nodded and did as he instructed with the train from the cardinal's robe, and Elias tied the other end around himself. "Sébastien, do you know how to tie yourself to the boat using a bowline knot?"

"Aye, aye, Captain." The boy saluted Elias, and took the long piece of the robe Elias held out to him.

"Father Charles, are you comfortable assisting if I need to right the boat?"

Father Charles nodded. "Yes."

Elias turned to his mother and gave her two strips, leaving a piece of rope draped over his arm. "Mother, tie yourself and Astley in as well. If anything happens, don't panic, I will be right here." She scowled as if panicking was beyond the pale, but her fear was evident in the way her eyes darted toward the violent surge of the water rocking their tiny craft.

The cardinal held out his hand, waiting for a strip of his cloth to tie himself into the boat.

"My apologies, Your Eminence. All I have left is the rope I will be tying to the boat, so that I may pull it." Elias didn't sound the least bit apologetic.

The cardinal nearly choked on his objection. "What am I supposed to do?"

"I suggest you cut off a piece of your hassock, say a prayer for all of us, and make sure you stay close to the boy. If he goes down, so will you."

The cardinal's skin turned pasty, but he didn't wait to see if Elias would change his mind. He reached for the hem of his hassock and began tearing the black material with red piping as if his very life depended upon it.

"Take off your shoes, they'll only pull you down." Elias took off the soldier's jacket and began stripping from the waist up, as Máira removed her shoes and placed them in the boat behind Father Charles. She turned to find her husband looming behind her, his strong muscular physique made that much more imposing by the exquisite backdrop of Mont Saint Michel.

He lowered his voice. "I'm going to tie myself to the bow hook with the rope. If something happens, use your knife and cut the sash between us."

"You mean the rope?"

"No, Máira. The sash. You will not be able to cut the rope quickly enough. Cut the sash and swim to shore."

"But—"

His voice took on the authoritarian tone he had used on her aboard ship on their way to France. "You will not go down with this boat. Understood?"

She nodded in agreement, but secretly, she would never adhere to his directive. He had never been her captain. He was her lover, her husband, her life. She would not allow him to go down with the ship alone.

Elias pushed the boat into deeper water, and together they waded into the wind-roughened bay, their most violent adversary yet.

Twenty

My darling Iseabail,

I have located your dearest treasure, and after a short sojourn for minor repairs, I will return it to your loving care. I cannot, however, guarantee that I won't throw the thief into the sea before this journey's end.

Congratulate your sister for me. An annulment may not be ideal, but the groom has agreed to seek one.

Your ever-devoting husband,
Nash

—A discreet letter from Nashford Xavier Harding, the 8th Duke of Ross, to his wife Iseabail Blair Handcock Harding, Duchess of Ross, regarding locating the duchess's sister on the coast of northern France.

Mon Dieu. Elias had never been so grateful to see the shore. His muscles twitched with fatigue when his feet gained purchase in the silted sand that still had the propensity to swallow his feet if he didn't keep moving. He reached over and grabbed Máira's arm to help her ashore. For a small woman, she had been a remarkable swimmer, matching him stroke for stroke. She may not have held the strength he had behind each pull, but she had more stamina than most of his sailors, especially considering some had never learned to swim prior to him demanding it. She'd made the journey in trousers and a shirt, which were plastered to her form and causing his loins to stir at the delectable sight. The last thing he wanted was for anyone else to get a look at that intoxicating view. Her long locks had fallen from their pins making her look as alluring as any siren he could have imagined, until she shivered.

"Go ashore. I will get your shoes and my shirt for you to wear."

"But you'll need help with—"

He leaned over her, the pull of their attraction driving him to let his body touch hers despite the audience a short distance away. "*S'il vous plaît, mon cher.* That wet shirt is giving me ideas I don't want the cardinal to have."

She glanced down between their bodies and he was certain he could see the heat of her blush pinken her cheeks even in the darkness. He counted himself blessed when she untied the red strip of satin from his waist, rolled it up with the one from her waist, and said, "I can think of ways to use these later."

"Later I will act upon those ideas."

She gave him a quick kiss before she headed toward the grassy shore.

Damnation, but he would never get tired of her unprecedented knowledge of what a man desired. More importantly, he could not wait to use that fine strip of cloth to tie her to his bed aboard the *Maribelle.*

"Stop your wool gathering and come help us."

He shook his head and returned to the boat Father Charles had pulled up upon the muddy shoreline. He reached in for his shirt and her shoes and then held them out to Sébastien. "Take these to my wife. She is cold from our swim."

"*Oui, monsieur.*" The boy assisted the cardinal from the boat, and then ran for where Máira stood in the distance.

Astley's skin glowed with translucence and pallor of death. He had only met the earl once, but on that occasion the earl's complexion had been much darker, and much richer. "How is he?"

"He breathes. Beyond that, I could not say," his mother replied.

"Could not or would not?"

Aventine bristled, yet the question was a valid one. Then she shrugged and lifted the nobleman up and away from her body for Elias to take hold of him. It was at that moment Astley chose to wake. "Where is Sébastien?" His gaze frantically searched the area, confusion marring his face. "Sébastien! Sébastien!" He pushed upward, batting at Elias's arms as he tried to lift himself from the boat.

"He's with us," Elias replied, but Astley continued his frantic search. "He's here, Astley. We did not leave him. He's with Máira on shore."

Astley's gaze speared the grassy coastline, his eyes finally pinpointing the spot where the two stood, and Sébastien raised his hand in greeting. The affectionate grin that began to form on the earl's face instantly dropped into stark fear. "No!" He struggled to stand, his lack of strength and balance threatening to dump the boat as his mother also yelled, "Elias, look!"

Two horsemen charged toward Máira and Sébastien.

"Máira!" He raced to her, the distance between them too great as horses drew to a stop and she placed her body between Sébastien and the invaders. She raised one hand with her knife to ward off an oncoming blow, and Elias roared. Everything in him focused on getting to her fast enough to kill the bastards threatening her.

The distance he had told her to take was now his enemy. She was farther on shore than he'd expected, and before he could reach her, a man who matched his size and breadth, but not his fear or anger, jumped off his horse and attacked, his massive arms enfolding her. Sébastien pummeled him with tiny, ineffectual blows from his fists as Elias raced with vengeance and murder flowing through his veins—as Máira disappeared from his view. Absent, as if she'd been swallowed whole by the assault.

Elias sensed rather than saw the second assailant leap from his horse and knew he would have to defeat him first. Despite every fiber of his being wanting to rip her assailant limb from limb, he had to face this second interloper first. He charged without thought, letting his instincts take hold as the man squared off, embraced for impact.

Elias struck iron, his impact driving the two of them to the ground, and Elias wasn't about to give up his advantage of being on top. He raised up, his fist reared and ready to deliver a punishing blow—only to freeze when he recognized the face below him.

"T-Tomás?" His voice stuttered with shock.

"Elias! Elias, stop!" Máira's sweet voice raised in panic caused him to push off his mother's thug and turn toward his wife. Her sweet face framed by the glow of the full moon as the damp tendrils of her blond hair radiating in its light. That was all he wanted to see. Healthy and unharmed, he wanted to kiss her and wrap her in his arms, yet her assailant stood behind her with an expression of murder on his face.

"Touch her and I'll kill you," the man growled, as if his English threat meant something in this land. He held a combative Sébastien at arm's length with a palm to his head. Sébastien's fists swung at the air, his feet striking out with little success. Then Astley coughed and the boy immediately stilled. He looked from Máira to Elias to the hand that held him in place, and ran for the earl, and the Englishman's hand fell to his side to ball in a fist.

Elias grasped Máira's wrist as he attempted to pull her behind him in the same manner she'd handled Sébastien, but the Englishman held her other arm firmly in his grip. He didn't under-stand why Tomás was with this man, but he knew with absolute certainty Tomás would not hurt his wife. The man in front of him, however, was an unknown entity.

"Your instruction means very little on French soil, wandought. Release my wife."

"Elias—" Máira started.

But the man whose nostrils flared and shoulders squared interrupted. "You believe me feeble and impotent?" He wore a smirk, but the look in his eyes held anything but humor.

"You couldn't hold onto a child," Elias taunted, as he nodded in Sébastien's direction.

Máira pulled at his arm. "Elias—"

"Not now, Máira." He needed all his attention on the threat in front of him.

"You're the one being a wandought, you ignorant fool." This latest insult came from his mother, who was helping Father Charles set Astley on the ground, while Sébastien knelt at the ailing man's side. The shivering cardinal kept his distance from them all.

His mother continued. "What is the meaning of this, Tomás? You are supposed to be at The Happy Hag."

"It burnt to the ground," Tomás replied.

Elias spared Tomás a glance before returning his gaze to the man in front of him. "You burnt her tavern?" he accused.

"No." The man drew out the word as if he were speaking to an imbecile. "French soldiers did."

"What?" The shock resonating through his mother's voice made him want to go to her, but at that very moment, he could do nothing but listen as Tomás explained.

"After you left, *he* came." Tomás nodded his head in the other man's direction and continued, "Then he began asking questions all over town about the Miss."

"My wife?" Elias clarified.

Tomás moved next to the Englishman. If Elias didn't know better, he would have thought he was siding with the man, but

Tomás had been at his mother's side since a few days after his father died. He was also the one who'd smuggled Elias to England to live with his uncle. The thought of Tomás betraying Aventine was as foreign as the man in front of him. Still, he kept his guard up and listened for holes in his explanation of events.

"Yes, your wife, and then soldiers came looking for him." Tomás tilted his head toward the stranger once more. "I had to smuggle him out the back, and when they couldn't find your mother or him, they burnt it to the ground." He looked at Aventine, his expression full of remorse. "I am sorry."

Aventine didn't miss a beat. "Was it my father?" she asked, her voice as hard as stone.

"Oui."

That left one question still unanswered. Elias directed his query to the stranger. "Who are you, and why do the French want you so badly?"

"Because he's the Duke of Harding, my brother-by-marriage."

"And I've come to take my wife's sister home." The duke's jaw tightened as if Elias were the prey, and the duke a starving beast ready to tear his head off with jagged teeth.

Bloody hell.

"I was trying to tell you."

"My apologies, my dear. I was caught up in my own thoughts of destroying your brother-in-law because I thought he'd accosted you."

"I believe the opposite is true, and for that—"

"The opposite is not true and you will not be calling out my husband." Máira's voice was made of iron and he had to admire her mettle. The duke was an imposing man that would make most men cower.

"There are things you don't understand—" the duke started.

"I understand more than you give me credit for, Your Grace." If her words did not explain exactly what she understood, the slow caress of her breasts against Elias's arm told the duke exactly what she understood about marital bliss.

The duke's brow rose in question before his scowled deepened and his angry glare turned once more on Elias. It was Tomás who stopped him from lunging.

"You gave your word you would not ruin her!"

Elias couldn't help but admire the way the handsome visage of the man was heightened by his desire to tear him limb from limb. He tried to soothe his brother-in-law's ire. "I did."

"Father Charles," the cardinal hissed and motioned for the priest to retreat.

"You are not good enough for her," the duke ground out, and turned toward Máira. "I'm sorry, Máira. I didn't want to tell you like this, but they leave me no choice." He ran a hand through his hair in a manner only a duke could make appear as if he was in a ballroom and not in the middle of fight for a lady's honor. "He lied about his identity. He is not the Earl of Dorset. He is a privateer and a recovery agent whose loyalty to the Crown is questionable. I left a Bow Street runner, Johnathan Payne, on his ship, and ordered them to the port of Carnac."

"Peter set sail for another port?" Fury and indignation laced his words. "How dare you order my ship to sail!"

"Your ship was to be burned."

"What?" A quick nod from Tomás confirmed the duke's proclamation. His gaze captured his mother's.

She shrugged as if it was of no great import. "Your grandfather would do it."

"Bloody hell," he muttered under his breath. "I knew the dangers he posed, but I'd not thought he would murder me in cold blood. I've been sailing under the wrong impression for years. You never told me of his mercenary heart," he accused.

"He killed your father in front of you."

"And I hate him for that, but he spared me."

"Did he? Or did he condemn us both?" The bitter hatred in

her voice startled the cardinal even further, and he clutched at Father Charles. "I sent you to England to be raised by a stranger. I would think that would be enough of explanation of the danger he posed. What mother would send her only child away after losing his father?" Aventine asked, and a distant memory surfaced.

His mother on the docks telling him goodbye and the sound of a sob escaping her throat as Tomás led him away. He had not seen her again for several years. Nor had he received any letters or correspondence from her in the years he had lived under his uncle's cold tutelage as a member of His Majesty's navy. Throughout the years, he had come to accept his mother had mourned his father's death, but not the loss of her son. That's what his uncle had led him to believe—all the lies. Years of emptiness. Even after he returned to France. He had seen her aloofness as an uncaring woman...from the look of despair deep in her eyes that she finally allowed him to see he'd been wrong.

"I would have never sent you away if I believed you to be safe from my father. You were not, and I could not travel to England because of him. There had already been one attempt to kidnap me as leverage against my father by the British Crown. We were doomed to separation the moment I married your father. I was just too naive and in love to realize it." Her eyes brightened with tears, but like the strong, indelible woman he knew her to be, any sign of her tears disappeared before they could drop.

His parents' marriage had been destroyed by their differences, their love defeated by politics. The same politics that were at play in his marriage to Máira. She was a woman of station, sister-in-law to a duke. He was a man with a questionable past and an even more questionable future. Máira may know the truth about his lies now, but she did not understand how fate would tear them apart.

He was a complete fraud, a scoundrel, and for the first time in his life, Elias felt the truth in that statement. He was not good enough to clean her shoes. Máira belonged with a gentleman, not a privateer or a recovery agent always putting himself and his crew in danger. She was too good for him.

The duke continued with his argument against their marriage as if Elias and his mother had said nothing. "There are three gentlemen en route to Caerlaverock as we speak, ready and willing to marry you."

Máira's voice did not waver in her reply. "I am already married."

"Your marriage is to be annulled." the duke explained.

"No." Her brow drew as she shook her head in denial.

In that moment, Elias knew the duke's chosen path for Máira was the right path for the woman he loved. Releasing her from a lifetime of strife and uncertainty was the least he could do. She deserved more than what his mother had endured for love, and releasing her from their sham of a marriage was the right thing to do. The duke had arranged for Máira to marry someone respectable. To lead the life she was born to lead. It had been part of his plan as well...before he'd gone and bedded her like the scoundrel the duke had correctly named him to be.

Máira glared at her brother-in-law, her anger rising above anything Elias had witnessed from her. "My marriage is real—"

Elias spoke before she could announce that they had consummated their marriage in front of God and everyone else. "Our marriage was never meant to be anything but a ruse to allow me passage to France. His Grace has taken the path which I planned to take upon our return." He said it with the ring of truth she needed to hear—he left out his change of heart from the moment he bedded her. It would only make her push harder for something that wasn't meant to be. Nor did she need to know that he planned to honor his vows until his dying breath. She deserved better than a mere knight who put her life in danger at every turn.

Máira's gaze turned to him, her blue eyes looking bruised and battered with his painful words. He wanted to take them back, but he couldn't afford for to her resist an honorable and good match the duke had arranged.

"But we—" Her cheeks flared with embarrassment, and Elias knew he had to drive his knife deep into her chest.

"We enjoyed each other's company. That is all. It is time for you and me to return to our own worlds. I am not a man who stays with one woman for long."

Máira's eyes filled with tears at the same time her shoulders straightened, ready to receive the kill shot she didn't want him to deliver. "What we shared—was it just an act...to...to...?"

He released the killing blow, guaranteeing her hatred. "I have shared many moments like that with many women."

A tear spilled down her cheek, and Elias wanted to kiss it away and admit it was a lie. He had never shared such intimacy with anyone but her, and he would never again feel that depth of love for another human being as long as he lived. It just wasn't possible to replace one's very soul.

If he'd thought he'd fueled Máira's scorn, it was nothing compared to the fire his words lit in the duke's veins. His anger roared to life and he hit Tomás like a crazed bull, his shoulder ramming into his midsection with enough force to bust through a castle door. Tomás flew through the air and landed on his back in the briny muck, as the duke charged Elias. Elias knew he deserved the beating the duke was determined to deliver, and because of that, he did not fight or defend the blows. He would thrash any man who threatened her honour in the same manner as he just had. Punch after punch he endured as Tomás came to stop the assault. Máira yelled and his mother drew a blade from her boot, no doubt ready and willing to deliver a deadly throw in his name, but before he could stop her, someone else put an end to the beating he endured.

"Enough!" Astley bellowed, shocking everyone into silence. The duke paused and looked back at the earl as if he wasn't certain what he'd been doing. Astley slumped against Aventine, his breathing labored. "Sébastien has seen enough violence."

Máira chose that moment to throw herself over Elias's body and stare up at the duke as if she would shield him from further assault.

The duke stepped back, his bloodied fists flexing, his own breathing coming with the heavy rise and fall of his chest.

"Who...who is Sébastien?" the duke asked, his chest heaving from the exertion.

When no one knew quite how to answer the question, including the boy who hugged Astley's side, the earl responded, "My son. Sébastien is my son and heir. His mother died and I came to France to bring him home."

It wasn't true. Every person present knew its duplicity, except perhaps the cardinal. Yet no one said a word in denial. Sébastien clung even more desperately to the earl, as if he too accepted the statement as truth and was thankful for it. The boy had no idea what the earl had just done for him with that statement, because if Astley died...

"Máira," Astley whispered, and she turned in his direction, unaware of what Elias knew was to come next. "I would be honored..." The earl coughed with the strain the last several hours had placed on his battered body. When he continued, Elias closed his eyes. "If you would become the next Countess of Astley."

Twenty-One

Your Eminence,

I am en route to Rome with Cardinal Jean-Frédéric Linguet. I found him in remarkably good health considering the ordeal he has suffered. No doubt it was his faith and the blessing of the Lord that kept him healthy while many others in the community suffered a grave illness. I am told Pope Pius VII has continued his travels through the Continent as the guest of Napoleon.

Your servant,
Abbé Charles-Michel de Moidrey Mill, France

—A letter from Father Charles at Moidrey Mill, France, to French Cardinal Andre Cattaneo, who continued to defy Napoleon and refused to legitimize the emperor's second marriage to Marie Louise. Pope Pius VII would remain in forced exile in France until 1814.

Astley did not die. Not that night or the next. Not on the dangerous journey to Carnac where they boarded her husband's—Elias's ship, the *Maribelle*, in the dead of night. Nor did he die during the voyage back to Scotland, but a piece of Máira did.

Especially when Elias did not come to his cabin. Instead, she shared it with Aventine and Astley. It would have been unseemly if anyone of the *ton* knew of their circumstances. An earl sleeping in the same room as two ladies, one of questionable reputation and the other with a reputation ruined beyond repair. Aventine merely shrugged, and Máira couldn't raise up enough emotion to care. The distance of her separation from Elias had never been greater than the door in which he did not enter and she did not exit. She poured all her energy into Astley's care. The ship's cook and doctor had set several of Astley's broken bones, his arm and collar bone, his left calf and ankle, and had rewrapped his broken ribs. His pinky had healed incorrectly and would forever look disfigured; the others would hopefully heal. She marveled at how he'd pushed his body up the wall as she'd grappled with the very bones the French had broken.

Máira had washed old wounds on his face and torso that should have been stitched, including a nasty gash in his left eyebrow that seemed to split it in two. The same eye was so badly swollen, Cook had instructed her to lance the festering wound on his eyelid to drain it to heal. Cook couldn't determine if Astley would lose the eye or not.

Máira prayed he did not; it was his one feature she and her sisters had agreed upon—Simon's eyes were the color of rich, dark, island coffee, full of a vibrant shot of life that would make any woman feel a jolt of heat in her blood. He had used that charm at the first breakfast he'd shared with the Blair sisters at the duke's London townhome prior to Ross marrying her sister. Simon's charisma and dreamy eyes had stunned them into silence.

Breakfast after breakfast he'd enthralled and flirted with every one of them, or rather all of them except Caillen. She had promptly ignored the earl after their very first meeting. Even her admission about his eyes being "*somewhat exceptional*" had been given grudgingly. Every other Blair sister had lost a piece of her heart to the untamable bachelor.

Tears bleared her vision as Máira gazed upon the sleeping earl, who seemed nothing like that carefree invincible man at the breakfast table. She wasn't sure how he had survived his rescue to this point or if he would continue to live once upon shore, but the fact that he still breathed after the depravity of his captivity was a miracle.

During the journey home, she'd busied herself spoon-feeding Simon broth, cleaning his wounds, and wiping his forehead and body with cool cloths to keep his fever at bay. Elias had insisted she not be the one to tend to her "betrothed's" more *personal* needs, and when she'd protested that they would expose more of the crew to Astley's illness if he or another member of the crew tended to him, Elias's anger spewed forth in French—giving her hope that he did care. He wouldn't be angry if he were not jealous, would he?

But Sébastien had stepped forward and said he had survived the sickness and had been tending to Astley's needs for over a month. That nearly caused her heart to stop.

What her sisters had once described as glorious cheekbones accentuating his strong jaw, were now so prominent, Máira was certain she could determine what Astley's skull would look like years after his death. The cardinal may have escaped the prison without catching the ague that had killed so many, but Astley had not.

Aventine had then stepped up and told Sébastien that it would not do for him to be in closed quarters with a man and his intended. She would take care of Astley, and Sébastien could assist the duke with his injuries. The duke had scoffed, Sébastien scowled, but both relented when during one of his few moments of consciousness, Astley had heard the conversation and agreed with Aventine. "Do as the ladies bade, Sébastien. It does not pay for a man to argue with a woman." Then Astley had winked with his one good eye that momentarily sparkled with merriment. It was the first sign of hope they'd all been praying for.

During the voyage Máira found herself becoming more and more comfortable with Aventine, and found it ironic that only after she was no longer to be her mother-in-law, did she not fear the woman. Several times Aventine had told her to take a break and go on deck to get some fresh air, but the one-time Máira had, Elias had refused to look at her. He didn't demand she get below deck despite the angry clouds rolling in on the turbulent seas. He had looked right through her as if her appearance meant less than an errant rat risking death by falling overboard. No, she had not gone above since. His lack of concern cut too deep.

Yelling woke her when she hadn't realized she'd fallen asleep. She looked up from her pallet on the floor to see Aventine looking out the small cabin window.

"Are we in port already?" she asked, as her damaged heart went into palpitations.

"Yes." Aventine turned toward the earl. "I need to prepare Astley to disembark."

She had to see Elias...panic nearly seized her as she jumped to her feet. In the early morning hours Elias would be on deck, especially as they arrived in port. Frantically she wrapped Astley's battered body in blankets, and when the knock came on their door, she ran her hands through her messy hair and tried to flatten out the wrinkles in her shirt and trousers before she opened it.

Peter greeted her. "Mornin', me lady. The captain wanted me to give you and Hag—I mean Mrs. Drake, these dresses to wear. He said you would need proper attire."

Her smile faltered as she looked past the first mate. Elias wasn't there. Only two members of the crew carrying a stretcher stood outside the captain's quarters with the first mate. She took the packages from Peter's outstretched hands and laid them over the desk as numbness began to wrap around her heart.

"We also need to gather the patient to take him ashore."

"He's almost ready," Aventine said over her shoulder, as she began gathering some of the bedding to cover Astley, who began another coughing fit that hurt his ribs, his shoulder, his lungs. The spasm lasted until he seemed to pass out from the pain and exertion, and Máira said a silent prayer that he recovered.

Peter stood with his hat in his hand. "Miss, again I'd like to offer me apologies for not delivering you to The Happy Hag."

"You should be groveling at her feet, Peter." Aventine added, as she wiped Astley's brow.

"If'n that be what you want, Miss—"

"No, Peter. You have apologized enough. Thank you." She squeezed his arm in reassurance. "Most ladies only dream of such an adventure. I get to tell my children about the time I was kidnapped by pirates—"

"Privateers," the three pirates corrected.

She smiled and nodded. "Of course. Privateers, and then I helped rescue a lord from Napoleon himself."

Peter's smile dropped as did the grins of the other pirates.

"Miss, you can't tell anyone about the earl's rescue. Didn't the captain explain that to you?"

He hadn't said a word to her—he'd avoided her, but this was the perfect opportunity to ask him. "Oh, well I'm certain he planned on telling me all the do's and the don'ts of the mission. Can you take me to him?"

Her question not only made the first mate's frown deepen, his brows drew together as well, and she knew immediately what he was going to say. She put up her hand to stop him. "He's already gone ashore, hasn't he?"

"Yes, Miss."

She put on her best society smile. It didn't fool anyone, least of all herself."Thank you, Peter. I believe His Lordship is ready. Is Sébastien still aboard?"

"Yes, Miss. He's waiting on deck."

She nodded. "We'll be up right after we change."

They transferred Simon to the stretcher, and she thanked God he was no longer conscious. It may be a sign of how dangerously ill he was, but it also meant he didn't have to suffer through the pain. Once he was on his way above deck, Máira closed the door and began changing her clothes.

"I'll need your assistance with these contraptions. I haven't worn a corset in over a decade." Aventine held up the undergarment and shuddered.

"I can honestly say, I am not looking forward to putting one back on," Máira confessed.

"Then let us go without." Aventine suggested.

Máira couldn't help but laugh despite her heart breaking. "It is not done in England."

"Are we not in Scotland?"

"Currently we are in England."

Aventine sighed. "Very well. Let the torture begin."

As the two women served as the other's lady's maid, Máira had to ask the question that had been plaguing her since their escape from Mont Saint Michel. "How did you find us at Mont Saint Michel?"

"I knew the Comte Legrand was on his way to execute the earl, so I borrowed a horse so that Tomás would not be implicated if I was caught. When the Comte crossed the bay, I tied the horse up in the woods and followed his horse's tracks. He knew the way very well." She lifted her chin with pride. "I did not sink once."

Máira thought about Aventine crossing the muddy bay alone and in the dark. All to warn them. "You risked everything for us."

"I risked everything for my son. One day, you will understand why."

Máira tried to smile, but couldn't, because she wouldn't. Children were not in her future.

They made their way to the deck, and she squinted against the harsh brilliance of the sunlight partnered with the jovial spirits of the crew. Their merry banter was in direct opposition to her mood as they went about their duties before taking leave on shore. Máira shaded her eyes and looked up to the quarter deck. Her heart dropped when she only found the second mate standing on the port side yelling orders to the crew. She scanned the rest of the deck to no avail. Her husband, ex-husband, she wasn't sure what to call him except the owner of her heart, was conspicuously missing. He was gone and had no plans to say goodbye.

Aventine was talking to Tomás and Sébastien, as he walked next to Simon's stretcher holding his hand. The sailors carried the unconscious earl down the gangplank and onto the docks. She hesitated, waiting...wondering...

"He left early this morning. He had an appointment with the War Office. He told me to tell you goodbye." She turned to find Ross gazing at her with pity and sorrow in depths of his eyes that brought back all the memories of her childhood. Her brother-in-law wore the same expression the servants had worn when the Blair sisters had left their childhood home. From their gardener, who handed each girl a rose to leave at their father's grave, a grave filled with questions and no answers, to their nursemaid, who had taken them home and cared for them, never explaining why their oldest sister was living with their new guardian while they stayed in the country in little more than a one-bedroom house. They had not wanted for food or clothing, but they certainly hadn't dressed or lived as they had when their parents were alive. They were hidden from the world, and the world had been hidden from them. She should have stayed hidden.

She gave Ross a half smile. "I'd heard he went ashore."

"Astley was serious about his proposal."

"He is the best of men," she admitted.

"You could never go wrong with a man like Astley for your husband."

"So why didn't *you* marry him?" she asked.

Ross smiled. "My heart was already taken."

"So is mine." A pang reverberated through her chest as if her heart had started a beat of its own that her body wanted to reject. Elias was not content with just breaking her heart, he had to grind it into pebbles to be trampled on for decades to come. How Ross could think she should hide behind Astley's name as his wife or widow, she didn't know.

"Your sisters are waiting in town. Including Caillen."

She grabbed Ross's sleeve. "Truly? She's there?"

"She is, but I would not expect her to stay."

"Why not? What are you not telling me?"

Ross took her hand and wrapped it around his arm and led her from the ship. "The tragedy has changed her—perhaps you, of all of your sisters, will be able to reach her."

"I would imagine watching the love of your life murdered before your eyes would change a person."

"I imagine it would, and I pray the rest of us never find out."

She nodded in agreement. It was better that Elias was alive and had the opportunity to marry someone he truly loved. It still didn't stop her wounded heart from bleeding. "I can't retell this story for my sisters. Could you do it for me."

Ross squeezed her hand. "Of course I can. You take the time you need."

"My carriage is waiting to take us home," he said, in a soft voice meant to ease her pain. Astley was being loaded into a carriage as they spoke. Ross's gentle understanding had the opposite effect.

"Home?" She laughed...it was either that or break down and sob, yet her voice held a bitterness it shouldn't. Máira lashed out in a manner she never had in her life. "You mean to Urquhart? My *real* home, the one you stole from my family?"

He had the good grace to wince at her attack. He did not deserve her ire. He had restored their family home and turned it into a family country estate. Any of the sisters could visit at any time they wished. The home would be entailed to the Harding dukedom, but Nash had done what he could and more to undo the sins of his father.

She swiped at the tear that dared to drop down her cheek. "I'm sorry, Ross. You didn't deserve that."

"But I did—"

"No, you didn't. You can't control your past any more than I can mine. I will return to the townhouse with you and make sure Simon is settled," she said with all the certainty of a woman of the *ton*, the one she was born to be. She stiffened her spine and took charge of her life for the first time. "After that, I would like to stay at home, though, if that's alright."

"Of course." He held out his arm once more.

Máira shook her head. "At Urquhart. I cannot marry Simon or any other suitors you have lined up for me. I had one wedding. I will not marry another man."

Nash looked over his shoulder and pulled her toward his carriage. "Máira, I understand that you are hurting, but you will be ruined if you do not marry Astley."

Her smile was small and held no joy. "I was ruined the day I was born—just ask anyone of the *ton*. I'm just one of those Blair bastards—a whore like my mother—"

"*Bâtarde*?" It was her mother-in-law's voice that interrupted. "Who says such a terrible thing? I will cut his throat if any man, lord, or sailor, dares to call you that." Aventine reached for her boot, but Tomas stopped her and she scowled up at him.

"I appreciate you wanting to protect me, Aventine," she said, "but I'm afraid this is where you and I say goodbye."

"No. Not *adieu*, but *au revoir*. We will see each other again. Until then, I give you this." Aventine furrowed her brow at Tomás who held up his hands in surrender and did not stop Aventine this time when she pulled her knife from her boot. "If anyone dares to use that vulgar word, you cut out his tongue."

A lump formed in Máira's throat. She would have loved to have gotten to know her mother-in-law better if given the chance. She took the blade and placed it in her reticule, the same one Elias had given her as a wedding present. "Thank you." Then she hugged Aventine, who stiffened at the embrace and then returned it.

Oh, how she would have loved to see that wall around Aventine's heart crumble, and just as she was about to release her, Aventine whispered in her ear. "Do not give up on my son. He loves you."

Máira bit her lip. She truly wished he did, but it was all a lie.

Twenty-Two

Sir Elias Drake,

She was honoured by my proposal but rejected my suit. She is with child.

Astley

—*The third letter written by Simon Benjamin Clark, Earl of Astley, to Sir Elias Maximilien Allistair Drake, when Lady Máira Blair Drake refused his proposal of marriage. The first two letters were thrown into the fire when Elias determined them to be illegible, as he drowned himself in alcohol.*

Urquhart Castle was empty. There were servants going about their daily tasks, but the silence was enough to drive her utterly mad. She missed the chaos of her sisters, the teasing, the laughing, even the fights would be better than the clock ticking away the time as if nothing mattered.

Because something did matter. The babe in her stomach meant the world. Iseabail had been the first to recognize her symptoms.

When she'd first become ill and lost her breakfast, everyone began to panic about the sickness spreading through the London town-house. Then she recovered within a couple of hours, and a huge sigh of relief went through the family and staff. Except it happened again the next day, and the next, until Iseabail pulled her aside and asked if it was possible she were pregnant. She'd broken down and cried in Iseabail's arms from heartbreak and misery and fear. Then her tears turn to ones of joy and happiness, as she realized she'd been gifted a piece of the man she loved.

The next morning she'd gone to see Simon and turned down his proposal of marriage. She was almost certain he wouldn't remember. His fever had been high, and he appeared to fall asleep mid-confession. She could not allow him to raise another man's baby, not after the scandal his family had suffered. She refused to do it to him. She followed up the rejection by throwing up most spectacularly in an antique vase in the earl's bedchamber. Caillen had come in and banned her until she was better.

She ran her finger through the moisture gathering on the glass of her library window overlooking the hillside. She wrote her favorite phrase over and over as if she were learning to write it in the nursery. Sitting in the window seat, staring out at the vast green hills, she wrapped her arm around her stomach, she leaned her head against the cool glass and sighed as she caught a glimpse of herself across the room in the floor-to-ceiling-length mirror.

"Miss Máira you have a visitor."

Máira swung her feet to the floor, slipped them into her shoes, and frowned. Her nearest neighbor was a good half-day's ride away. "Who is it, Ward?"

"He says he's the Earl of Dorset, your husband."

Her heart skipped. "I don't have a husband."

"Aye, lass, you do." He stood in the doorway to the library, dripping on her floor as if he'd been in the rain for days. His long curly hair was plastered to his head, and his body was covered in mud.

"Don't talk like you're a Scotsman, you dirty Sassenach French bastard."

He smirked. "I don't think Aventine would appreciate you saying that."

"It has nothing to do with your mother, and everything to do with the man traipsing muck into my home!"

He looked down at the trail of mud behind him and sat down in the middle of her floor and began removing his boots. Then he addressed her butler. "Apologies, Ward. I was just anxious to see my wife again."

Ward nodded in understanding.

She looked toward heaven for patience and sanity. "Don't bother taking your boots off, you're leaving."

"I'm staying, *mo ghaol*," he said softly.

"Stop talking as if you know Gaelic. You are not a Scotsman, and you are not an earl. You are a bloody, lying Sassenach French bastard who doesn't know the meaning of *mo ghaol*. And don't help him remove his boots, Ward!"

Her order was too late. Elias's second boot was off and making her pristine butler filthy. "Sorry, Countess," Ward said, as he backed out of the room and closed the door.

"I'm not a bloody countess!" she screamed.

Elias grinned as he stood and turned the key in the lock.

"Get out."

He waved his index finger at her as if she were a naughty child. "I'm not going anywhere, Wife."

"You had our marriage annulled."

"I did not."

Her heart skipped a second beat and she found it difficult to swallow. "You don't love me."

"I do. I lied."

"Exactly. You lied. Everything out of your mouth is a lie."

"Not anymore."

"And how am I supposed to tell if that's a lie?"

"I swear on all that is holy I should have never let you go." He continued his advance.

"You're not a particularly religious man. You threatened to throw a cardinal out of a boat."

"He valued his dress more than a life. I would say he was the one who wasn't a religious person."

"I still don't believe you."

"I swear to our unborn child, I love you with everything that I am."

"Yet you left me."

"I thought you deserved more than what I had to offer. I am sorry I hurt you. I was trying to do what was best for you."

"And what is best for me now?"

"To remain married to the father of your child, who will spend the rest of his days making up for the sorrow he caused you."

Her heart seized. He knew, and he was just saying that because he wanted his child. Her child. "I will not let you take away my child. I will use Ross's power as a duke to destroy you or anyone else who tries to take my child from me."

"Good."

"Good?"

"Yes, good. The woman I love would never let anyone take away our child."

She stared at him, wanting to trust his words but not daring to trust him with her heart. "You're not an earl."

"I am an earl, thanks to your brother-in-law, Ross, and Sir Robert Williamson of the War Office. They petitioned our Regent with my heroism in rescuing Astley. They were quiet about rescuing the cardinal. Ross believed the real reason His Majesty granted me the title was their timing. Our Regent was preoccupied with his mistress, and he wanted them gone. He expelled them from the Buckingham Palace for the next year. Ross is heartbroken."

"I don't love you," she blurted out.

Elias grinned as he slowly crossed the library to where she stood. "You are a terrible liar, *mo ghaol*."

She lifted her chin in defiance. It was her last line of defense against his charm and smile and those damn kissable lips. "It's true."

"Your writings on the window say otherwise."

She looked over at the window and found herself in his arms before she could deny the truth once more. A tear ran down her cheek, but she couldn't look away from the damning words she'd written just moments before. *I love him. I love him. I love him.*

"Say it," he whispered.

"I love you, but—"

His lips were on hers, and for the first time in what seemed like forever, she was home. When she was in his arms, nothing else mattered but the two of them together. This was where she belonged. Where she'd known she belonged from their very first kiss.

His lips were strong and dominating and he tasted like everything she'd ever dreamed a man should be, as he pushed her against the bookcase. His cock hardened against her, reminding her of the everything he could do to her body. He groaned as she pressed into him, lifting her hips to create more friction. Her fingers slid through his wet hair as her nails dug into his scalp and she pulled his head down to deepen their kiss. What this man did to her was madness.

He pulled her hands from his scalp and wrapped them behind her back as his lips trailed down her jaw and neck. She bent her neck to the side giving him more access as he sucked on her pulse point, making her body respond in a way only Elias could.

"Oh, God, don't stop."

"I don't plan to."

She should have thanked the stars, the moon, the rain for allowing her to feel this way again. Intoxicated, drunk, thoroughly foxed on her passion for Elias—until she wasn't.

"Wh-what are you doing?" She tugged on her wrists, only to find them tightly secured behind her back. "Elias?"

He lifted his head and grinned a devious smile that on any other man would be frightening. "I told you I would use the cardinal's robes to tie you up."

She gasped. "We can't..." She hesitated and arched her back to look over her shoulder at the neatly tied sailor's knot securing her hands together with the red silk fabric of the cardinal's robe. She whispered, "We can't have sex while I'm tied up with a priest's holy clothing."

"Want to place a wager on that?"

"How did you get it?"

"You dropped it on shore when Ross found us. I picked it up and kept it."

He was out of his clothing in seconds, not minutes, and then he was pushing the shoulders of her gown down and lifting her breasts from her half corset, exposing her to his gaze.

"Holy hell," he swore.

"Don't say that!"

"You're more beautiful than ever." He caressed her, stroked her, admired her flesh as he pushed and plumped, and finally took one nipple into his mouth and groaned a throaty noise that spoke of desire and need. "God, I've missed these."

"If we..." She gasped as his tongue circled and teased. "If we get struck by lightning it's your fault."

"Mmmm."

He switched to her other breast and continued teasing the first nipple between his thumb and forefinger. Rolling it, then pinching it as his teeth grazed the other. Máira could do nothing but moan as she arched into his mouth and absorbed every touch and stroke he gifted her. Material ripped and her gown was gone. His nimble fingers unlacing her corset faster than any maid. She heard the ripping of more fabric as her shift fell away and then he was kissing her once more. Their naked bodies rejoicing in their nudity as he directed her away from the bookcase toward the settee.

He broke the kiss and turned her around, his chest to her back as he reached over the settee and grabbed a pillow.

"What are you...oh, holy hell."

"It seems we will both be to blame if we are struck by lightning," he whispered into her ear.

She didn't have to look over her shoulder to see what he was doing, because the full-length mirror on the wall gave her the most erotic view of her life—their naked bodies aroused for each other. Elias placed his hand in the middle of her back as they watched each other in the mirror, and he slowly bent her over the back of the settee, making sure her ribs were protected with the pillow and that she could see what he was going to do to her in the mirror.

He grinned when he had her right where he wanted her. "Don't move."

"I don't plan to."

He kissed her spine, tracing the ridges with his tongue, every inch feeling like a new dash of ecstasy. His fingers caressed her arse, massaging her flesh, stroking so close to her center, only to retreat time and time again. She squirmed as she watched his mouth trace over the globes, his tongue circling her most intimate place until she was a ball of aching need.

"Please, Elias," she begged, and he was on his knees, his cock pointing to where they both wanted it to be. "I need your cock," she insisted.

"I need your pussy," he responded, right before he spread her legs wider and lapped her wetness. "Mmmmm," he moaned, and did it again and again.

He licked, and tormented, and tantalized to the point Máira was unable to watch. She closed her eyes and let her orgasm take over as he sucked her clit, and her body quaked with spasm after spasm of pure bliss.

"Open your eyes, *mo ghaol*."

She complied and saw his beautiful body in the mirror. His knees bent, his glorious cock going between her legs to nudge at her core and she was on the brink once more. He entered her with one hard thrust, his head falling back and his exquisite hair brushing his shoulders. He was the vision of a Roman god, making love to her.

"This is heaven," he groaned. "I don't ever want to leave."

She flexed her core in response.

"Devil woman," he growled, and slapped her arse, shocking them both. She whimpered and his eyes widened as he sought her gaze in the mirror.

"Do it again," she begged, and watched his jaw tighten and his eyes light with desire.

His palm met her arse once more and she groaned, her pussy spasming around his length as he rubbed circles into the red mark of his hand. His desire took over, he pulled out to drive up into her hard and fast, one hand gripping her hip, the other splayed across the middle of her back. The carnality of it all as he stroked in and out, the red satin tickling between the globes of her arse, was enough to drive her to insanity. Her pants urging him on as a bolt of pleasure shot through her body.

"I've missed you, Máira. I was a husk of a man without you." Their bodies moved in perfect harmony.

"Then don't leave me again." Her voice became edgy as her hands curled around their silk binding and she moaned in rapture.

"Never. I. Love. You." Each word a slap of flesh meeting flesh, and a rumble traveled through his chest as she fell over the edge of arousal into complete ecstasy. She watched as he pushed in and out, his neck straining, the muscles of his legs showcasing his strength and masculinity, and Elias followed her into to the paradise of the two of them being one.

His chest heaved as he stood there, his muscle quaking.

"What are you doing?" She laughed between pants.

"I told you I didn't ever want to leave."

She giggled and flexed her muscle around him, and he groaned in pleasure. His body draped over her as he kissed up her spine and her neck.

"You are the most amazing woman I've ever known."

"You are the most talented man I've ever known."

He drew back and looked at her. His brows drawn together. "Are you saying you've known more men since we've been apart?"

"Would it matter if I did?"

He thought about it for a moment before shaking his head. "No. I love you. Nothing will change that."

"Then you won't mind if I continue seeking out other men?"

That created a scowl on his handsome face. "Over my dead body."

She giggled. "You are the only man for me now and forever."

He pulled her up from the settee and gently untied the silk as he ran kisses across her shoulders. "You are a minx."

"I am your minx."

A triumphant smile passed his lips. "And I am your 'dirty Sassenach French bastard' now and forever."

She winced and wrapped her arms around his neck. "Don't ever tell Aventine I said that."

"Never, beautiful wife of mine."

Epilogue

Dear Sir Robert Williamson,

It was no accident. His last meeting was with Viscount Pembrock. Then six children were orphaned.

Astley

—A letter penned by Baroness Caillen Griffith to the Sir Robert Williamson, War Office, London, England, for the severely sick Simon Clark, Earl of Astley.

Caillen was not meant to be a nursemaid. The injured and sick earl lying in front of her dying was testament to that. She was not meant to be anything. She had no purpose. No goals. No feelings. Except...

Astley had said the death was no accident. She wouldn't have thought too much about his insistence she write his dying testimony to Sir Williamson at the War Office if he hadn't mumbled, *six children were orphaned.*

Six children were orphaned.

Astley had six siblings—not children. He had one son and he'd made her promise to take Sébastien to his own mother when he died. If he died. She prayed he wouldn't, but it didn't look like those prayers would be answered. His fever had lasted for days, and she didn't know how much longer his body could fight.

She rinsed out the cloth in the wash basin and returned to the man in the bed where she began sponging off Astley's brow. His dark skin held the pallor of death, yet the angles of his cheeks and jaw still showcased the most handsome face she'd ever seen. Careful not to push too hard around his swollen eye, she wiped down the bridge of his gloriously straight aquiline nose that now had a new bump in the middle it had not had the last time she'd seen him. She continued down across his full, split but masculine lips.

She worked her way down the cords of his neck and thought about his long hair she'd had to cut. She'd come close to crying as she'd lopped off the snarled mass that had once been silky smooth. She worked the cloth across his Adam's apple and down across the wide breadth of his chest. She smiled as she remembered the first time she'd seen Astley's chest ten days earlier. She'd never seen her husband's chest and was rather shocked to see Astley's nipples and the light sprinkling of hair. He'd lost a tremendous amount of weight, yet she could still see the strength of his muscles across his entire torso. She worked her way down his stomach and hips, marveling at the trail of hair to his—she froze. Her gaze flew to his face to find him still sleeping peacefully. She looked again at his manhood, shocked to see him aroused for the first time since she'd begun taking care of him. Even that part of him was markedly different than what she remembered of her husband. In his entirety, Astley was beautiful, despite the bruising and cuts and broken bones. The exact opposite of what she had looked like when he'd rescued her from similar circumstances.

A knock at the door made her throw the bedclothes over the earl, only to see a large tenting in the middle from his hard manhood.

"Blasted. Do you always have to bring attention to yourself?" she cursed.

"Caillen, may I come in?" her sister asked.

"Just a moment!" Caillen ran across the room and grabbed another blanket and tossed it over the earl's midsection. "Control that damned thing, Astley," she whispered. She stood back and looked at her handiwork. Now only an experienced woman would know what the rise in the blanket meant, and she prayed Iseabail had not explained everything to her younger siblings yet.

She grabbed the cloth and said, "You can come in now."

Her younger sister Robina entered the room with a bowl of broth. "I thought you'd never let me in. How is the earl today?"

"The same." Lie. He was worse.

"Do you think he's going to live?"

No. "I don't know." She rinsed the cloth out in the basin and wondered if a man's appendage became hard when they were about to die.

"Are you ever going to talk to us again?" Robina whispered.

"What would make you ask that?" Caillen wrung out the cloth and folded it.

"Because you don't engage in conversation with us. You just spout out answers that are meaningless."

"I'm just preoccupied with Astley." And I have nothing to say, except... "What can you tell me about Viscount Pembrock?"

Robina put the tray down next to the bed and folded her arms across her chest. "Why do you ask?"

She bit her lip before she said something that would start an argument. "One of Astley's sisters is interested in him. I wanted to make sure he was a good person."

Robina snorted. "He's the last person you would want your sister to be around."

Caillen thought about the day her husband was killed. "Probably not the last person."

"Oh, most definitely the last. Don't you read *Whispers of the Ton*?"

"No." She didn't care about gossip.

Robina sighed then crossed over to the chair and plopped down.

Blast. That was the last thing she wanted her little sister to do. She wanted a quick report, and then she wanted Robina to leave her in peace.

"He is said to be a bigger rake than Astley."

"Not possible."

Robina shrugged and looked at her fingernails. "He's vastly wealthy, owns much of the land that the canal is being built upon, and he's said to keep a mistress at each one of his estates. Can you imagine how expensive that would be?"

She was going to scream. Robina had to be the nosiest, most talkative sister in the bunch, but she was telling her nothing of import. "Are there any rumors about his involvement with the underworld?"

Robina laughed, her gaiety so loud the earl flinched.

"Shhh," she admonished.

"The *ton* might consider dabbling in trade as the *underworld*, but if you're talking about criminals, no. Unless...did the earl implicate him? Is Pembrock a French spy?"

"Don't be ridiculous," she hissed as she leaned over the earl's body toward her far-too-intelligent little sister.

Robina's eyes widened. "It's true! Wait until —"

"Say one word and I'll box your ears so hard, you'll never be able to listen in on another conversation."

Robina grinned as she stood up and skipped across the room. "It's nice to see my sister again."

As the door closed behind her, Caillen closed her eyes and took a deep calming breath.

"I'm not sure what's worse. Having the information that is supposed to go to the War Office in the hands of your little sister, or not being able to respond when a beautiful woman washes your body."

Caillen's gaze shot to Astley and her cheeks heated. "You were awake?"

His lip quirked. "Could a man sleep while his body is being caressed?"

"I did not caress you! I bathed you like I've been bathing you for over a week!"

His brows drew together. "I've missed an entire week of erotic hands doing wonderful things to my body?"

Caillen's lips thinned as she pressed them together. "If you even think about touching me, it will be the last thing you ever do."

"Damn, all that passion wasted."

She was going to hit him.

He grinned for the first time. It would have been wonderful if...

"You can't hit a dying man."

"Actually, I can."

His grin grew. She wanted to celebrate until he said, "My cock still needs to be washed."

A Note from the Author

Dearest Reader,

I hope you enjoyed Máira and Elias in *The Rebellious Countess*. It was necessary for them to travel to France for the series to progress, and I needed a historic prison. After some research, I discovered Mont Saint Michel to be the perfect backdrop. I took some creative liberties with the abbey, later known as the *Bastille of the Sea*, and how Máira and Elias were able to pull off a rescue.

The abbey was built in the 8th century, but began to fall into disrepair during the Reformation period. It became a political prison during the French Revolution. In 1836 there was a public push to restore the abbey as a national treasure. Victor Hugo was one of the prominent individuals pushing for its restoration, and because of that, I wanted to pay homage to him in *The Rebellious Countess* even though he was only nine years old at the time of my story. The prison was finally closed in 1863.

In Chapter Six I also paid tribute to my husband's favorite female singer from his childhood, Karen Carpenter. You'll notice a description of Máira's "hair glistening in the moonlight as if sprinkled with angel dust," and referencing going utterly mad over "moon dust." Both are inspired by the lyrics from *(They Long to be) Close to You* by Burt Bacharach and Hal David. It was the perfect inspiration for Elias's feelings.

The story also required an elite fighting force to be at Mont-Saint-Michel, and the French Hussars under Napoleon were the perfect fighting force to go up against. General Antoine Louis de Lasalle was a charismatic leader of these forces, with fascinating idiosyncrasies, and I modeled General Alexandre Baptiste Reynard Legrand after him. Lasalle was a talented soldier and leader responsible for countless French victories, but he was also uncompromisingly brutal to the enemy. He believed a Hussar who lived past thirty was a scoundrel, despite he himself living to the bright old age of thirty-four. Lasalle was known to carry a smoking pipe into battle, but I had my General Legrand carry a pipe as an additional weapon that Aventine could use against him. I also used a quote from Lasalle's farewell letter to his wife because it was so incredibly powerful: *"My heart belongs to you, my blood to the Emperor, my life to honor."*

Pope Pius VII was kidnapped from Rome by Napoleon's army and held prisoner for five years from 1809-1814 due to the Pope's refusal to acknowledge Napoleon's second marriage and church appointments Napoleon made in the Catholic Church in France. After three years, the Pope was moved from Savona, Italy, to the Palace of Fontainebleau in France. Pope Pius VII was kept in isolation, but never in a political prison.

Thank you for all your support, and I hope you will join Caillen and Simon in the next *Scandalous Sister* adventure, *The Wicked Baroness*.

Warmest regards,

Helene

Also by Helene Matheson

The Scandalous Sisters

The Ruined Duchess

The Rebellious Countess

About the Author

After following her childhood dream to serve and protect, Helene retired from public service and began a new dream—creating happily ever afters. First publishing in mystery and romantic suspense, she decided to add her love of travel and history to her personal oeuvre. From the first page to the last, Helene promises to take you on a journey to arouse your imagination and capture your heart.

When she's not writing or researching her next novel, she can be found rummaging through antique stores, estate sales, and flea markets looking for that next piece of inspiration.